WHERE THE DEAD MEN GO

Liam McIlvanney was born in Ayrshire. He is the author of *Burns the Radical* and *All the Colours of the Town*. He lives in Dunedin with his wife and four sons.

Praise for *All the Colours of the Town*:

'An authentic, atmospheric and ambitious debut.' Val McDermid

'McIlvanney is deft at weaving the language of politics, both of the hearth and of ethical reportage, and the jargon of journalism into a thriller that is bolted together by both . . . The book's real heft lies in delivering a gripping, unflinching meditation upon the suspicions that still twitch in the Northern Irish air like the proverbial net curtain. McIlvanney has flair and assurance and executes a powerful tale with all the dexterous sensitivity and ballsy swagger the subject is due.' *Scotland on Sunday*

'*All The Colours of the Town* is a distinctive and striking debut. One quality that makes the novel stand out is Liam McIlvanney's portrait of the deep-rooted tribal tensions in Glasgow and Belfast.' *Times Literary Supplement*

'There is nothing like a thriller done really well and *All the Colours of the Town* is a perfect example of why talented writers ought not shy away from tackling genre novels. Noir doesn't need to be pap; this is a smart and engrossing crime novel.' Francesca Segal, *Observer*

'This is a bold, impressive debut. Its best writing turns the conventions of noir fiction on the politics of devolution to find individuals compromised and nations wanting.' *Telegraph*

By the Same Author

Burns the Radical
All the Colours of the Town

Where the Dead Men Go

Liam McIlvanney

faber and faber

First published in this edition in 2013
by Faber and Faber Limited
Bloomsbury House,
74–77 Great Russell Street,
London WC1B 3DA

Typeset by Faber and Faber Ltd
Printed and Bound by CPI Group (UK) Ltd, Croydon CR0 4YY

Epigraph lines taken from 'Lunch with Pancho Villa' from
New Selected Poems 1968–1994 by Paul Muldoon,
published by Faber and Faber Ltd, 2004.
Reproduced with kind permission from Faber and Faber Ltd.

A CIP record for this book
is available from the British Library

ISBN 978-0-571-23985-6

2 4 6 8 10 9 7 5 3 1

For Andrew

'Do you never listen to the news?
You want to get down to something true,
Something a little nearer home.'

Paul Muldoon, 'Lunch with Pancho Villa'

Prologue

You wake in the half-light, fleetingly lost, the strange room assembling itself, the extra bed, the smudgy big mirror, the pitch-dark desk and chair. From the strip of sky between the half-closed curtains you can tell that you've barely slept, a matter of minutes, the lightest doze. You are lying on top of the bed in your clothes, no sound except the breath in your nostrils. If you closed your eyes right now you would sleep.

This is how it affects you. Some people get wired, jumpy, they can't settle till it's under way. With you it's different, your heart-rate slows, your breathing shallows, your body seems to be shutting down in stages.

You rise from the bed and draw the curtains.

The room is on the fourteenth floor and looks out onto traffic, eight lanes of motorway in a deep concrete trench, a tangle of slipways and off-ramps and flyovers. You watch them shifting lanes, the cars and buses, the big boxy lorries, busy in both directions. Wherever they are headed they will hear it tonight, in their living rooms, on their kitchen radios, the thing you are about to do.

Beyond the motorway is a school. The playground is bare. Light glints off the puddles on the sagging bitumen roof. Off to the right you see the spires of the West End, the snow-topped Campsie Fells. To the left is the river and the great shape of the crane, the vast hammerhead structure, a handgun trained on the city.

You imagine how a tourist would see it, what a tourist would notice, watching from this window. After all this time away, your years of exile from these begrudging streets, you're a tourist here too.

In the shower you drag a razor up your shins, the smooth skin gleaming in the overhead spots. Then you stand for a while under the spray, let the water punish your bowed head, fall in runnels off your limbs.

Afterwards, you dress in a thick white bathrobe and use its fluffy cuff to rub a porthole in the steamed-up mirror. Your things are laid out along a shelf of frosted glass and you use them in turn, ending with a dull red lipstick that you blot on a plucked square of tissue that floats down into the waste-paper basket.

Your eyebrows are a mess but you lack the energy to fix them.

Your clothes are laid out on the bed. As you smooth the ten-denier over your legs a hangnail catches but as the run is high up on the thigh, it won't matter. You button the midnight blue wet-look blouse, slip the side-split black pencil skirt over your hips, fumble for the zip. With two hands you flip your hair over the fake-fur collar of the short wool jacket.

You step into your heels, feel your skirt tighten against your buttocks, your calves stiffen as the tendons strain. Facing the full-length mirror you look at yourself as a stranger would, twisting your head, frowning, appraising. You have seen better, you have seen worse. It's cold out there so you knot a silk scarf at your throat, lean forward to check your front teeth for lipstick.

You are almost ready. Almost but not quite. You cross to the safe and key in the number, take the Model 36 from its folded rag. You set it on the desk where the light from the window traces the contours of the blued steel, the grooved cylinder, the fuzzy strip on the barrel where the serial number's been filed away.

The cylinder carries five rounds. You stand them up on the desk like little lipsticks, the gold tubes with the blunt-edged copper-coloured heads. Semi-wadcutter .38 Specials. You slot them home, snap the cylinder shut.

You heft it by the wooden grip, watching your ghost in the mirror. The two-inch barrel makes it look like a toy. You need to get close, with a barrel this short, five yards or closer, point and shoot, no sighting, no headshots, aim for the torso. But not so close that the target can jump you, kick it loose, smack the gun from your hand.

The revolver fits snugly in your handbag, the little square purse on its thin leather strap. You put it in now, slip the bag on your shoulder. It weighs a lot but looks normal.

You cross to the window again. Parents are gathering at the gates, little clusters of mums, the dads standing sparely alone, busy with their mobiles. School will be out soon, the kids in winter jackets and hats, scattering, running, buoyed up by the early dark, the nearness of the holidays.

You close the curtains, lie on the bed, your heels on

the satiny coverlet, your hand on the bag at your side.

Twenty minutes from now you will leave the hotel. There is a taxi-rank by the hotel entrance but you will walk the three hundred yards to Central Station. You will enter the station by the side entrance and exit by the main front doors, where another line of taxis waits. One of these will be yours.

Inside the cab you will smooth your skirt, settle your handbag beside you on the seat. You will smile at the driver's eyes in the rear-view mirror. You will give an address. You will sit well back and watch the streets spool past, the festive city, the Christmassy windows, the shoppers and partygoers, the women with buggies, the buskers, the bucket-rattling charity collectors in their Santa hats. There will be time to sort it out later, how you feel about this, a time to keep and a time to cast away.

The address you will give is three blocks short of your destination.

Chapter One

'You think it's deliberate? Do they time these things to fuck us up?'

Driscoll was shaking his head. A dummy was up on the screen, tomorrow's splash, my first front page in a month: *Yes Camp Poll Boost*. A YouGov survey pegged support for independence at forty per cent, up five points since June. The real poll – the one that mattered, the be-all-end-all referendum – was still two years off but the shadow war would keep us in headlines till then. Assuming the paper survived that long.

On screen was a headshot of Malcolm Gordon, the Nationalist First Minister, with his schoolboy haircut and lopsided grin, looking like the man who broke the bank at Monte Carlo. '*Who'd bet against him?*' was the caption, a quote from an unnamed Westminster frontbencher. There was a sidebar giving analysis of the figures and a paragraph of comment from a rent-a-quote politics boffin at Strathclyde Uni. The page was toast anyway, if Driscoll got his way.

'You'd start to take it personal. Jesus. Do they time it to fuck us up?'

He ran a hand through his too-long hair, rubbed the back of his neck.

'They timed it to coincide with a football match, Jimmy.'

Driscoll scowled at me. My eyes were suddenly stinging: Maguire's acrid perfume. She'd been upstairs for a meeting. Sixth floor. The suits.

She held up her hand as Driscoll started to speak.

'Gerry.' She never even looked Driscoll's way. 'This shooting. What do you think?'

Driscoll sagged. He looked away, shaking his head, and then back at me. Blank, bagged eyes. Slack jowls. Roll of belly over the waistband.

'It's an inside lead, Fiona.' I spoke to Maguire but looked at Driscoll. 'Page six. Four at best. What do we know at this stage anyway? A guy's been shot on a football field. "Gang-related." That's it. Nothing's coming out between now and deadline.' I shrugged. 'Lift it from the wire. Top and tail it. No one's scooping us on this.'

My eldest son had a piping competition that afternoon in Ayrshire. I'd promised him I would make it. Try to make it. Once I filed my copy I was finished for the day.

'*Six?*' Driscoll was shaking his head. 'Fucking six? This is the splash, Fiona. The *Mail* will fucking bury us with this.' He turned to me. 'No one scooping us? It's all over Twitter, photos from the locus.'

Maguire frowned at the screen. Before she got the big chair, Maguire had been news editor. She'd done Driscoll's job for seven years. But the game was different now. You couldn't appeal to precedents. We were dropping five per cent, month on month, year on year. There were no precedents for where we were now.

'Make the call, Fiona.' Peter Davidson spoke, production editor, hovering at our shoulders. 'We're off-stone by eight. Make a fucking decision.'

This was Glasgow. This was the *Trib*. We'd like to be quality, the paper of record. We'd like to cover the world from a West of Scotland perspective, reporting far-flung conflicts from every angle and on every front. Correspondents in five continents. But we didn't have any money. And the readers we retained had other priorities. Celtic and Rangers. The Neils and the Walshes. The city's tribal battles, on and off the pitch. That was our métier. Bigotry and violence. Football and crime. Maguire had been upstairs, talking numbers. The current figures had just come out. I didn't know what they were but I knew they weren't good.

I sympathised with Maguire. The last editor I worked for at the *Trib* – the guy who fired me four years back – was Norman Rix, a cheerful brutal Cockney who did his stint among the Jocks and went back home to edit the *Indy*. Between Rix and Maguire the *Trib* had gone through three editors. Time was, *Tribune* eds reigned like monarchs – whole epochs passed by under one man's dispensation. Now they were football managers, turn it round in eight or nine months or face the bullet. It made them nervous, made them prone to bad decisions.

'It's page one. Gerry, you're on it.'

Driscoll wheeled away, the smirk of glory pasted to his face.

'Fiona.'

Maguire was already walking, striding past the sports-desk.

'You're on it, Gerry. Take a snapper.'

'And the splash?'

I was almost trotting beside her, the caustic perfume sizzling in my airways.

'It's not the splash any more,' she said. 'It's page four. Subs'll finish it.'

'Fiona, come on.' I glanced over at Moir's empty chair. 'This isn't mine. At least let me try and get hold of him again.'

'Gerry, you're not listening.' She nodded at the empty chair. 'Your mate's AWOL. Again. But Martin Moir's whereabouts is my problem. Your problem – *one* of your problems, your most immediately *pressing* problem – is to get this story.'

'Aye but, Fiona—'

She stopped in her tracks, turned to face me, fists on hips. Here we go, I thought. I could see it in her eyes before she opened her mouth.

'This is the gig, Gerry. If you didn't want it, why'd you come back?'

She stared in my face for a count of three and then bounced into her office.

'I must have missed you,' I said to her freshly slammed door.

I slumped into my chair, took a pull of lukewarm Volvic. I looked around the floor. Neve McDonald was scowling at her screen, her burgundy lips primly twisted. Kev Carson at the sportsdesk was hunched over his keyboard, fingers stabbing, his nose six inches from the screen. I craned round in my seat. All across the newsroom, the heads were bent, the fingers busy. The insect tick of keyboards, the patient drone of Sky News. It must have been somebody's birthday: a little string of balloons was pinned to a partition over by Accounts.

Why did you come back? In various forms and inflections, this question had dogged me for the past year, since I threw up my life on the run at Bluestone Media and shuffled backwards along the escape tunnel to my cell at the *Tribune on Sunday*. Fiona Maguire posed it most weeks, in her snidely rhetorical fashion, but other people were genuinely stumped. The answer wasn't obvious, to me or to anyone else. Like every Scottish title, the *Trib* was in freefall, bleeding readers with every quarter. Anyone with a chance to leave seized it. Mostly they went into PR. The world and his managing editor left to set up companies called Impact Media or the Cornerstone Group, each one promising to 'manage' a client's reputation with 'experience gained at the frontline of news and political reporting' or 'skills developed at the pinnacle of British journalism'. I had written some of this horseshit myself: *A bespoke team will guide you through the media minefield. We will minimise the impact of negative stories.*

I'd been back six weeks when the paper was sold to an American media conglomerate. Lay-offs started soon after. Now the empty workstations dotted the newsroom like foreclosed houses.

Often, when a workstation went suddenly bare, I could no longer picture its occupant. The colleague whose Blu-tacked snaps of ringletted twins or bounding black labs had clogged their monitor's rim, whose summer suit jackets and winter coats had draped their chair-back, who offered tight little smiles and theatrical shows of professional briskness when you stood behind them in the queue for the fax machine or the copier; that person was now a ghost. I felt bad about this, but who could you ask? It was like the Disappeared in Chile or Argentina, people vanishing overnight, leaving oddly stark chairs and denuded blue partitions, and we carried on as if nothing had happened.

There was one empty chair that stood out from the rest, a chair that marked a presence, not an absence. This was the chair of Martin Moir, the King of Crime, Investigations Editor for the *Tribune on Sunday*, Scottish Journalist of the Year in 2009 and 2010 and probably – the envelope would be opened at the Radisson Hotel in a fortnight's time – 2011 as well. The chair was empty because he was out on the job, rooting out stories and standing them up, boosting the circ, saving our jobs. The chair was empty because he was out on the piss, lining up voddies and knocking them back, missing his deadlines, risking our jobs.

I slugged some more water and watched the snow clouds settle on the Campsie Fells. Moir was a mate – the best mate I had. Stories, fights, five-a-side football triumphs, five-a-side football disasters, lost weekends: we'd shared a lot and went back a long way. When Moir first came to the paper I looked out for him, fed him stories, shared my contacts. For a couple of years we worked as a team. Four years ago in Belfast he saved my life. But people change, we both had, and we'd done barely more than pass the time of day since I'd started back at the *Trib*. Moir was rarely in the building. When he did show up he was curt, aloof; the backhand wave, the guarded nod. Moir was the talent: he didn't want reminding of the days when he'd featured further down the bill. I didn't want reminding of them either, truth be told.

I looked sourly at his workstation. The blinded screen of his iMac. Autumnal foliage of notelets on his partition walls. Papers and books. A can of Diet Coke, open. It had been there since Thursday, the last time Moir's cosseted arse had parked itself on his blue swivel chair. Beside the can of Coke was a framed photo. His girls; six and four. Perfect. Blonde. Sun in their hair. What did he need their photo for? He got to see them every night.

I checked the PA wire. Standard shtick from a 'police spokesperson': *We are investigating the fatal shooting of a 26-year-old man in the East End of Glasgow at 11.20 this morning. The man was pronounced dead at Glasgow Royal Infirmary. This shocking incident took place in broad daylight in a busy public park. We are appealing for anyone with information, no matter how irrelevant it may seem, to contact us.*

No point calling Pitt Street. What I needed was a proper cop, not a desk-clerk with a 2.1 in media relations from a former poly. A proper cop: *A source close to the investigation revealed.* What I needed was Moir's tame cop. All the crime boys had them. You couldn't write the stories Moir did without a cop in your pocket. Maguire, then? Maguire still had contacts. I could knock on her door and ask but I sensed, somehow, that this was a test, that she needed me to fail, prove to us both that my days at the sharp end were

11

finished. I was on my own.

Elaine answered on the second ring. The kitchen phone, I thought: she'll be fixing lunch. She didn't ask why I was phoning. She didn't need to. She didn't say anything, just a rasping sigh then she called his name. Roddy knew, too; the way he said 'Dad?' when he answered. I didn't tell him I would make it up to him because you can't. You don't make it up with cinema tickets or a football strip or a new game for the Nintendo. You make it up with time. You put in the hours. It's that or nothing.

'Will I still see you tomorrow?'

'Try and stop me. What are you playing?'

'Today? *Bloody Fields of Flanders*.'

'You got it down?'

'I think so. Want to hear it on the chanter?'

Driscoll was crossing the newsroom, hard eyes, set mouth. I swivelled my chair round to face the screen.

'Not right now, son. That's a good choice, though. Play an easy tune well not a hard tune badly, that's the ticket. Watch the grace notes.'

'Okay, Dad.'

I opened my desk drawer, started raking through the debris, the old memory sticks and Post-its, bulldog clips and lidless biros, index cards and telemessage sheets, the paper hankies, strips of aspirin. Lewicki's number was in here somewhere, this month's number. I'd lost my phone the week before, the trusty Nokia, my contacts gone. Such as they were. A stack of business cards and two ancient address books stood on my desk. I was transferring the numbers in my spare time in batches of eight or ten, tapping them into the iPhone I bought in a fit of up-to-dateness.

Driscoll appeared at my desk, breathing through his nose. I could see his belly out of the corner of my eye, resting on the desk. I kept looking for the scrap of paper, swept my hand through the drawer, made as much noise as I could. He spoke softly.

'Want to tell me what that was about?'

Nothing was easy with Driscoll. The prick bore grudges from previous papers, previous lives. He hated me. He hated me because I took the big stories straight to Maguire. It's what everyone does but Driscoll took it as a personal slight.

'It's called a professional disagreement, Jimmy. Never had one?'

'Telling me how to do my job?'

I found the bit of paper I wanted, stuck it in my shirt pocket.

'Nah, mate.' I stood up, shouldered into my jacket. 'Take too long. I've got a story to write.'

As I waited for the lift I tapped the number into my contacts and then tapped to dial. It's pronounced Levit-ski. He's a second-generation Scottish Pole. When I first met him I was the *Trib*'s crime reporter and Lewicki was working out of Aikenhead Road. Now he was an Agency cop, part of Scotland's FBI. He carried two mobiles – his Agency smartphone and a pre-paid Motorola for talking to people he shouldn't have been talking to. He changed the Motorola every month.

'Uh-huh?' The voice was cagey, he wouldn't recognise the number.

'It's me,' I said. 'It's a new phone.' I didn't tell him I'd lost the old one: five or six of his former numbers were in the contacts list.

'Okay, Geronimo. Do you and your new phone have a question?'

'We do. This thing out east, Maxton Park: you hear anything?'

'Since when are you back on crime?'

'Since the Boy Wonder went AWOL.'

'This is Moir we're talking about, your mate Martin?'

'Aye. Except he thinks he's Dean Martin now. Three-day benders, drunk on the job. Been on the skite since Thursday.'

'Tsk. What's he got, "issues"?'

The lift yanked to a halt then eased the final inch. The doors shushed open.

'He's got a very understanding boss, Jan. That's what he's got.'

'Okay, Ger. See what I can do.'

It was a measure of the city's struggle with its tabloid image, its lurid heritage of razor kings and hard men, its hatchet fights and ice-cream wars, that a public act of violence struck you first as a piece of theatre. *Well, of course, that's exaggerated*, was your reflex response; *Glasgow's not like that any more, it's an outdated stereotype, it's not realistic.* You had to remind yourself that the crime had actually happened. That a man's toe-tagged, traumatised frame was laid out on a brushed-steel tray at the City

Morgue on the Saltmarket.

William Swan's corpse would be heading there now, but the focus for the moment was the scene of the crime: Maxton Park in the city's East End.

The duty snapper was next door in the coffee shop: McCann, a new guy, English. I rapped on the window, tapped my wrist. He nodded, rolled his eyes and drained his pail-sized carton of coffee.

'East End,' I told him. 'Maxton Park. A shooting. One of Neil's boys.'

The sun had gone in and the sky was low as we headed up the Gallowgate in McCann's Jeep Cherokee. Past the Saracen Head and the shabby cluster of Celtic pubs with their tricolours snapping in the wind. Purple clouds squatting on the Barrowland.

'Christ, it looks like snow.'

McCann craned out of the windscreen, grunted. Chatty bastard. When I tried to give him directions he cut me short. His ponytail shook when I offered a smoke. I sparked up a Café Crème and punched the button to drop the window. The wind blew the smoke back into the car. McCann shook his head, like he was the only man in the car with someplace he'd rather be. I should have been driving to Ayrshire now instead of playing fireman for Martin Moir.

'It's a piece of nonsense anyway.' We were out on the Shettleston Road. 'I'm supposed to be Politics.'

McCann frowned out of the window, scanning for street signs.

'This is Politics.'

The fuck would you know about it, I thought, but he was right. They acted like feuding states, the Neils and the Walshes. Renaissance principalities, petty republics. Mostly it was border skirmishes. Beatings. Arson attacks. Street dealers robbed at knifepoint. But now and then there was a call for grander measures, grievous acts of revenge, the ghosts of 2005 out for a lick of blood.

McCann was slowing, flicking the indicator.

'Here we are.'

An apron of grass opened out on our left. The little crowd, cops in yellow jackets, the Mobile Incident Unit like a stranded bus. The quivering ribbons of blue and white tape.

A cop stepped into the roadway and waved us down. I had my press card out as the window dropped.

'Gerry Conway, *Tribune on Sunday*.'

The cop leaned down. Ginger moustache. Wedge of gold between his two front teeth. He looked past me at McCann, who smiled with his lips closed. McCann was wearing his snapper's vest, all zips and buckles, D-rings and pockets. His camera case was on the floor between the seats.

'OK, lads. Park at this side of the pitch. You know the drill: keep back from the locus.'

They had taped off the grass, a patch of nothing, ten metres square. A canvas tent had gone up, white, tall, with a pointed roof, like something from a medieval tournament. SOCOs in their white moon-suits were traipsing in and out. An officer guarded each side of the square. Within the tape the detectives stood around with their hands in their pockets, poking at the turf with their dress shoes. They wore dark shirts, metallic ties, black overcoats. As we crossed the grass I spotted Bobby Ireland, a DI from Stewart Street; another guy from Baird Street who I knew but couldn't name. They looked like Mafiosi at a funeral.

Behind the far goal was the MIU, a big white trailer with a short row of steps to the door. Another yellow jacket by the steps.

The chopper was churning the air as McCann strode ahead, appraising the scene, squinting at the sky, rummaging in his shoulder-bag. He was conscious of the onlookers, avoided their eyes. The professional at work. There was a zip to his movements, a military crispness. He fitted a lens. He shot the tent, the SOCOs, the cop in front of the MIU, the football pitch and the high flats.

He shot the crowd, huddled like some faithful remnant. They seemed to expect this, looking incuriously at the lens or staring morosely into space. The killer liked to haunt such scenes, standing at the edge of the crowd, craning to witness his own absence. It paid to take a picture, just in case.

And then he was off, sending a curt nod my way as he shouldered his bag of tricks and skedaddled across the park. I envied him his finite task: in, out, squeeze off some shots; the crisp, moist click of the shutter. They would use a frame of a lone cop on tomorrow's front page, the visored eyes, the resolute jaw, the solitary watcher standing between us and the chaos that takes place on the other side of the incident tape. I would have to turn it into words. I turned up my collar, set off across the freezing grass.

I spotted Gallacher from the *News of the World* chatting to one of the cops across the incident tape. In the shadow of the high flats was a news crew, Manda Levitt from *Reporting Scotland*, sexy-severe, talking to camera. I half-expected Moir to show up, his long dog face and floppy hair. He'd been following this feud so closely for so long he could sense where the next eruption would come. Moir was like a water-diviner for gangland violence. When the last victim – Jason 'Jackie' Stewart – was dispatched in an Asda car park, Moir was on the scene within minutes, interviewing witnesses, taking cellphone snaps of the shot-up Audi.

I should have worn better shoes. I flexed my toes, they were turning numb in my thin-soled oxfords. What was I doing here? Let Moir talk them up, these neds and hard men. A city fixated with hoods and blades. Why add to it? This was terrible journalism, the worst type of pandering. It wasn't hard, it didn't take special talent to get murdered in Glasgow. We had the worst per capita homicide rate in Western Europe. You had to travel far – Vilnius, Detroit – for a city that could top us. Thirty killings a year. But the perps weren't gangsters. They were friends and flatmates, fractious neighbours. They plunged their mates with bread knives at drunken house parties in flare-ups fuelled by supermarket booze. And the victims; what did we give them? A wing column, two pars on an inside page. I spat on the grass, pressed on towards the trailer.

My plan was to chivvy a quote from the duty detective

– it would be warmer in the trailer, at least – and then cab it back to base, but I didn't make it that far. A teenage boy was coming towards me, baseball cap, scarf round the face, hands in the pockets of his snow-white track-top.

'My maw saw it all,' he said. 'She saw the whole thing.'

'Aye? Where is she?'

He pointed at the high flats. 'Fifth floor. Fucking grandstand view.' He had his phone out, waved it at me. 'Want me to see if she'll talk to you?'

'How much?'

'Fifty.'

'Fuck off.'

'Twenty.'

I nodded. I stamped the stiffening turf as the boy made his call. How the mighty have fallen. Foreign jollies. They sent me out to Hong Kong in '97 to cover the handover. I remember the rain. The pipes playing 'Auld Lang Syne' as the Black Watch paraded past in their white dress jackets, their spats raising splashes from the flooded esplanade. The piece wrote itself. The massed umbrellas. Patten standing hatless to the rain. A kiltie with a folded Union flag, the pibroch slow and lonely as he stepped across the concourse.

That's what I wrote, but what I really remembered was waking the next morning in my tiny stylish hotel room, high above the streets. The rain had stopped. The day was dawning fine – it wasn't yet six – and below me, ringed by skyscrapers, was a public garden, a little disc of green. It had trees and paths and a children's playground with little pagoda roofs, and there were people, standing, raising legs and arms in slow, balletic arcs. Even from my window, hundreds of feet in the air, I could sense their composure, the figures in the canvas trousers, baggy shirts; they were self-possessed, indifferent to the rousing city, the new dawn, the fresh dispensation. In the centre of the garden was a pond, a deep green eye, where the tiniest orange smudges flashed and died.

'Big man.' The boy was loping towards me, waving his mobile. 'It's sorted. Come on.' We set off across the grass to the high flats.

The lifts were fucked. Rain started falling as we climbed the stairs, big windblown squalls that shook the landing windows. Stink of piss and cooking oil. The walls were finished in some hard metallic render and the slap of our palms on the black plastic handrail echoed round the stairwell.

Fifth floor. SHEPHERD in yellow on a tiny Perspex nameplate. A short woman in a dark hallway, she grunted at the boy. The boy didn't stay. I heard him clattering down the stairs as I followed his mum down the hall.

The living room was cold but I was sweating from the climb. A big window gave onto the pitch. I sat on the sofa opposite her armchair. There was a print above the fireplace, something Highland and greenish, gloomy hills, a fringed cow.

Her face was puffy and coarse. Lank orange hair. Late fifties. She was wearing a man's fleece, zipped to the neck, its sleeves folded back into gauntlet cuffs.

'Mrs Shepherd—'

'My name's Duncan,' she said.

'Mrs Duncan.'

I could see my breath. There was a coal-effect electric fire in a fake-brick fireplace, its three bars dead and grey.

'Mrs Duncan, your son tells me you saw the incident?'

'Uh-huh.' Suspicious, truculent. She looked too old to be the boy's mother. Deep creases on her upper lip. Smoker's face. Giving nothing away.

'Could you describe what happened?'

I set my Sony UX on the coffee table.

'What's that?'

'It's a kind of tape recorder. It saves me having to take notes. Is that alright?'

She frowned at the black oblong with its glowing orange screen. Her fringe hung down like the cow in the painting.

'Mrs Duncan, I'm not the police. You don't have to talk to me if you don't want to. I thought that was clear.' I took out my wallet and found a twenty, laid it down beside the UX.

She looked at the money and stood up, pushed at the too-long sleeves. 'Come here.' I followed her to the window. The detectives had gone, but the uniformed cops kept their guard beside the dwindling crowd. The rain had stopped but the droplets shone on the pane.

'That was all in shadow.' She wiped her hand across the foreground. 'The sun was out this morning but this bit was in shadow. Most of the folk watching were on the far side, in the sunshine. There was nobody really on this side. Couple of wee boys, just. And the man.'

21

'You noticed him? You got a good look?'

'Aye. He was standing right there with his hood up. This pointy hood. Kind of scary-looking.'

'You didn't see his face?'

The red fringe shook.

'Naw. When the ball got kicked out just here he ran back to get it and the hood came down but he was wearing a hat, a baseball cap and I couldn't see his face. He got the ball and I thought he would kick it back but he didn't. He just stood there with his foot on the ball. And when the player came towards him he wanted it back, he was waving for the guy to kick him the ball and then bang, he's down.'

She shook her head, slower, seeing it again.

'You see the gun?'

'Naw. I didn't even know he'd been shot. I heard the noise but I didn't know what it was. I saw the guy running away and the football fella sat down. He didn't seem that bothered. Then he's on his back and the rest of them come running. And ten minutes later the ambulance comes right across the pitch, siren going. I didn't know he'd been shot till I heard it on the wireless.'

We stood looking out at the scene, the locus. Not yet four but the light was failing, shadows on the grass, yellow headlights on the Baillieston Road. From this height you could see the tracks in the grass, the ambulance's treadmarks. The crowd had thinned by now and the yellow jackets stood impassive. The window was turning glassy, reflective. She jerked her chin at my reflection, pushed the hair out of her face.

'That any use to you?'

'Aye.' We turned back to the room. 'Tickety-boo.' I lifted the UX, put a tenner down on top of the twenty.

I left the flats at a clip. The boy peeled off from a wall and caught up with me, walking in step.

'Go alright, big man? Get what you wanted?'

I nodded, kept walking.

'Square me up, then? Finder's fee?'

'Ask your grannie.'

The mobile rang and I dug it out. Lewicki. He'd spoken to the CID at Baird Street. They were playing it close, Jan said. Wouldn't tell him anything, just that there was footage, some camcorder shots of the gunman. 'Watch the late news,' he told me.

The rain was coming on again, thickening into sleet. I flagged a cab on the Baillieston Road. I'd had enough of the celebrated Glasgow banter to see me through the winter but it wasn't finished yet.

'See that carry-on this morning? Guy shot dead on the fitba park?'

The driver put his wipers up to double speed. The sleet had turned to snow, big flakes streaming at the windscreen, whipping past like stars, like passing galaxies. It gave me a feeling of vertigo, as if the cab was falling through space.

'It was nothing-each when it happened.' He caught my eye in the mirror and grinned. 'First shots on target all day.'

The cab kept falling through snow.

Chapter Two

I wrote it up and filed it. Fifty minutes' work. 'Man Shot Dead in City Park.' I used a quote from the woman in the tower, the statement from the police. I wrote it flat and dry. No tricks, no gimmicks. Sent a four-par précis to tribune.com. We put the paper to bed at half past eight.

In the Cope, I pushed through the crush and found a stool at the bar. Joe Gorman turned for the Lagavulin bottle.

'Saw the splash' – he nodded at the city edition on the bar-top, tipping a quarter-inch of smoky gold into a tumbler. 'Been a while.'

'Cheers, Joe. Yeah, for what it's worth.'

'Moir sick, is he?'

'Fuck you.'

Joe turned away, smirking. I added some water from the tap on the bar, scanned the crowd for Moir. He was usually here at this time. I took my phone out. There was a text from Roddy – *2nd place* and a smiley face. I tapped out my answer: *Go get em! Congrats + sorry. Work stuff. See you tomorrow.* Since I'd bought him the phone, Rod was like a different boy. The silences, surly pre-teen huffs were gone. He texted me three or four times a day. 'Sup.' 'Hey.' 'Later.' Meaningless little tweets but I was glad to get them. I thought about my own dad, after the divorce. A week, ten days between calls. The pips. Cursing and fumbling as he fed the slot. The coins shunting home. He lived in a bedsit when he left us, a student place on Kelvin Drive. Shared toilet. No phone. *I'll have to go*, he'd say; *there's a queue of people outside.* I used to picture it. The red phone-box on the city pavement, a boxed oblong of yellow light. Dad holding the door for the next user, the little nod of acknowledgement.

I texted Moir – *Come in Number 3, your time's up*, I wasn't angry any more – and put the phone away.

The words 'White Russian' cut through the buzz. I recognised the order, then the voice. Neve McDonald was beside me, purse in hand. We'd had a thing, briefly, three weeks of fucking before they fired me for the Lyons piece. I broke it off but I can't imagine she was heartbroken. That was four years ago. Since I'd come back to the paper we'd kept our distance.

'Back in the old routine,' she said.

'Sorry?'

She leaned across me, her left breast grazing my bicep, lifted the folded paper from the bar-top. She spread it out.

'Gerry Conway, ace crime reporter.'

I'd been on crime in my early days at the paper. Court reports, mostly.

'Can't keep a good man down.'

My arm was tingling where her breast had touched it.

'So I hear. You tweet it yet?'

'What?'

'The story. Gallacher's trending already. He's got pics from the locus. Quotes. Do one now you'll get some of his traffic.'

'Traffic?' I shook my head. 'Jesus Christ, Neve, a man's dead. Dead, okay? I boiled it down to six hundred words. You want me to tell it in 140 characters? To do what – steal "traffic" from that prick at the *News of the World*?'

'Fine.' Neve's hand was up, shutting me off. 'Do I give a fuck if you tweet it or not? Tell Driscoll. Tell Maguire. Jesus, sorry I spoke.'

'Okay, Neve. Look, let's – I'm sorry, alright? It's rubbish, anyway – paper of record splashing on a city killing, local neds. It's freesheet stuff. Never have happened under Rix.'

She breathed out slowly through her nose, took a swig of her drink, licked her milky moustache. 'No one ever tell you you're hard work, Gerry?'

I sipped my whisky. 'Someone might've. Few years back. But I knew she was joking. The way she said it, I could tell she didn't mean it.'

She paid for the drinks, slotted her change into the big charity whisky bottle on the bar. 'Mari okay? The wee fella?'

'Angus,' I told her. 'Brand new, thanks.'

'Good.' She collected her drinks in a little diamond formed by her fingers and thumbs. 'We're in the back booth.' She jerked her head across the pub. I could see Maguire talking to Davidson, Driscoll lifting a pint to his lips.

'I've got to get back.'

'Aye. No doubt.' She squeezed back into the crush, her drinks held high, hips swivelling.

I lifted the paper from the bar-top, tucked it under my arm. The night was cold and clear, the clouds gone, the pavements icy. I crossed the bridge, stars ablaze in the glossy Clyde. I looked up to see if the scattered pricks of light would resolve themselves into a constellation – a bear or a plough or one of the others – but they held their random stations. My heels rang on the walkway of the bridge as I crossed the river and set off into town.

In some ways the gloom was cheerful, the gloom that enveloped the trade, that pervaded our weeks from conference on Tuesday morning to the Cope on Saturday night. At least we had the benefit of foresight. We knew that our business was on its way out. We were the scattered remnants, the last of the clan. Okay, let's go out with style, make the last days count. The past few weeks as I rode the subway to Ibrox I'd been happy, I relished my job more than ever. I was like a man recovering from a life-threatening illness; every day was a bonus.

The weather helped. I always think of winter as a hopeful time, a season of quiet graft and preparation, of groundwork and hidden diligence. Summer makes me nervous, fretful, I feel life passing me by. The sunny days are like an accusation. When the shortest day has passed I feel bereft, wrong-footed, like I've missed the boat again. But with the winter coming on, with November around the corner, with a hard blue sky in the mornings and a silver glint on the pavements and the cold air punching your lungs everything seems ahead of you. The future seems assured, even when it's not.

I was glad I'd come back from PR. PR is where you go to die, or where you go when your paper does. I stuck it for three years before I staggered back like Lazarus, back to my old desk, my old beat, my old contacts and adversaries. Only everything was new. The title on my business cards – Scottish Political Editor, *Tribune on Sunday* – was the same, but now I was writing for the daily as well as the Sunday, writing for the website as well as the paper, writing news as well as Politics. And Politics wasn't Politics any more.

I'd come back in time to cover the last election and I was still recovering. The losing party can go off and lick its wounds, regroup, elect a new leader. But the hacks who get it wrong? We have to sit down and write next week's copy, pretend we know what we're talking about. For months, it seemed, I'd been covering a different country. On 5 May the Scotland I described in my weekly column – that chippy, chary, toe-testing land, where the generations voted Labour from fear and from habit – turned out not to exist. It was a Narnia of my own invention. Maybe it was already passing into folklore in 2007, when the Nationalists won by a whisker. But now the old Scotland was finished, sunk like Atlantis. I kept a map of the constituency results on my partition wall. Except for some atolls of red around Glasgow and two spots of blue on the border with England, the whole bloody country was SNP yellow. Every seat in the Highlands, every seat in the North-East, every seat in Aberdeen and Dundee, four out of five in Edinburgh, five out of eight in Glasgow, all seats bar one in Ayrshire and Fife: the Nats had taken it all. Seats that had been Labour since 1945 had crashed like rotten redwoods. This was the map of a foreign country, one I knew nothing about.

There was solace in getting things utterly wrong. You had to start over, relearn whatever you thought you knew, start from the bottom, take your first steps like everyone else.

The night was getting colder and I flagged a cab. Both the fold-down seats bore the logo, the green 'G' in its coloured rings: 'Glasgow 2014. XX Commonwealth Games.'

Because I missed it? Was that the answer? Because I got sick of PR? Because this was the only thing I was halfway good at? Because, despite the evidence of my senses and the actions of my colleagues, I still thought papers mattered?

The cab climbed Hope Street. Saturday night. Lassies' legs in the headlights. The lads strutting up the roadway, cropped heads and rolling shoulders. Black-clad bouncers with earpieces, satin jackets shining in the lights. Maybe Maguire was right. When you go you should stay gone. Coming back was always an error.

We turned into Clouston Street, stopped halfway up. I signed the chit. Inside the flat I checked on Angus, listened for the breathing, tucked his left leg back under the blanket, tugging the cuff of his pyjama trousers over his plump calf, upped the heating a notch.

'Here it is,' Mari shouted.

I got a Sol from the fridge and plumped down beside her on the sofa.

They led with it. *A man has been shot dead in a Glasgow park in what police suspect is a gangland execution.* Shots of the park, the MIU, the yellow jackets guarding the incident tape, the murder squad standing round chatting. A shot of the chopper, filmed from below, an asterisk in the sky.

William Swan, known as 'Blackie', was killed by a lone gunman during a football match in the city's Maxton Park. Headshot of Swan, cropped from a squad photograph, black-and-blue stripes at his shoulders. Grinning, tanned – the heedless victim.

They had no more details than we had. A cop was interviewed, mild, media-trained, hatless but in uniform, North of England accent. *Want to reassure . . . obviously unusual . . . visible presence . . . everything we can.*

Then they showed the footage. I sat forward, set the bottle on the floor between my feet. It was shaky, coarse-grained, dark. Hard to make it out at first. A jumbled crush of bodies and then a striped shirt blocking the lens. When the stripes move off the ball has squeezed out for a throw-in on the far side. At this point the camera swings round sharply to the touchline: a guy with a greying crewcut mugs a grimace, blows a kiss to the camera. You hear the shots just then – two flat cracks like someone snapping a desk with a ruler – and the camera jiggles nervously and fumbles for focus. Grass. Sky. A muddy blur then the camera steadies, finds it.

A figure on the grass. A dark shadow sprinting away.

The camera tracks the runner, loping off towards the railings. As he reaches the park entrance he turns to look back. We get a still of this, the gunman caught in mid-stride, the torso twisted. Black parka slipping off his shoulders. Baseball cap with the bill pulled down. They'd tried to refine it, enhance it, bring out the features, but the face was still a blank. You'd recognise the gait, the stance, before you clocked the face.

Police are looking for anyone who saw a dark-coloured car parked on Baillieston Road between 11 and 11.25 a.m. Digits on the screen: the incident room at Baird Street; the Crimestoppers number. Please call.

Mari gathered her drawings, slipped them into the portfolio and zipped it. She slapped my thigh, leaned over to kiss my forehead.

'Don't be long.'

I waggled my beer-bottle, two-thirds empty.

'Right behind you.'

A dark-coloured car. Good luck with that. I heard a noise above the news, a muffled crump as though a war report was encroaching on the previous item. I muted the telly and caught it again, the crackle of fireworks. Glitterburst of purple in the window. Guy Fawkes was two weeks off but they jumped the gun a little further each year, the local neds, terrorising the pets of Kelvinside. I necked the dregs of the Sol and fetched a final bottle from the fridge, thumbed a wedge of lemon down the neck.

I flicked through the channels and back to the news. *Ground was broken today on a 36-hectare riverfront site that will house the Athletes' Village for the Commonwealth*

31

Games in 2014. Camera flashes. A fat man in a hard hat, resting his foot on the lip of a spade. Close-up of his fleshy, grinning face, the green 'G' on his yellow hat: Gavin Haining, leader of Glasgow City Council. Cut to artist's impression of Scandinavian-style houses in tasteful clusters, puffy green trees, pedestrians on walkways.

'This will bring the East End back to life,' Haining was saying. 'Nearly eight hundred homes. Eco-friendly. State of the art.'

I knew Haining a little. I'd been to my share of civic receptions, shared his table at charity dinners. A big ebullient figure with a mooing laugh, a clapper of shoulders, a barer of teeth in bonhomous grins.

'And what happens, Councillor Haining, when the Games are over; will these houses be sold as private homes?'

'Some of them, yes. But four hundred of these homes will be reserved for rental accommodation, providing the kind of high-quality social housing this city so desperately needs.'

The reporter said that a grouping of construction firms – the Kentigern Consortium – would oversee the building of the village, but that contracts for sub-contractors would be awarded over the coming weeks and months. There were two more items – a fatal collision on the A9 and a missing Glasgow prostitute – before the anchor handed over to the sports reporter, a fizzy blonde in a tailored jacket, risky inch of cleavage.

The mobile rang, my new iPhone, the ringtone still unfamiliar.

'You see it?'

Lewicki.

'Not exactly Zapruder, is it? Missed the money shot.'

'Yeah. Well.' Lewicki's voice had the belligerent edge. Drink taken. 'We know who it was anyway.'

The football results were coming up on the screen. *If you don't want to know the scores, look away now.* Could be the caption for my life over the past couple of years, I reflected: *Look away now.*

'The shooter?'

'Fuck the shooter. The shooter's immaterial. We know who *did* it.'

We'd beaten Hearts two-nil. The Huns had drawn with Motherwell. Put us four points clear.

'Everyone knows who did it, Jan. Maybe they should claim responsibility. Like they did in Ireland in the old days. Passwords and codenames. P. O'Neill. Still,' I said. 'Happy days on the South Side. Dancing in the streets of Pollok.'

'Shitting their pants is more like it.'

'Payback?'

'You don't shoot a guy playing football. Saturday morning. His old man watching from the sidelines.'

'Swan's dad was there?'

'Aye.' Little kisses came down the line as Lewicki got a cigar going. 'Billy Senior. Hamish Neil's first cousin. They'll feel it down there. Jesus. Shitstorm that's coming.'

*

I walked down to the twenty-four-hour garage for the other Sundays. Papers getting fatter as their readership thinned. Walking back across the bridge in the sharp cold air I checked my phone, scrolled down my Twitter feed:

Kevin Gallacher @kevinrjgallacher1h
Batten down the hatches. Hope I'm wrong but this cld be worse than 2005. Last thing Glw needs w Commie Games arnd corner. #gangwar

Hope I'm wrong. Like fuck you do, Gallo. I checked Moir, too, in case he'd mentioned the killing, but his last tweet was two days old.

Back at the flat I slapped the stack of newsprint onto the table and fetched a final beer. The English qualities had nothing. Not a wing, not a par. There was a page six lead in *Scotland on Sunday* (*Killing Sparks Fears of Gangland Feud*). But the redtops gave it a show. GANG WAR was Gallacher's splash in the *News of the World*. He quoted a source close to 'underworld kingpin Hamish Neil' saying reprisals were certain: 'The Walshes won't know what's hit them.' Aye they will, I thought: Hamish Neil.

But Torcuil Bain in the *Mail* had pissed on us all. They'd splashed with a photo of Swan in a Rangers jersey: soccer starlet slain. Swan was twenty-six; hardly a 'starlet'. But it turned out he'd trialled for Rangers. Bain had dug it up, Swan's football career. Schoolboy international. The teenage trial with the 'Gers that didn't work out. Signed for St Mirren: a leg-break crocked him for a year, cost him a yard. Free transfer to Morton. Dropped down to the Juniors. By this time he was an enforcer for Maitland, but he kept turning out, skippering the local team. On an inside page there was the squad photo of Blackhill United, Swan with the captain's armband, a strip of suddenly sinister black, as if he was in mourning for himself.

A gangland execution with Old Firm overtones. Driscoll would be spitting. We'd led with Swan but the *Mail* would bury us anyway. I looked again at the front-page photo. The bleached-blond spikes. Silver sleeper catching the light. The royal-blue jersey with the lager logo splashed across the chest. He must have been useful, to try out for the Huns. He'd skippered Blackhill to last year's Junior Cup Final. I thought of the weekly write-ups, the match reports in trundling soccerese, *some good work down the left saw Swan release Cunningham.* It wouldn't be hard to target Billy Swan. No need to monitor his movements, study his habits, establish a pattern. All you needed was next week's fixtures, there in black and white in the local paper.

Bain's piece had another scoop: *According to eyewitness reports, the killer was dark-complexioned, possibly of Eastern European origin.* From the footage you could hardly tell a thing about the killer, but I knew what Bain was doing. You never lost sales by blaming the Roma. But a stopped clock's right twice a day and according to Lewicki one of the Roma gangs in Govanhill was working with the Walshes. Frighteners. Disciplinaries. General enforcement. The Walshes farmed these tasks

35

out to their Slovak buddies. Maybe hits were being sub-contracted too.

I pushed the papers away. The TV was still running in the living room. The weather forecast. More snow. Snow in October. I thumbed the remote and killed the picture. There was an ominous rumble in the flat, low throbbing knocks like a rumour of battle. I snapped the box-room light on. The tumble-drier. The clothes flopped in drunken heaves, collapsing onto each other and chasing round again. I watched Angus's vests, the days of the week in a tangled swirl, and padded through to bed.

Chapter Three

I woke up at seven and jumped in the shower. I don't sleep in on Sundays, never need the alarm. Sunday's my day with the boys and my body clock knows it. I've got two sons from my failed marriage. Roddy and James. Nine and six.

I kissed Mari's temple and lifted my keys. Angus's door stood slightly ajar and I eased it open. Little moon face, ghostly in the half-light. I dropped my hand into the cot, felt his breath on the backs of my fingers, laid my knuckles on his cheek: chilled. I slipped two fingers under the collar of his babygro; his back was warm. The baby thermometer on the wall had gone from 'Just Right' to 'Cool'. I settled his blankets. The central heating would be clicking on soon.

White flakes were sifting down through the waste-ground trees. My shoes left black dance-steps on the thin snow. The car started first time. Down Great Western Road, past the lighted minimarts, the headlines under lattice frames: GANGLAND SHOOTING, SOCCER STARLET SLAIN. I thought of people waking up, going out for the paper, fixing brunch with the radio on, chewing toast, reading my piece on the Swan murder.

Moir should have written it. Moir was the expert. He would know the whys of this killing. He knew the language, the precise level of insult offered by the corpse of Billy Swan. When he came back to work he would follow it up, chart the feud when it all kicked off. I big-footed Moir in the old days; now he would bigfoot me. For the moment, though, it was my story and it wasn't the worst feeling in the world to have ended Moir's monopoly on the front page, if only for a week. As the car joined the motorway I put the foot down. Even in my prim, begrudging prose it would boost us by four or five thousand.

The snow had lain on the Fenwick Moors and the whiteness rolled away on either side. I thought of my dad in his coffin, the white billowing satin lining, the tight yellow skin of his nose, the folds of his neck above the white tieless shirt. It was last winter, nearly a year since we travelled this road, the same road in the same weather. He died before I came back to the *Trib* so he never got the chance to ask me: *Why did you come back?* His own question was different. Though he never put it in words, the gaps in his conversation, his non-committal grunts and downcast eyes when I spoke of my new job, asked it for him: *Why did you leave?*

He was a high-school English teacher who dreamed of being a journalist. I was fulfilling his ambition when I signed on at the *Trib*. His hero was George Orwell. Not the novelist, not the visionary allegorist of *Animal Farm* and *1984*, but the hack reporter, the jobbing colum-nist for the *New Statesman*, the *Observer*, the *Manchester Evening News*. He kept the four volumes of *The Collected Essays, Journalism and Letters* in an alcove shelf beside the fireplace and you counted it a lucky day when he didn't say 'Listen to this' after tea and read a passage from 'Revenge is Sour' or 'Books v. Cigarettes' in his correct and earnest reading voice. When I was handed a photocopy of 'Politics and the English Language' on my first day at the *Trib* I was able to hand it straight back. I could probably have recited it from memory, and though I doubtless flouted them in everything I wrote, its rules – 'Never use a long word where a short one will do'; 'If it is possible to cut out a word, always cut it out' – were as familiar to me as the lines on my brow.

My father's paper was the *Tribune*. Every night after tea, before he started his marking, my father sat down with the *Trib*. He would vanish behind the big pages, the vast crackling sheets that only a grown man could manage. You didn't interrupt him. I would watch him in the telly's reflection, his arms spreading as he turned the pages, as though the paper were a set of chest expanders.

When he'd worked his way through to the sports pages he'd close the paper, fold it against the crease and fold it again, fish a biro from the jacket he'd slung on a kitchen chair-back and tackle the crossword.

One night he opened the paper and gave a short laugh. 'Come here,' he told us, 'come and see this.' It was a letter he'd written. They'd printed it there on the letters page, a thin jaggy column of type. He'd written to complain about an editorial branding the striking miners 'fifth columnists'. We looked over his shoulder, my mother, my sister and I, at the words my father was reading aloud. His name was printed beneath the letter, in darker type: Hugh Conway. Our address was there, too: 25 Ellis Street. For the next few days I looked at them both – my father, our house – with new eyes, as if their appearance in print had altered their nature, lent them, however faintly, the glamour of news. My first byline gave me the same sense of magic and even now, when papers mean little to anyone and I recognise my thrill for a childish superstition, I can't suppress that fizz of pride when I see my name in print.

My father died last year, on Christmas Eve. Three months later I was back at the *Trib*. If you think there's a connection between these events, you're probably right. It wasn't quite a dead man's wish, and I didn't go back out of filial duty, but I had plenty of time to think in the small, sky-blue room in the Southern General where my dad's corrupted lungs kept him pinned to the bed when he wasn't dribbling into a cardboard sick-bowl. CONWAY, it said on the chart at the foot of the bed – as it says now on the pink marble stone I have visited twice – and it seemed like all the epitaph he'd want. The name mattered to my father. Though a second-generation Scot, he had the immigrant's sense of the family narrative, the arc of the generations. As if this was America and not the Scottish lowlands. As if the name were bound to rise. Eamonn Conway scraped a living as a pedlar. Michael Conway howked coal in the Ayrshire pits. Hugh Conway stuck in at school and earned his teaching diploma. The logic of the story called for another ascent. Had three generations struggled and toiled in this black-hearted land so that I might frame elegant lies to boost the profits of Scottish Power or the Royal Mail? So I chucked PR and went back to papers. As if that was any better. In almost every way you could name, my action was pointless. The man I was trying to impress was dead. The paper I came back to was dying. The job I took up wasn't the job I had left. It was too late. Everything was too late. But I still went back.

The traffic was sparse, I was making good time. I passed the Covenanter's memorial, the old Celtic cross. I was almost in Ayrshire and the snow had gone, green fields displacing the white moor. The boys would be out of bed now, spooning Sugar Puffs into their mouths, the glare of cartoons dancing in their eyes.

It was nearly eight. I punched the button for the radio, news on the hour.

Strathclyde Police have confirmed that a man killed in Glasgow yesterday had links with organised crime. William Swan, an enforcer for the Neil crime family, was shot dead yesterday morning as he played football at a public park in the city's East End in what police are describing as a gangland execution. The gunman, described as of medium height and dark-complexioned, wearing dark clothes, a white baseball cap and a red tartan scarf, escaped in a waiting car. Commentators have warned that this killing could spark a gangland vendetta similar to the feud that claimed seven lives in the so-called 'Sunbed Wars' of 2005. David Ancram is a true-crime author with extensive contacts in Glasgow's criminal underworld: 'The worry is that this could escalate. The Neils will hit back, there's nothing surer. It's about saving face but it's also good business. They've put a lot of effort into getting where they are and they're not about to give that up without a fight.'

New Scotland, I thought. The early days of a better nation. But Glasgow's civil war ground on, a city like a failing state. The regime controlled the centre and the West End, the good suburbs, the arterial routes. East and north were the badlands, the rebel redoubts, where the tribal warlords held their courts and sacrificed to their vengeful gods. The M8 was the city wall, keeping out the barbarian hordes.

Concerns have been raised that the Yes camp could outspend the No by a factor of two to one in the lead-up to the 2014 independence referendum. While tight spending limits will be imposed on both camps for the official campaigning period, there are no limits on what can be spent in the run-up to the poll, which is still more than two years away. The Nationalists have been buoyed by the recent donation of £1 million to the independence campaign by lottery winners Chris and Margo Chisholm of Saltcoats, which follows an earlier bequest of £1 million by Scotland's late national poet, Cosmo Haldane. A Scottish Labour spokesman accused the Nationalists of attempting to 'buy' the poll. Meanwhile, a former Scottish Secretary has warned that the No campaign may be hampered less by finances than by the lack of a credible leader. Campbell Bain, who served as Scottish Secretary in John Major's cabinet, told an audience at St Andrews University that Malcolm Gordon might carry all before him if no 'big beast' stepped up to lead the pro-Union cause.

I punched the button, killed the radio. The sign for Ayrshire flashed past. Big beasts in the fields, black and white Friesians, not brown-and-white Ayrshires. You never saw Ayrshires any more, not even here. Mureton was coming up shortly, my home town. I thought of it in the past tense; it was the kind of place you left when you hit sixteen and never went back. But Moir lived there, now, the King of Crime. He moved out from the city a year or two back, when their second girl was born. I thought of looking in on him, getting off some gentle gloating over today's front page, but I passed the Mureton turn-off and kept going.

You could smell the sea now, even with the windows up, and when I crested the next rise the town lay before me, the blue roofs of Conwick and the brown sandstone spires, the green hills on one side and the bright dancing firth on the other. Every time I drove down here I felt it more keenly, that pang of regret for the life I had left. At some level – at most levels – I hoped we'd get back together, Elaine and I. Even when I met Mariella and she moved into the flat, even when Mari got pregnant and Angus was born, even then it was hard to envisage a future in which Elaine and Gerry and Roddy and James did not comprise a unit.

She'd been with Adam for four years. They got married last June at Culzean Castle. Roddy and James were Adam's groomsmen. Mari and I were at the second top table, seated with Adam's cousins and Elaine's strident aunt who kept assuring me, in a loud sherry voice, that I would always be her niece's true love. Angus cried through the speeches so I took him out, but even in the bar, jiggling the boy on my shoulder as I stole sups of

Stella, I could hear Adam gamely including Gerry and Mariella ('for their marvellous help and friendship') in his vote of thanks.

I drove down the High Street. The billboards propped outside the Spar had the same headlines as the city. GERS STARLET MURDERED. GANGLAND SLAYING. But down here it was a feelgood story, the kind of thing that made you glad you lived in the boondocks, among the red pillar-boxes and crow-stepped gables, the spry retirees walking their terriers.

Inside the Spar, the papers were stacked on their racks. Billy Swan's face grinned up from the tabs as if he knew he had finally made it. The boy who pissed away his talent, who blew his chance at glory, had got himself shot and killed, an accomplishment that put him, being also a minor functionary in a criminal syndicate, on four front pages. Who else had died in Scotland yesterday? What useful lives were overlooked, what deaths unmarked, so that this little prick, this no-mark thug who had courted his death, could enjoy his redtop ovation?

I bought a loaf and a carton of milk and drove up to the house, thinking about numbers. Seven. That was the figure to beat. Seven lives had been lost in the Sunbed Wars so this one would have to be bigger. The actual logic of the conflict didn't matter, they couldn't stop till the body count was up there, eight bodies, nine, any fewer would be a let-down.

The bell on my old front door gave its usual sardonic clank: one of the chimes was broken. I stood on the doorstep and nudged the loose tile with my toe. I'd never

44

got around to fixing it and Adam hadn't either. This house meant a lot to me, our lives had been good here for a while, but I wished Elaine had bought a new place when she remarried. It's about continuity, she told me. At a time like this the boys need stability, familiar surroundings. I could see her point, but it felt as though everyone's lives had carried on the same, only I'd been replaced, like the male lead in a soap. *Bewitched* with Dick Sargent instead of Dick York.

'Dad!'

The door slammed back on its hinges as James launched himself at me. He buried his head in my belly, threw his arms round my back. Roddy hung back, his hand raised in greeting. 'Hiya, Dad.'

'Hey, guys.'

'Is it snowing, Dad? Is it snowing in Glasgow?'

'It is.' The snow never lies in Conwick. It's too near the sea. The Gulf Stream waters keep the temperatures up. There are palm trees in the gardens of the shorefront B & Bs. 'Yeah, it's lying.'

'How deep?'

'I don't know.' I measured a couple of inches between my palms. 'About that much.'

'Can we bring the sledge?'

'Of course you can. Bring your togs too, we'll go the pool.'

I made a coffee while the boys got ready. Elaine and Adam were still in bed. There was a new picture on the kitchen wall, a framed poster from the 'Glasgow Boys' exhibition at Kelvingrove: a wee girl in muddy boots herding a line of geese. I shouted through as we left and Elaine shouted to wait.

She came through in her dressing-gown, took the boys' heads in her hands, kissed them in turn. Her face had the soft, slept-in look and her hair was unbrushed but she still looked good.

'Heavy night?'

She shook her head. 'Heavy week. Heavy life.'

I didn't ask.

'Can you have them back by six? Roddy's got pipes.'

We spent the morning in Kelvingrove Park, sledging down the hills, rolling down bankings, lying on our backs making angels, starring the flanks of an equestrian statue with pelted volleys of snowballs. We warmed up and dried off in the museum, wandering round the Scottish Wildlife room, craning up at the Spitfire suspended in the entranceway. We ate lunch in the Silverburn mall, browsed in the games shop and then I drove us to the swimming baths.

We spent the next hour on the flumes, slapping up the spiralling concrete ramp and hanging onto the overhead bar till the green light sent us plunging, one after another, down the gloomy, translucent tube. The boys laughed and started back up the ramp, moving lightly on the balls of their feet. I saw how little they needed me now, how much they'd grown, though it seemed to me to be no time at all since they'd clung to my neck as we entered the water, their legs gripping tight round my torso, their toenails scratching my sides.

Before we left they dragged me across to the diving

boards. I hate heights. Climbing the stairs I stamped to quell the tremor in my knees. The middle board was four metres high but it felt like the top of a building. The swimming-pool noise – all the echoey shouts and splashes and cries – seemed to rise from a fabulous distance. A yard from the edge my soles wouldn't lift from the board so I slid the last few paces. The diving pool looked too dark, its water a deep marine blue, not the light sunny turquoise of the other pools. But my sons were stamping and shivering behind me so I closed my eyes and stepped off.

The rush of bubbles seemed to go on forever but I finally reached the bottom of the plunge, that long silent interim when you're not sinking or rising or floating but just suspended in water like a bubble in ice before the reverse gravity sucks you back to the surface. I kicked to the side and held on, watched my sons' pale bodies drop through the air.

We were driving back to Conwick, the car stinking pleasantly of chips and pickled onions, Muddy down low on the Bose – 'Goodbye Newport Blues' – and the white fields rolling away under a black sky.

'Dad?'

'What?'

'Does Angus not like the swimming baths?'

'Yeah,' I said. 'He does. He goes with Mari sometimes. "Tadpoles." It's a mother-and-baby thing.'

We drove for a bit.

'*You* should take him,' said Roddy. 'Or bring him with us.'

'I do take him. I take him sometimes. Anyway, this is your time. You don't want to have a baby around all the time.'

'He's nearly two, Dad. He's my brother.'

I watched the road. Roddy craned round in his seat.

'I just think you should spend more time with him, Dad.'

I reached out a finger to the sound system, turned Muddy down even further.

'Did Mariella ask you to say this?'

'I'm eleven years old, Dad. I can think for myself.'

'That's not what I asked you.'

'We spoke about it. Mari thinks you should spend more time with Angus. And I agree.'

He popped a chip into his mouth with a rhetorical flourish.

'Okay, Rod. Well. I appreciate your concern.'

'Good.'

'I'll bring him next time.'

'Good.'

*

Within the hour I was back up the motorway, back in the flat. Mari was Facebooking her Kiwi friends. I was giving Angus his bath. I had soaped his hair when I heard the phone, then Mari coming through. She knelt down beside Angus while I took the phone through to the living room.

'Gerry.' I couldn't place the voice for a minute. I was

48

still thinking about Angus, how I hadn't rinsed his hair. 'Gerry, it's Fiona Maguire. I've got some bad news.'

For a second I thought, *she's going to fire me again.*

'It's Martin Moir,' she said. 'Gerry, he's dead. Martin's dead. They found his body in Auchengare Quarry.'

Chapter Four

A climber had called it in. The quarry's a popular spot with local craggers. Early on Sunday a hospital administrator called Mark Alexander was scaling the main buttress. Low down, at ground level, you can't see into the water. All you can see is the glare, or the surface shirred by the wind. But the higher you climb, the deeper you see. Halfway up the route the climber starts to notice something between his boots: a white shape, a milky cube in the bottle-green deep. He knows it's recent; he'd climbed the same route the week before. When he gets to the top he calls the police. It's the white roof of Moir's CR-V. The frogmen find the body in the car.

'Jesus.'

'Yeah.' Maguire looked at me, a question in her eyes: did you know something about this? Are you holding out on me here?

I shook my head. We were in Maguire's office, the corner suite with its views across the river to the Finnieston crane, the Armadillo, the latticed façades of the north bank hotels.

I turned to look out at the newsroom floor.

Everyone knew. You could tell from how they carried themselves: something angular, a tightness of the limbs. Little knots of people at the desks, gathering to share the news. The furtive eyes, the rapt looks, greedy. How they touched each other when they spoke, hands resting on forearms. The office was buzzing with Martin's death.

Maguire sucked a breath between her teeth.

'We'll make an announcement.'

I nodded. There was something else, too, I thought, looking out on the floor. Not just grief but professional embarrassment. How did we miss it? Moir's death was pitiful, shocking, cruel. It was also a story. A story that every paper would carry tomorrow morning: it was here in this room and we missed it.

'Ten o'clock,' she said. 'Niven's coming down to the floor.'

'That's good.'

Back at my desk I clicked through my bookmarked sites – the Beeb, Scottishwire, the Scottish and English dailies – but my eyes kept straying to Moir's blue chair, his abandoned can, the smiling blonde heads of his daughters. When Maguire had phoned me the previous night I'd gone out for a walk. It was cold – the snow had mostly gone but a freeze was starting, the puddles were chewy and creaked like floorboards – and I crossed the bridge and started up Great Western Road. I was trying to remember Moir's age, thirty-four, thirty-five, he was younger than me by five or six years. I turned into West-bourne Gardens, passed the Struthers Memorial Church. The houses here had a rich honey hue, the stone glowing warm in the yellow streetlights. There were curtains undrawn, still-life living rooms with opulent blood-red walls, bright blurred Peploes and Cursiters, bookshelves

51

of deep seasoned wood. There was nothing of Moir or myself in these rich framed rooms, just the mystery of unknown lives, the pathos of domestic space, but I had to pause for a spell on the pavement, beneath one of these bright yellow squares, leaning on the smooth iron railings.

At ten o'clock we stood by our desks beneath the muted TVs as Niven emerged from the lift. Teddy Niven was the *Tribune* group's Managing Editor. You rarely saw him in the newsroom. He was a distant figure, up there on the sixth floor, a short man with brittle hair and small pointed teeth that he bared in a strained smile. If you met him in the lift he just nodded and looked away; below the level of editor, he didn't know anyone's name.

When he spoke to his staff it was always through his editors – Maguire at the Sunday, John Tulloch at the Daily. The fact that he was here, awkwardly by the vending machine, twisting his wedding ring, meant that it was serious. He stood in his shirtsleeves, a small dapper fellow in scarlet braces, like someone impersonating a newspaperman.

As he waited for silence we shuffled back, making sure those behind us could see. An atmosphere of punctilious politeness had established itself in the newsroom. We knew what Niven would say, but we wanted to be equal to the moment, standing in our reverent circle like mourners round the grave.

Finally Niven spread his arms, twisting his torso from left to right, surveying the heads, his dainty paunch nosing over his waistband.

'You have all heard the news.' He spoke low – or at least he didn't raise his voice – so that we all craned forward to hear. 'Martin Moir, Investigations Editor on our Sunday paper, was found dead at the weekend. His body was recovered from a car in Auchengare Quarry on Sunday morning.'

He paused then, looking down at his shoes. The gesture looked rehearsed, but Niven's face, when he raised it, was blurry and flushed, aswim with emotion.

'We do not yet know – and neither do the police – what happened to Martin. Whether this was suicide or—' His raised hand waggled in the air for a second then dropped to his side. 'Or not.

'There will be rumours.' He cleared his throat. 'There will be speculation. In the canteen. In the Cope. From your colleagues on other papers. I ask you now, for the good of the paper, and out of respect for Martin, please do not add to this. Don't gossip. Wait until we know the facts.'

The word *facts* he gave a peculiar, cushioned emphasis, almost breathing the word, as if facts were such fragile, furtive creatures that the smallest unruly sound might scatter them.

At his elbow, Maguire frowned fiercely, her specs flashing green in the overhead lights.

Niven kept twisting his wedding band.

'Over the coming days, Strathclyde Police will visit the building. They may want to question some of those who worked closely with Martin. We will of course co-operate in every way we can with their investigation.'

He scanned the faces again. He smiled an odd tight smile.

'For the next few days, this newspaper' – he pointed at the floor beside his feet; 'this newspaper is part of the news. It has happened before; it will happen again. We will not lose our heads. We will go about our business and we will do our jobs to our usual high standards. We will report Martin's death in tomorrow's paper. Sunday staff, you will wait to see how things develop. We will want a feature on Martin's career and, of course, obituaries in both papers. John and Fiona' – the cone of his belly turned on Maguire – 'will fill you in at conference.'

He stood there glancing nervously round. We wondered if he was finished. A phone rang at a far desk and we had started to break up when he spoke again.

'This is a difficult time,' he said. We shuffled back into position. 'A difficult time. For all of us. Martin Moir was – well, you don't need me tell you what kind of journalist Martin Moir was. He was a great investigative reporter in the finest traditions of this newspaper.' He looked round sharply at that point, as if he expected someone to contradict him. 'But be that as it may' – he wiped it all away with a languid hand; Martin's death; his standing as a journalist; the words he'd just spoken: 'Be that as it may, we have work to do. The best tribute we can pay to Martin is to keep making this paper as good as we can make it.'

This time he was finished. He gave a brief, military nod and clipped back to the lift. There were two or three disjointed claps but nobody took them up.

When Niven left it broke the spell, released the grief that had massed in the air. We hugged each other. We wandered the newsroom, patting shoulders and gripping elbows, clapping each other's backs. It was like the HQ of the losing party on election night. But there was something else. A little flicker in the eyes. A charge of static in the air as we resumed our desks. This was a story. This was our story. What kind of a spike would it give to the sales? Even in death Moir would jockey us one last boost. The *Scotsman* would take a tanking tomorrow.

Two hours later I was writing the obit. Conference had been short. Maguire raced us through the schedule. The referendum, house prices, the new anti-sectarian bill: Driscoll, the News Editor, flagged up Sunday's leads. Neve McDonald gave her curt, bored preview of the magazine. Carson, the new sports guy, ran through his roster of Old Firm transfers, manager profiles, flagged up a rumour about the taxman chasing Rangers for using EBTs.

'EB whats?' Maguire screwed her face up.

'Employee Benefit Trusts.' Carson consulted his notes. 'It's an offshore thing. You pay players without paying tax on top. It's how you afford the big names.'

'Cheating?' Maguire said. 'Financial doping?'

'Well. Probably come to nothing. I'll keep you posted.'

'Do that then. Nothing else? Good. Let's talk about Martin.'

We did. Seven days earlier he had been sitting at this table, eating Marks & Spencer sandwiches with the rest of us. Now he was the news.

As Niven had observed, we didn't know the facts. We still didn't know if it was suicide or a drunken accident. But whichever door opened, something nasty would come out. Secrets and sins. The old unforeseeable mess. The kind of stuff we dug up about bent councillors and access-peddling cabinet ministers.

We are the news. I looked round the polished table, the troubled faces. They didn't like it. The telescope was the wrong way round and it made them uneasy. Working at a paper, you think you're bombproof. You visit chaos on other people. Chaos doesn't visit you.

It didn't bother me. I'd been there before. Four years back a gangster I exposed in a front-page lead turned out to be an undercover cop. I looked a little stupid for a couple of weeks as my failings were rehearsed in a dozen blogs and columns. Even at the time, though, it wasn't that bad. Disgrace. Obloquy. It wasn't so awful. What I mainly felt was relief. At not having to be right all the time, not having to pretend to know it all. Hands up. *Mea culpa*. I got it wrong.

'If anyone knows anything,' Maguire was saying, 'now would be a good time.'

Her gaze rested on me for a moment and I stared her out. There was a general crossing of arms and sucking in of lips around the table. Maguire looked around the vacant faces.

'Okay,' she said. 'But no surprises, people. If Martin was in trouble, if he was involved in something, it's better we break it than somebody else. If there *is* an issue and it turns out that one of you knew—' She flicked her wrist to indicate some swingeing repercussion further down the line.

By four o'clock that afternoon I was proofing the obit. I had gathered Moir's cuttings for the past six months. I had phoned his former editor at the *Belfast Telegraph* and spoken to some of his colleagues there. I was trying to do him, I want to say 'justice', but where's the justice in taking a man's life and boiling it down into eight hundred words? I was on the final par when I raised my head to see a man pointing at me from Maguire's office as Maguire and another woman followed the line of his finger. Then Maguire poked her head out and beckoned me over.

Jesus, that was quick, was my thought as I crossed the floor. Maguire passed me on the way in. There were two cops, a woman and a man. They were using Maguire's office for their interviews. The woman was in charge.

She nodded at the door and I closed it. I eased into the vacant chair.

'We're sorry to take you away from your work,' the woman said. She was leafing through papers. She didn't look sorry.

'That's alright,' I said. 'I could use a break.'

'Good.' She clasped her hands on the desk. 'I'm Detective Sergeant Gunn and this is Detective Constable Lumsden.'

Lumsden and I nodded at each other. He was big, prematurely bald, with an ugly prop-forward's mug. He wore a rumpled lilac shirt and leather jacket. His silver and purple tie was ugly too. Gunn was neat and pretty, fair hair back in a scrunchie.

'You're the Political Editor, right?'

'Yeah. On the Sunday.'

'What are you working on?'

'You mean right now?'

'Right now. What are you writing?'

Maguire would have told her.

'I'm doing the obit, Martin's obituary.'

She looked young to be a sergeant. Certainly she was younger than I was, younger, too, than the gloomy Lumsden.

'You knew him well, then?'

Lumsden had his biro out, elbows spread on the desk.

'I don't know. I thought I did.'

Her accent was hard to place. It wasn't Highland but the vowels had a lightness and bounce. It might have been Canadian but it wasn't that, either.

'Your editor says he was closest to you. Out of all the employees.'

I shrugged. 'That's not saying much.'

'You mean he didn't have many friends among the staff?'

'I mean he wasn't here much. He worked from home a lot, when he wasn't out on a story.'

She nodded, looked down at her notes. 'When did you see him last? Outside the office, I mean.'

DC Lumsden looked stolidly on, the point of his biro pressing his pad. He looked like a waiter taking an order.

'Two weeks ago. I took a present down for his

58

daughter's birthday.' I paused. 'She's my god-daughter.'

'You're godfather to Martin Moir's daughter?'

I nodded.

'That sounds pretty close.'

I shrugged. 'Yeah. Well it wasn't close enough, was it?'

She smiled at the desk and tucked a loose strand of hair behind her ear. She enjoyed her job – you could see that. I don't mean that she relished the power over others or that proximity to murder and calamity thrilled her – though that may have been true. She enjoyed the game, that's all – the challenge, the pursuit. I almost wished I had something to hide, to give her the pleasure of teasing it out.

The face was composed again when she raised it.

'He ever speak about problems? Debts? Marital issues? Depression?'

I snorted. 'The guy was an Ulster Prod, officer, nobody tell you that? They're not big on confession.'

'Never sounded off? Not about anything?'

I frowned. 'Piss and moan a bit in the pub. Like everyone else. He had it pretty good, though. He didn't have too much to complain about.'

'Special treatment,' she said. 'The star turn. Lot of professional jealousy?'

'You mean me?' I smiled. 'Was I jealous? Yeah, probably. Might take a little more than that, though, to drive a man to suicide.'

'Right.' She was looking through her notes again. 'What was his actual job here: he was chief crime reporter?'

'Yeah. He was Investigations Editor. He went after the big players.' I paused. 'Did a better job than your lot.'

59

'Yeah, well.' She smiled again. 'Knowing who did it's generally the easy bit, Mr Conway. Hard bit's proving it in court. So Moir got results?'

'Now and again.'

'Piss people off?'

I shrugged. 'It's in the job spec.'

'Someone in particular?'

'What?'

'He piss off any players? Southside? East End? The Walshes, Neils?'

There was something wrong here. I looked across at Lumsden.

'Hold on. This was suicide, right?'

The cops exchanged glances.

'We don't know, Mr Conway.' Gunn was looking at her papers again. 'We haven't determined that yet.'

'But it might be murder?'

She nodded. I looked across at Lumsden again and back at Gunn.

'What makes you think it was murder?'

'We don't think it was murder.'

'But you think it might be.'

Gunn exchanged another glance with Lumsden. It was Lumsden who spoke.

'He was tied to the wheel.'

'What?'

Lumsden's pen skittered onto the table. He held up his hands with the wrists turned out, like a man wearing handcuffs.

'Ligatures round his wrists. His wrists were lashed to

60

the steering wheel.'

'Jesus Christ.'

The image came unbidden. The car smacking the surface, water surging in, the body thrashing and bucking, trying to wrench free.

'Someone tied him to the wheel?'

'We don't know. He might have done it himself.' Gunn stood up from the table. 'It's not uncommon. You keep the hands close together, tie the knots loosely. Pull them tight with your teeth.'

'Oh Christ.'

She gathered her papers, slipped them in a folder. Lumsden stood up too and tucked his notebook into his inside pocket. In his bulky, shapeless jacket he looked like an upright bear.

'Thank you for your time, Mr Conway.' Gunn put a business card on the table and slid it across. 'If anything comes to you.'

'Of course. Aye.'

The two of them left and I sat there for a minute, my hands flat on the table. Could Moir have been murdered? Could a *Tribune* reporter of fourteen years' standing, the current Scottish Journalist of the Year, could a man like this have been taken out? I thought of the offices of the *Sunday Citizen* in Belfast, a narrow room down an alley in the Cathedral Quarter, a building with security doors and bullet-proof glass. Four years back I stood in an alcoholic haze while the editor – who'd been standing me drinks for most of the afternoon in the Duke of York – showed me the polished brass plaque on the wall. It bore the name of the *Citz*'s Special Reporter, Brendan O'Dowd, a guy with three kiddies. He was shot in the head by Loyalist paramilitaries, murdered for writing the truth. That's what happened in Belfast. Not here. Not on the mainland, things were different here.

I heard Maguire come in, close the door behind her.

'You hear this?' I said. 'They're saying it could be murder.'

'I know.'

A look passed between us: *Could be a bigger story than we thought.* I looked down at the table. Maguire turned to the window, fiddled with the roller blind.

'Let's sit on this for the moment, Gerry. Let's not get carried away.'

Back in my chair, I added Gunn's card to the pile on my desk.

*

At dinner that evening I cut Angus's gammon into tiny cubes and quartered his potatoes, quartered them again, pretended to salt his food when I salted my own, trailed a bootlace of ketchup over the lot. He set to work cheerily with his blue plastic spoon. Mari talked about work, how busy she was, how challenged, how she loved being back. Six months ago she'd started back part-time at an architects' firm on St Vincent St. The firm had been great. When she took the job she got pregnant three months later. That was three years ago but they kept her job open, they were glad she was back. The Commie Games was in the offing and the bids had begun – they were working flat out on plans and costings and could use all the help they could get. Mari's main client was a firm bidding for the velodrome contract, parts of the athletes' village.

I tried to stay focused, nodding and grunting, chewing my food, but I kept thinking back to Niven's talk. Wait till we know the facts. That used to be our job, didn't it – finding the facts? What facts would the cops find out? What facts did we miss, what facts might have shown us that Moir was in trouble, edging towards that hole in the ground? And how come his friend and closest colleague, his daughter's godfather, failed to spot them?

After dinner I scraped the plates, ran them under the hot tap, stacked the dishwasher. I sprayed the worktops and wiped then down. I ran a bath for Angus, washed his hair without getting water in his eyes, let the mirror steam up while he dunked and emptied his plastic cups, puddling the bathroom floor. I dried him in front of the living-room fire, read his little stack of picture books, put him to bed. I dug the Blue Mountain out of the freezer, made a pot of coffee, took a cup to Mari. Eventually, you run out of things to do, ways to put it off. You tip some Islay into your coffee and sit down at the table, punch the numbers.

A woman answered. Posh voice, Scottish, touch of English: the sister up from Manchester. Clare was sleeping. She'd been sedated, she couldn't come to the phone. I wasn't sorry. How do you talk to a woman whose husband has done what Moir had done? I'd done enough death knocks to know how it worked: grief, bereavement, the hunger for blame. Blame themselves, blame the victim, blame you. I asked the sister to pass on my condolences, tell Clare I'll call in a couple of days.

Chapter Five

Sunday evening. A back-to-school feeling pervaded the flat. The boys had been with us all day. It was time to take them back, to drive Rod and James down to Conwick. James was playing on the carpet with Angus, building little towers of coloured bricks that Angus would joyfully smack to pieces. Some kids were riding a motorbike on the wasteground across the street, the engine's whine rising and receding.

'There's your phone, Dad.'

Rod was slumped on the couch, the black hyphen of his Nintendo DS barring his eyes.

'What?'

'Over there.' He pointed with his stockinged foot, the game still fixed before his face. 'I left it on the bookcase. It's needing charged.'

'You had my phone?'

'Yeah.' He sat up a little from his horizontal slouch, worked himself up with his shoulders. He glanced up blankly. 'I must have put it in my pocket when I used it last weekend. Remember I was out of credit and I phoned Mum?'

'Jesus, Rod.' I turned the phone over in my hands, as if inspecting it for damage. 'I've just spent four hundred quid on a new one. You couldn't have let me know?'

'Sorry, Dad.'

I shook my head. There was more to say but I bit it back. We'd be leaving for Conwick in half an hour, there was no point in picking a fight.

I drove them down to Ayrshire after tea. When I got back to the flat, Angus was down and Mari was making inroads on a bottle of Merlot.

'There's a glass on the breakfast bar.'

We watched *Newsnight* and *Newsnight Scotland*. Mari went to bed and I found Season 5 of *The Wire*, put it on while I tanned a couple of beers. It was one o'clock when I drained the last Sol. As I turned off the kitchen light I saw the phone, the bright square of its display window, on the breakfast bar. I had plugged it in before taking Rod and James back to Conwick. It would be charged by now. I flipped it open and turned it on and stood there in the dark. I would do the voicemails later; for now I scrolled down the messages.

To call it a premonition would be wrong. But as I thumbed down through Maguire and Mari and the others, I knew it was coming. Moir almost never texted me, he preferred to phone. And yet here it was: 'MM'. I checked the date: 9 October, 7.56 p.m. Fifteen hours before the climber found him.

Ger I had 2 do it tell C Im sorry 4 it all MM

I laid the phone down on the breakfast bar. I could hear the clock, the hollow knocks of the second-hand jerking round, and then the fridge thrummed loudly as the cycle changed. I stood in the dark for a few minutes longer. Then I turned off the phone.

*

In the morning I called DS Gunn and by nine o'clock she was thumbing the buzzer.

Mari had just left for work and the nursery run. I was clearing away the breakfast dishes and half-listening to Sky News on the telly. I opened the door and heard them climbing the stairs, Gunn and the lumbering Lumsden.

They trooped through to the living room. Nobody spoke. The cold came in on their outdoor clothes.

I found the message and passed her the phone. She looked at me when she read it, no expression, passed the phone to Lumsden. Lumsden nodded and passed it back; he was sweating from the climb. Gunn held the phone in her palm as if weighing it. They looked at me.

'He forgot,' I said. 'He's a ten-year-old kid. I thought I had lost it.'

Gunn looked away at the television and then back at me.

'It could have been a murder enquiry,' she said. 'We hadn't ruled it out. And you're sitting on the crucial piece of evidence. A week goes by and now you produce it?'

'Yeah, it's not ideal. I understand that. I'm sorry.'

She was shaking her head.

'We'll need this.' She dropped the phone into a plastic wallet, slipped the wallet into a document case, got me to sign the production label. 'And you weren't close.

He sends you his suicide note but you weren't close.'
She shook her head. *Orkney*, I thought: the accent was
Orkney. I pictured a garden-sized island, treeless turf, a
whitewashed cottage in a raging gale.

They turned to go. I followed them down the hall.
Gunn paused on the threshold.

'That's everything is it?'

Lumsden was already on the stairs but he stopped to
hear my answer.

'Everything what?'

'No more surprises, no last-minute revelations?'

'I've said I'm sorry, Sergeant. You think I did it on
purpose?'

She shook her head again, the ponytail twitching.

'He's a ten-year-old boy,' I said to her back. 'They forget things. It happens.'

'We'll be in touch.'

They scliffed off down the stairs.

And that was it. Moir had killed himself. His death
no longer mattered. His death was now an annoyance, a
waste of time. They had squandered a week on Moir, a
week they could have spent on deaths that counted.

I made a coffee and phoned Maguire.

'There's a note,' I told her. 'He left a message on my
phone, the night he died. It was suicide, Fiona.'

I told her the message. I could read the silence as if she
was speaking. The big story was gone; Moir wasn't
murdered, that dramatic splash wouldn't happen. But the
message, that was a story in itself – tragic journo's last
words.

'You want to write it?' she said.

'No.'

'No, you're right. I'll get the Desk on to it.'

*

I stood at the window to finish my coffee. The wind was whipping through the wasteground across the street, lashing the long grasses, agitating the trees. There was a sad little patch of allotments at the far side, started by the local community group, the kind of upbeat, cargo-panted young parents who referred to the wasteground as 'North Kelvin Meadow'. Kids from Maryhill hung out there at nights, built their fires, smoked blow, smashed Buckie bottles on the scout-hut walls. It was another dead space in the disintegrating city.

Moir had reached out to me after all. Not for help – he was past the stage of helping – but to pass on the message. His final words. It was a scoop of sorts, a last sad exclusive, though the words didn't sound like Moir's. I couldn't hear his voice, couldn't place his Ulster vowels in the choppy text-speak: *Ger I had 2 do it tell C Im sorry 4 it all.* All what? Maybe at that stage 'all' is all there is. All or nothing, and nothing to choose between them.

I was sorry, too. Sorry to learn that Moir had taken his life. Murder would have made more sense, would have measured the worth of what he did, a job so important it cost him his life. His stories might have survived him then – stood apart from his death, served as his memorial.

But suicide changed all that. In killing himself Moir had killed his stories. They weren't his legacy, they were just another feature of the world he threw away, they were part of the 'all' for which he was sorry.

And if Moir's were worth nothing then what about mine? Had I written a proper story since I came back to the *Trib*? Had I even tried? I tried to write well. I took as much time as my deadline allowed. I transcribed my interviews faithfully. My facts, such as they were, got checked. But the real job – the job of finding stories that needed to be told, of bringing truth to light, of telling people things they didn't know: that was a job for somebody else.

Martin Moir had been doing that job. At some level, it seemed to me, he'd been doing it for both of us. Back in the Nineties Moir had come to the *Trib* to work beside me. I brought him on, schooled him, taught him his trade. I felt responsible for Moir, as if his current work could be chalked up to my credit. And now that he was gone, that fiction was over. I was just me, Gerry Conway, no-mark jobbing journo.

I finished my coffee and drove to the gym, spent a weary half-hour on the treadmill, another half-hour with the weights. After a shower I drove to the office. Monday was my day off but so what? We'd have days off in plenty when the paper went under, when the *Tribune*'s last issue hit the stands. Lately I'd been spending more of my Mondays at the Quay. I wasn't trying to look keen or impress the Yanks – it was too late for that. I just liked to sit at my desk in the newsroom, staring at our ghostly reflections in the window. Being a journalist while I still could.

I looked in at the Cope on the way home. Carson, the new Sports Ed, was stood at the bar, getting a round in.

'Jesus Christ, Gerry.'

'I know.'

He was shaking his head.

'You heard about—'; he held out his wrists, like a prisoner being cuffed.

'Aye.'

'Jesus, eh? He wasn't kidding on.'

'It wasn't a cry for help.'

'That's for fucking sure.'

I ordered a pint of Deuchars, took a booth at the back, next to the dartboard. Professional jealousy? I'd lost count of the hours we'd spent in booths like this, bad-mouthing Martin Moir. At first, when people bitched about Moir, I took his part. Moir was the talent, he was shifting papers, he was keeping us all in a job. It wasn't a million years since I'd been the golden boy and I felt a kind of nostalgic solidarity with the Ulsterman. But there's limited fun in defending a man whom your peers have determined to hate, and I'd noticed that lately, when someone mouthed off about Moir, I busied myself with whatever I was doing and stayed silent.

I was jealous. Not of Moir's perks, I don't think; not of the Lexus in the car park or the long lunches or even his arrogant freehold on the front page. I was jealous of Moir's job. His brief, his beat. When I started at the paper I wrote crime. I sat in the High Court and the Sheriff

71

Court and took my shorthand notes and I wrote up my stories of murder and mayhem. I met cops and liked them and they liked me. I was happy. Then the day came when John Fyfe called me into the office and gave me the news. I was moving up. Political Correspondent. In a few years' time I could be Political Editor. I took his fat hand in mine and let him clap me on the back but even then, as I smelled his rank cologne, I knew it was a comedown. I'd left the pure realm of story for the palace of lies.

There were ghosts that evening when I got home from work. The first one rang the bell as we finished dinner. Angus held my legs while the ghost stood in our kitchen and took three attempts to complete a limerick. His friend was a vampire with a knock-knock joke. There were two more posses of neighbourhood kids – zombies and Hobbits, buccaneers and superheroes. We gave them lollies and chocolates, dropped fistfuls of monkey nuts in their supermarket carrier bags, and they trooped down the stairs with their swag, their voices ringing in the stair-well.

Later that evening I sat at my desk, checking the PA, the Beeb, Slugger, Scottishwire, the reputable blogs, the disreputable blogs. Nothing on the Walshes: Hamish Neil wasn't trick-or-treating down Govanhill way or out in Pollok. Nothing on the referendum. The Glasgow pro was still missing, six days and counting. A roadside bomb in Helmand province had killed two British soldiers.

Chapter Six

'That's your idea of a story, Fiona? Nothing's happened yet. "The news is there is no news." How is that a story?'

'A blog post, then. The mood on the streets. Climate of fear. A city holds its breath.'

'It's like we want it to happen. We're egging them on. *Gee the fuck up and start topping each other. We've got papers to sell.*'

Maguire was smiling. 'Gerry. Thing is, I'm not pitching this. I'm not inviting a debate. I'm your editor. Now go and fucking write it.'

At least it wasn't snowing. I drove along Paisley Road West, down Eglinton Street, parked the Forester on Westmoreland Street. Maguire's idea was to do a feature on the communities who would suffer the brunt of Neil's revenge. What did it feel like in Govanhill, in Pollok, waiting for the sky to fall?

It felt like anywhere else in the city as I left the car, took to the mid-morning southside streets. For years, now, Govanhill had been the city's blackspot, the rancid backdrop to all the crime reports we couldn't stop reading. In scores of exposés, some of them written by Moir, the name had acquired an aura, the tinge of stigma. The irony here was that Govanhill looked alright. A little shitty and shabby, but this wasn't one of the Sixties misadventures,

73

the no-go zones of broken lifts and gangland murals that pitted the city. Externally, at least, this was solid Victorian Glasgow, street upon street of bluff orange tenements.

I turned the corner onto Allison Street. A gorgeous Pakistani woman was striding towards me in a sky-blue sari with silver tassels, silver-lamé high heels, stepping through the dogshit and burst cardboard boxes, the pigeons nipping at the spent kebabs.

I walked on, past the bookies, the Jeddah Food Store, another bookies, a Western Union and the Queen's Park Pawnbrokers. I stopped under the Guinness sign and the plastic Sky Sports banner of Neeson's Bar.

Years ago Govanhill was Irish. When the Pakistanis moved in, the Irish moved out – to Newlands and Shaw-lands – but they kept their pubs. When the Pakistanis traded up to Pollokshields they kept their shops and their buildings. The landlords here were mostly Pakistani and their tenants were the Pakistani poor and the white Scottish poor and the city's most recent wave of poor migrants: A8s from the accession states, Czechs and Slovaks, mainly Roma.

Neeson's was quiet. Two old boys sat side by side at a scuffed table, long-nursed pints of lager before them, heads craned to watch the racing. I ordered a half of Guinness. The barman poured it and went back to his paperback. It would be fair to say that a climate of fear had yet to establish itself in Neeson's Bar. Climate of fear about your pint not lasting till lunchtime. Climate of fear about losing your pound each way on the 3.15 from Goodwood. I sank the black and left them to it. Maybe

Pollok would be more promising.

I drove down Pollokshaws Road, took the Barrhead Road through the golf course and into Pollok. I hadn't been in the scheme for eight or nine years. The old Pollok Centre had gone, replaced by the shiny new Silverburn Mall, but the streets round the Haugh Hill featured the same old white-harled four-in-a-blocks and three-storey flats. Pollok was the oldest of the big four peripheral schemes, built in the Fifties to house the families cleared from the central slums. The Walshes were the powers-that-be around here but you didn't see them at weekly surgeries, you didn't see them in constituency offices on the Crookston Road. What you saw, on a weekday lunch-time, was the usual outer-urban cast of moochers, mums and toddlers, shuffling old men. There was no story here, no danger of a story ever happening. I pulled over and phoned Lewicki.

'A tout? I think you mean a CHIS, Gerry.'

'A what?'

'Covert Human Intelligence Source. All the best cops have them.'

He explained it to me. The Regulation of Investigatory Powers (Scotland) Act 2000 brought a new set of rules to the handling of touts. A tout now had to be registered. And a tout was no longer a tout, but a Covert Human Intelligence Source. Only a registered CHIS could be tasked to go out and find specific information. Only an approved officer could handle a CHIS, and only a seni-or officer – Assistant Chief Constable or above – could sanction an op. You had to show forms, permission slips, operational reports: every time you used a tout you had to drop half a week on the paperwork.

'And you do this?'

'Are you stupid, Gerry? Do I fuck.'

'So have you got one?'

He was quiet for a bit. 'Maybe. Call you back in ten.'

Lewicki's tout worked part-time as a janitor in the Community Centre on Langton Road. Within half an hour he was sitting in the passenger seat of the Forester, smelling strongly of turpentine ('I was varnishing the sideboard'), his thirty-quid fee in his boiler-suit pocket. He was a bit put out when he heard what I wanted.

'The *mood* of the place?' He squished round to face me, shaking his head. 'The fucking *mood* of the place?'

I had hurt his professional pride. He was used to being asked for a name. A time. Some precise piece of data only he could divulge. Not something anyone could answer.

I tried again. 'I mean, what are they saying about it, the Walshes? Are they nervous, scared? Are they taking, you know, precautions?'

Again the pitying look. 'Well they're not being silly about it. They're keeping the head down. But that's the wrong question, son.'

'So what's the right one?'

'Who killed Billy Swan? Because I'll tell you something, son. No one round here's got a clue.' He nodded importantly, tapped a finger on the dashboard. 'No one's got a clue. Maybe some of the young ones, or the gyppos up in Govanhill – maybe they did it on their own, make a name for themselves. But no one ordered it. No one

76

green-lighted it here. Alright, son? We done?'

I thanked him as he wrestled out of the car. This was as close to a vox pop as I was going to get. I watched him stroll down the hill, arms braced for action, the keelie roll. How did you make a mood piece out of this? A carnaptious old grass in a stained boiler-suit.

I drove straight home from Pollok, back to the cold empty flat. I'd set the fire that morning and now I lit it, watched the blue flames play on the firelighter cubes, the twists of newspaper flare and blacken, the thin ribs of kindling quicken and blaze. I stuck two blocks of larch on top. I found an old fleece and pulled it on and lay on the couch watching the flames pouring round the yellow blocks, and wondered why I couldn't get warm.

'Daddy!' The boy was slapping my shoulders, the crown of my head. 'Daddy! Wake up!' His grinning face, the bunched cheeks pink with cold. I could feel the outside on his anorak as I unzipped it and tugged it off. When I hoisted him onto my chest he buried his face in my neck, chilling my skin with his cheeks. His shoes bumped to the carpet as I pried them off in turn.

He was twenty months old. For months he'd been in the point-and-tell phase, striding around the flat like a diapered Adam, imperiously designating the objects in his path, drunk with the joys of naming. *Book! Car! Dada! Cup!* Recently he'd discovered the two-word sentence and a plangent note, a thread of yearning, had entered his pronouncements. *Doggy gone! All done! Want it!* There was a haiku starkness to these bulletins that I found appealing and that made me think of the words

77

we waste and of how we would fare if we were held to the two-word sentence. The gains would be striking. The lies, the excuses, the fudges and shams would all go. Job done. Enough bullshit.

Over the boy's head the day was fading in the window. I could hear Mari in the kitchen, putting the shopping away. Angus slithered down and skittered through to his mother. The fire was dying, the last logs blackened on top, still pulsing red underneath. I lifted the poker and opened the door in the latticework fireguard, keeping one hand free in case Angus came back. I turned the logs over and laid some kindling sticks crosswise over them. When I went to add a block of larch my hand jumped and the knuckle of my middle finger bumped the edge of the stove.

In the kitchen I ran the cold tap and watched Mari stacking cans in the cupboard. She glanced over as if to check what was blocking her light.

'How are you feeling?'

The water was cold now. I put my hand in the stream and let it play on the burn, a purple hyphen over the knuckle.

'Fine. I burnt my finger. It's OK.'

'No, I mean how are you feeling?'

I looked over my shoulder. She had paused with a can in her hand, as though weighing it for a missile.

'I don't know.' The knuckle was numb. 'I'm fine. I wish he had called, though. I wish he had let me know. I wish he'd done that.'

I dried my hands on a dishtowel, stopped to look at

them, the palms, the freckled backs, the pale strip where the ring had been. Could your hands do this, I wondered. Suddenly betray you? The little creatures that scampered to meet your every command, could they calmly tie the knots that lashed your wrists to a steering wheel, calmly tie and tighten them, send you to your death?

Then Mari was in front of me, taking my hands in hers, placing my hands on her waist, pressing against me. She pulled my head down till her lips were touching my ear. 'Give yourself a break, Gerry. It's not a reflection on you.'

I nodded. That I needed to hear this didn't mean that I believed it.

When we broke apart Mari clapped her hands, chafed them together. 'Anyway!' She was all brisk and business now: 'Looks to me like someone could do with cheering up.'

'Well it's not you.' She was struggling to stifle a grin. 'So I guess that leaves me. I'm open to offers. What did you have in mind?'

'Ah, I don't know.' She forced two fingers into her back jeans pocket and extracted a hinged strip of card. Two tickets. The Black Keys gig at the Barrowland.

'And dinner,' she said. 'Beforehand. At Ferrante's. That's the place you like, isn't it?'

'Jesus. Aye. What's the occasion?'

'We got it.' She shrugged. 'We got the contract.'

'The athletes' village?'

'The *velo*drome, Gerry.'

'Aah, brilliant.' I hugged her. 'Brilliant. Well done.' I

paused. 'What about his Lordship?'

She looked at her watch. 'Sitter's due in forty minutes. Get your arse in that shower.'

*

Ferrante's was busy with the pre-theatre crowd but we landed a nice two-seater by the aquarium. We ordered Glendronach Parliaments to celebrate Mari's news, and a bottle of Central Otago pinot to make her feel at home.

Though we always spoke about making time for ourselves we rarely did it. I'd forgotten how good it could be just to talk and drink and eat, enjoy the music of a conversation, be Mari and Gerry, not Mum and Dad. Mari was stoked about the bid, kept coming back to it. It wouldn't be officially announced till the New Year but they'd been tipped the wink that their bid was the winner. I was enjoying her elation, the wine, the nearness of her bare arms across the table, until halfway through the entrees I noticed Mari staring at something over my shoulder. She did it three or four times over the next two minutes. When she did it again I knocked my napkin to the floor and bent to fetch it. Three tables away. Big, good-looking guy in a pink polo shirt, the Kappa logo on his chest, the two naked women sitting back to back.

I tried to focus on Mari's words but the guy's big square grinning face kept swimming up before me. When she looked at him again I stopped eating, set my knife and fork down on the plate.

'Jesus.' I finished chewing. 'What the fuck, Mari – do

you know this guy?' I jerked a thumb over my shoulder. 'Do you want me to get you an introduction?'

She was still watching him, though her head responded to the tether of my voice and then her eyes followed, focused on me, puzzled at my angry tone: 'What? Yeah, I do know him. I was trying to work out where I'd seen him. It was with Bryan, he came to see Bryan last week.' Bryan Hamill was Mari's boss at the firm. She was smiling. 'Oh, that's sweet, Gerry. Were you jealous? A pink polo shirt? Really? The Magnum moustache? You're worse than my old man.'

Mari's father had once walked out of an amateur production of *Death of a Salesman* when he thought Mari's mother was flirting with Willy Loman.

'Listen, remind me to phone home when I get back,' she said. 'I need to talk to them. Mum and Dad.' She looked up quickly. 'It's six years since Josh. Since – you know.'

Mari had an older brother, deceased. He got killed in Oz, some shitty outback town, murdered, a mugging gone wrong.

'I never told you about him,' she said. 'Not properly.'

I knew Josh from the blurry snap of a blond, sardonic beach-bum in a wife-beater and yellow board shorts that occupied our living-room bookcase, and from the pious annual tribute that Mari's mum paid him in the photocopied round-up of Somerville family news that accompanied our Christmas card.

'No,' I said. 'You didn't.'

She drained the dregs of her whisky, took a slug of

pinot, leaned forward and started to talk about him. There were five years between them. Josh had been more like a cooler, younger father than a brother. He bought her little presents, taught her how to surf, throw a rugby ball. Taught her how to fight. Josh had been her best friend right through her childhood, walking her to school, vetting boyfriends – terrorising them, it sounded like – and generally looking out for Mari, in so far as a GP's daughter in a high-decile harbourside Auckland suburb needs looking out for. Then he left home. Bright but lazy, he finished school at sixteen, worked in a Huntly coalmine, played league on the weekends. He liked the life but the wages were shit and pretty soon he followed his mates across the Tasman, the big Kalgoorlie gold mine out in Western Oz. Big money. Coming home at Christmas with presents for everyone, laptops, digital cameras.

Then one Boxing Day morning Mari saw Josh coming out of the bathroom with a towel round his waist and a new tatt splashed across his back, a snarling bulldog in a studded collar and a scroll with MAD DOGS in flashy Gothic script. He laughed it off but the family learned later that he'd gotten involved with a bikie gang, he might have been patched, was probably dealing for them. And then he'd fallen out with the top boys. The cops' intel was that Josh had tried to stiff them on a hash deal but he might just as readily have said the wrong thing or looked the wrong way at someone's missus.

The family told people that Josh had been mugged but really he was murdered by his buddies. His Mad

Dog brothers. The Kalgoorlie cops found him round the back of a brick-veneer row-house in an Aborigine district. Beaten to death. His face stoved in. Choked by his own blood. Mari's parents flew over to identify their boy, bring back the body.

'Jesus. I had no idea. I'm sorry, Mari.'

'Yeah.' She poked at her salad. 'So, anyway. It gives you an idea why they act like they do, why they're keen for me to come back. They miss me, Gerry. They worry. Every time I phone they think something's happened.'

'Why would they worry when they know you're with someone like me?'

'Well, exactly.' She rolled her eyes. 'I can't imagine.'

She smiled and I was reaching out to grip her hand when a clatter at my elbow stopped me short. The waitress had dumped an ice-bucket down on a tripod. The dull gold shaft of a champagne bottle poked at a slant from the slushy ice. A waiter leaned across, twice, landing champagne flutes on the table, aligning them with little sweeps of his palm on the tablecloth, two fingers clamped round the stem.

'Sorry, no, we didn't order—'

'It's compliments of another diner, sir.' The waitress had stripped the sheath of gold foil from the neck of the bottle and was twisting the wire coil with sharp little flicks of her wrist. She nodded at the bar. 'Gentleman in the leather jacket.'

The little gunshot of the loosened cork sounded as I turned to look. The guy in the pink Kappa polo shirt, the guy Mari recognised, was on his way out, but it wasn't him. He was holding the door for a second man, the one who'd had his back to us at the table, a shorter, square-set fellow who pocketed his wallet, scooped a handful of mints from the bowl on the bar, tipped two fingers to his temple and aimed them at me on his way out the door.

'Who was *that*?'

Mari held her glass of brimming fizz. The waiter had withdrawn. The waitress lodged the bottle in the bucket, wrapped a napkin round its neck, left us with a little bow.

It was Hamish Neil.

'No one,' I said. I lifted my own glass. 'A guy from work. Owed me a favour. Cheers.'

'*No one*?' Mari frowned, held her glass as if she was proposing a toast. 'No one? You look like you've just seen a dead man.'

Chapter Seven

The funerals fell on consecutive days, Swan's on a Tuesday, Moir's on Wednesday. The Calvinist in me – even the Catholics in Glasgow are Calvinist, and Calvinism never lapses, it bites too deep in the bone – relished the prospect. Black suit laid out on the bed two mornings running, black tie draped on the wardrobe door. Shave against the grain with a fresh blade; virtuous sting of aftershave. I stood before the mirror in my stocking soles, folding a tie I'd inherited from my father, a tie I first wore to his funeral.

Mari came through from the bedroom, fiddling with an earring. She nudged me out of the way with her hip and stood frowning at the mirror.

She drew her upper lip over her teeth, checking her lipstick. She smoothed the front of her dress, turned to check the back view over her shoulder. I felt an incongruous stab of desire as I settled my Windsor and turned down my collar, watching the light catch the folds of her dress, the sheer tights, the glossy heels with the tapering spikes, and my cock nudged the fly of my trousers, once, twice: *It's not me who's died.*

'You okay?' She pulled me round to face her, brushed the shoulders of my suit, fiddled with my tie.

'I'm fine.'

'This is the real one today.'

'I know.'

The day before I'd stood outside the church with the other hacks, the crew from *Reporting Scotland*, the rubbernecking locals, and watched six gangsters shoulder Billy Swan down the steps to the hearse. I followed the convoy of cars to the cemetery and stood well back when the interment began, me and the snapper and the rest of the pack. They stood six-deep round the grave, it was a Neil show of strength. Plain-clothes men haunted the edge of the crowd and a pair of uniforms stood beside their squad car at the cemetery gates. But that was just work. Today was for real.

On the way down to Ayrshire we stopped for petrol. The cashier smiled, then she noticed my tie, passed me the receipt with a sympathetic grimace.

We parked at the railway station and walked down the hill to the church. Mari took my arm as we crossed the cobbles.

The Old High Kirk in Mureton is a squat grey box in the shadow of the viaduct. It looks like someone has fashioned a barn out of stone and then plumped a little clock-tower on top. I took an order of service from a teenage boy and we filed inside with the others.

The church was packed. The service wouldn't start for another twenty minutes but already the pews were thronged. We squeezed down a side-aisle and into our seats. I thought of Moir as a lone wolf, Johnny-no-pals, so it surprised me, the tight rows of mourners, the old kirk groaning like an emigrant ship. I felt sorry for my dead self, for the Gerry Conway whose boxed carcass would one day rest on trestles in front of a crowd far sparser than this. It feels a little hollow to be jealous of a dead man.

Mari read the order of service and I looked round for people I knew. The daily and Sunday were out in force – we'd left a skeleton staff at Pacific Quay – and my colleagues, unfamiliar in black, with their unknown partners and spouses, were dotted round the church. Maguire and Niven were up the front, conferring like plotters. Further back I spotted the fire-truck lipstick and red-rimmed eyes of Neve McDonald and a haggard-looking Jimmy Driscoll. Russell Spence, the QC, was shuffling along to make space for Lachlan MacCrimmon, the court reporter. A couple of TV presenters whose names escaped me were tossing their heads in the gallery. Peter Hewlett the Rangers striker was there, and Mark Halliday, who won the Open Championship at Carnoustie in a three-way play-off with Woods and Westwood and never won anything again, and a red-haired character actor from *River City*, tugging at the sleeper in his ear. Towards the back of the church was a restless clutch of thugs with squaddie buzzcuts: I took these to be villains, the career crims who found their chronicler in Moir. I clocked the meaty profile of Gavin Haining, his big square shoulders in the pinstripe suit, and the imperative cherry bob of Annabel Glaister, the Deputy First Minister. Lewicki was there – he tipped me a nod across the aisle – and Bobby Ireland, the DI from Baird Street. I looked for Gunn and Lumsden, the blonde ponytail, the hulking leather jacket, but Moir was no longer a case and I should have known better. Another batch of crop-haired men, some with moustaches, sat with their slight wives in the second and third rows and the consoling hands they planted on the shoulders of a man in the front pew – Martin's father, the retired RUC man, his grey hair looking freshly trimmed – marked them out as the relatives from Ireland.

The reading was Ecclesiastes. Martin's father rose from his place and stepped to the lectern. Before starting to read he rolled his shoulders and you sensed, in that ready-ing gesture, all the funerals he'd attended down the years, all the send-offs for fallen colleagues, the knottings of the black tie. 'To every thing there is a season,' he told us, in a booming, theatrical bass. 'And a time to every purpose under heaven. A time to be born and a time to die, a time to plant and a time to uproot, a time to kill and a time to heal . . .' There was no comfort in the words, no consola-tion. Just the tit for tat of his pendulum rhythm. A time for this and a time for that. His implacable Ulster vow-els: '. . . a time to embrace and a time to refrain, a time to search and a time to give up . . .'

I could see Clare in the front pew, her curls bouncing lightly as her shoulders shook. I was glad the girls weren't there. Their blonde oblivious heads might have set me off. Mari felt for my hand and squeezed it and I squeezed back.

The minister was a wiry, competent-looking woman with rimless glasses and a guilty smile. She looked like a distance runner. Her eulogy was nicely pitched. I'd been ready to resent it, to wince with scorn at her whitewashing of my friend's memory but she seemed to know Moir better than I did. She didn't hide from the fact – if fact it was – that Moir had killed himself. She spoke about his sometimes overbearing intensity and his 'irritating frankness' as well as his love for Clare and the girls and how stress can make us do unusual things. We sang a final hymn: 'Will your anchor hold in the storms of life?' Moir had been a sergeant in the Boys' Brigade, the minister explained, and this was the BB anthem. It was a proper hymn, very Protestant, with a thumping tune and a strong, uplifting chorus, and I felt the better for having sung it.

At the close of the service I stepped forward with the others and shouldered my share of the burden. At first it seemed we might buckle under the weight and I staggered a bit as the edge of the coffin cut into my neck, but we set off gingerly up the aisle, the undertaker beside us, counting our steps, like the coach of the world's slowest rowing crew. We carried Moir into thin yellow sunlight and laid him in the hearse. One of the undertakers slipped me a card with 'Number 4' printed on it. Later, at the graveside he called out the numbers and I stepped up: the end of a blue tasselled rope was placed in my palm.

The grave was black against the snow, and I thought again of my old man's coffin. 'Brace yourselves,' the undertaker whispered, and the six of us gripped our ropes as he slid the wooden staves from under the box. The cords snapped tight and our forearms trembled. The coffin pitched and wavered over the grave, but we steadied it and held it true, and wobbled it into the slot. Wet smell of earth. Same smell as Dad's. Same ache in my shoulders. It was delicate work, and the ropes seemed too slight for the job. The undertaker talked us through it in his low, steady undertone, tapping our forearms in turn when he wanted us to pay out more rope. The coffin jerked down in its narrow slot, tilting and right-ing, the head and now the feet pitching forward. Finally it bumped down onto hard earth. The undertaker bowed and we walked backwards to our places, hands clasped over our groins.

'You going to the hotel?'

Lewicki at my shoulder. There was a reception in the Goldberry, Mureton's only decent hotel. Halfway decent.

'I'll see you there.'

He clapped my shoulder, nodded at Mari, set off across the gravestones clutching his overcoat tight at the neck. At the car park I collected the flowers from the back seat. Mari stayed in the car.

*

At the reception Mari went off to the ladies and I joined the other suits at the bar. There were sombre nods, hand-shakes close in to the body, claps on the shoulder. It's always like this. We stand around sipping pints of lager tops, talking in low voices, the bar staff alert and respect-ful. Then the first round of whiskies appears. Someone tells a joke. We all lean in for the punchline and lean back laughing. The mood lifts and the reception has begun.

90

It's the camaraderie of the living. At the root of it lies the recognition that, try as we might to avoid it, death will find us out. But Moir hadn't tried to avoid death. Moir had rushed forward to meet it, and that rather spoiled the occasion. Standing at the bar, we had no way to deal with this, no joke that wouldn't have seemed tasteless, out of place. We nodded at each other and drifted off to the tables, to the little side-plates of sausage rolls and triangular sandwiches.

The Goldberry Hotel had changed. In the twenty years since I last crossed its doors the place had been tarted up. It was furnished in the tourist style, a tourist being someone who's a little hazy about the trajectory of the Highland line. A targe and twin claymores were mounted on the wall above the fireplace and the waitresses – local girls whose tattooed lower backs and pierced navels were hidden under starched white shirts and sober tartan skirts – marched the dark acres of Black Watch carpet.

The function suite was busy. Haining was there, the big beast, clapping backs, clutching elbows, working the room. He bicep-punched a man with silver hair and leaned to kiss a thickset woman. He scoped the room, head high, predatory, caught my eye over the shot glass, nodded. A silver tray bumped my ribs. Little orange breadcrumbed balls. I looked at the girl.

'Blue cheese and walnut truffles,' she said. Her hair was scraped back and tied in a bow. A man's shirt and tie under the apron. Tiny nick in the skin, just under her left eye.

'I'll take your word for it.'

91

When she moved off I spotted Lewicki, patting the pocket of his suit and heading for the fire-door.

The car park was full of smokers, gathered in little conclaves, refugee huddles. Flapping their arms, stamping in their thin-soled shoes. Breath and smoke in the frozen air. Lewicki had his head in his armpit, shielding the flame with his jacket.

'Thought you'd given up,' I said.

The head popped up. 'Hey!' He kept the ciggie in his mouth to shake my hand, clapped me on the back, our shoulders bumping.

I lit a Café Crème and rolled the chocolatey smoke round my mouth. We watched a hotel employee in a puffa jacket clearing snow from the driveway. The rasp of his shovel on the tarmac echoed crisply in the brittle air.

Lewicki had been 'my' cop since my days on the news-desk. But the fact that he was standing in this car park meant that he'd been Moir's cop too. Moir had inherited Lewicki along with my old job when I got fired for the Lyons piece. I felt another futile stab of jealousy.

'Did you know?' Lewicki was asking. 'You have any idea that this was on the cards?'

I shook my head. 'Hadn't spoken to him in months. Not properly. He was drinking, but you don't know that's a sign at the time. You just think he's drinking too much.'

'Enjoying himself,' Lewicki said.

We smoked for a while in silence. The chill wind stung our cheeks and the cars swept past on the Glasgow

Road and the thought we didn't speak, the question on both of our minds, took that moment to assert itself. It shouldered its way between us like an ill-bred dog. Lewicki looked away across the fields and his voice when it came was sly-like and quiet.

'You think he did it?'

I took my time answering, nodded slowly though Lewicki was still turned away towards the frozen fields. 'Looks that way.'

His head snapped round, there was spit in little bubbles on his bared teeth. 'I know what it looks like for fuck's sake. Do you think he *did* it? That's what I'm asking. Did Martin Moir kill himself?'

'No,' I said. 'No. I cannae see it.'

'That's the thing.' Lewicki's anger was gone, his voice had sagged, his features with it. 'I can't either.'

He dropped his smoke on the ground and a blackbird hopped over, stabbing at the fag-end with its yellow beak. Lewicki glanced to see how much of my Café Crème was left and then took out his packet again.

'I keep thinking how he would write things.' I poked the snow with a polished toecap, exposing a black slash of tarmac. 'When something happens, I keep thinking how he would write it. Like this missing girl.'

'The prozzy?' Lewicki said.

'Aye.'

Lewicki nodded. 'You'll be thinking it a lot more, would be my guess. Jesus, he's taking his time, though.' He pursed his lips. He was talking about Hamish Neil. 'When was the funeral?'

'Swan? Yesterday.'

That was the favourite time for reprisals. Revenge killings. You timed them to coincide with the funeral of the victim. The man is laid to rest as his killers are found in a car. Trussed. Bludgeoned. Shot in the back of the head.

'You imagine Maitland waiting this long?' Lewicki clicked his tongue against his teeth. 'Maitland would have hit them before the ambo came for Swan.'

This was Hamish Neil's fate, to be judged at every turn against the man he replaced, the man he ousted. What would Maitland have done? How would the old man have acted? Maitland had a name for being fast, for moving quick and bloody when the need arose. But he hadn't seen Neil – his top boy, his trusted offsider – setting him up for the fall.

'Not always the key thing,' I said. 'Speed. Slow can work, too. Slow and careful. Maitland been a little bit slower he might still be in the game.'

Lewicki spat on the snow. '*You'd* been a little slower he might still be in the game.'

Four years ago, before I even knew who he was, Hamish Neil brought me a tip-off, a photograph of Peter Lyons, the Minister for Justice, in the company of Protestant paramilitaries in Northern Ireland. By the time I'd chased the story to Belfast and back, I'd placed Lyons at the scene of a sectarian killing and fingered Walter Maitland as the UVF's chief armourer. The minister resigned and I got fired, but that was all collateral damage as far as Hamish Neil was concerned. The big prize – the thing

94

he'd aimed at from the start – was that Maitland went to jail, Maitland's sons fled the city and Neil took over as northside boss. He'd taken Maitland out with a minimum of fuss. As it turned out, fuss was required anyway – there were seven men dead before Neil came out on top – and the question now was why someone who could go to war to assert his control was taking so long to hit back over Swan.

'I've a tout down there,' Lewicki said. 'Across the river. The guy you met. Word is, Packy Walsh has gone to ground. Hasn't been over the door in a week. It's the waiting that does it. Neil should have hit them by now. The longer he leaves it the jumpier everyone gets. The waiting's worse than the actual hit.'

'Not if you're the one getting hit.'

'There's that.'

We smoked in silence.

'I missed you at the church,' I said.

He studied the end of his cigarette. 'Not a great fan of churches.'

'Yeah? I'd have pegged you as an altar boy at least.'

'I *was* an altar boy.' Lewicki was watching the traffic, the lorries and cars on the Glasgow Road. 'That was the problem. Saw behind the scenes, mate. Spoiled the mystery.'

'What, did the priest try to—?'

'Father Nugent? Naw.' He snorted. 'Naw, he was a good old guy. I just, don't know, took the hump with it. St Christopher was the last straw. When they bumped St Christopher, that finished it.'

He tapped the ash from his Regal, took another draw. 'We had a medal in our car, the old Ford Consul, hanging from the rearview. St Christopher wading through the waves with his big wooden staff in his hand, the baby on his back. My mum prayed to him every time my dad drove down to see his brother in Carlisle.

'I took it as my saint's name. At confirmation, like. Got a St Christopher medal along with my rosary. Same as the one in the car. Then Father Nugent gave it out at mass: it was all a mistake, he never existed.'

He frowned, remembering. 'No patron saint of travellers? Fuck. I mean if there's a saint for anyone it should be them. And the prayers? My mum's, all the others, they just vanished in the air? I thought, fuck you Father Nugent. You can keep God and Jesus, all the saints. Mary, the bastarding mass. I'm sticking with St Christopher.'

'And did you?'

He stuck two fingers down his collar, fished it out, the silver disc on its flimsy chain. He grinned. 'Figure he needs all the help he can get.'

'Aye. Him and me both.'

Lewicki's smile fell. 'Fuck,' he said, leaning forward. 'Three o'clock. Talk of the devil.'

I turned in puzzlement, half expecting to see the bearded ex-saint wading across the hotel car park, parting the smokers with a wooden staff, a wean perched on his shoulders. A man had stepped down from the fire-door, patting his pockets. An unlit cigarette in his mouth. Another man followed, bigger, black crombie,

96

and stationed himself at the door. The smaller man wandered over, the ciggie drooping from his lips, and mimed sparking a lighter. Lewicki passed him his cigarette and the man lit his own off it, passed it back.

'Jan,' he said. Lewicki nodded.

He turned to face me.

'And how are things, Mr Conway?'

I looked at him. He took off his dark glasses and smiled. The broad nose, the coarse skin, the wiry, black, receding hair, with a scurf of white at the temples.

'I've been better.'

He nodded, blowing smoke. Apart from that glimpse in Ferrante's it was three years since I'd seen Hamish Neil. He looked well. Broader, fuller, a little shorter than I'd remembered. He wore a black shirt and black silk tie, three-button suit. No overcoat. He rocked on his heels, tapping the ash onto the snow. The muscle watched from the fire-door.

Lewicki was coughing, doubled up. Neil turned to me.

'Enjoy your Moët?'

'I prefer Veuve Cliquot,' I said.

Neil nodded, smiled at his shoes. 'Sad day,' he said. 'Like fucking buses, funerals. That's two in two days.'

Lewicki finished coughing, spat on the snow. He straightened up.

'Expecting any more?'

Neil looked at him neutrally, looked at the mess on the snow.

'Kind of up to you, Jan, isn't it?' He looked off towards the white fields, the black ribbon of road. 'With all the specialised criminal intelligence at your disposal, you might have an inkling of who was to blame. Might want to make a move, take him off the streets while the tally's at two.'

Lewicki hunched his shoulders against the wind. 'You planning to boost it, like? The tally?'

'I'm planning to stay safe, keep my business safe.'

'Yeah?'

'You can't keep a thing safe, you don't deserve to keep it.'

He was looking at me as he said this. Lewicki dropped his smoke and I followed him inside.

Mari was talking to Clare. She had moved over to Clare's table and now clasped Clare's hands in her own, leaning in close and talking quietly in that low, steady way of hers. Clare was nodding, in short regular bursts, looking up at Mari and then back down at the table. I passed our own table and kept walking.

There were no Islays. The barman had the grace to feign embarrassment. His vowels were the broad, open vowels of Ayrshire, not the spindly whine of the city. I was pleased. After all, I thought, it still counts for something, that twenty miles of moor between Mureton and the city.

I plumped for a Macallan. A man appeared at my elbow, one of the cousins. We nodded at each other in the whisky mirror and then a big flat hand swum under my nose.

'Davey Moir,' he said. 'Martin's cousin.'

I shook the hand.

'Gerry Conway. Martin's colleague at the *Tribune*. Friend, too.'

'Conway, aye. Ronnie spoke about you, Martin's dad. You were over on a visit at some point, few years back? Across the water.'

'That's right.'

'Aye.' He hitched his trousers, braced his hands on the bar. He shook his head: 'Bad business, this.'

I tilted my whisky. 'Can't argue with that.'

The barman's raised eyebrows loomed before us. Davey Moir passed him a sheet of paper with a large order on it and the barman got to work, calling one of the waitresses over to help.

'His old man,' I said. 'He did well at the church. Bearing up, is he?'

Davey Moir glanced round at the tables.

'Ronnie? The whisky's bearing him up. The Black Bush's bearing him up.'

There was a hard, jaunty note in his voice.

'Well,' I twisted my glass on its mat. 'It's not every day you bury your son.'

'That's true.' He nodded. 'He's got a grand excuse today. It's the past twenty years you'd wonder about.'

I sipped my Macallan. I could see Neve MacDonald in the mirror at one of the tables, snuffling theatrically into a napkin. One White Russian too many.

Davey Moir grimaced, shook his head. 'Ach, I shouldn't speak ill of him. He's a good man. But weak, a weak dog. Been hitting the sauce since that business in Larne.'

He looked round as he said that, eyes narrowed,

checking that I knew what he was talking about.

'Shit.' He was digging into his pocket, passing two twenties to the barman. 'Sorry, I thought you knew. Ach, there was a thing in the early Nineties, an incident, Ronnie was a DI up in Coleraine. I don't know the right story, he did something he shouldn't have done. Anyway, they bumped him down to sergeant, put him back in uniform.'

'Jesus. Sore one.'

'Yeah.' He took his change. 'Fucked his pension, too. Look, this crowd'll be thinking I've absconded. Better get back. Nice talking to you – Gerry is it?'

'Yeah. Likewise.'

I helped him load up the tin tray. Three pints of heavy, a lager and lime, two vodkas and Red Bull, a gin and bitter lemon and a Baileys on ice. He'd hoisted the lot and was turning to go when someone bumped him in the back and he buckled forward, raising the tray like a judge's scorecard.

The noise was like a building coming down. There was a stunned lull in which the round tray wobbled off with a hollow silver whisper and clanged against the leg of a chair. I looked at the floor. All the pints had smashed. A dark pool was spreading on the Black Watch carpet, a paint splash of Baileys striping my shoes. We looked like we'd been fishing, Davey Moir and I, fly-casting in our best suits, wading in a river to the knees.

Before he could react I gripped Davey Moir by the sleeve. His teeth were bared and the back of his neck was bunched in bristled folds but I held his sleeve and clamped my hand on his shoulder till I felt him subside. This was his cousin's funeral, you didn't want fighting games at your cousin's send-off. The man who bumped him – tall, hook nose, late twenties – was apologising, he had his hands up and his fingers spread like a goalkeeper facing a penalty. Then his wallet was out, he was leaning across to shout another round, scooping bar-towels off the polished bar. He had long fair hair that curtained his face when he squatted down to help the waitress pick up the shards, mopping the carpet with the balled-up towels.

It seemed like a good time to bail. I collected our coats and we said our goodbyes. Moir's father was drunk, slurring the words 'Good boy' as he clapped my back, though whether it was Martin or myself who had earned this commendation I still don't know. Across the room, Hamish Neil stood under the crossed swords, leaning on the fireplace with a whisky in hand, as if this was his living room and we were his guests. He tipped two fingers to his temple in a slick salute. I kept my hand on Mari's shoulder and stared straight ahead.

Mari drove. It was too cold to keep the windows down so I put up the heating and angled the hot air onto to my legs. All the way back to Glasgow the smell of hops and juniper rose between my knees.

Chapter Eight

Nearly two weeks later I was driving down to Ayrshire again, low winter sun in my eyes, Warren Zevon on the sound system; 'Empty-Hearted Town'. The motor-way's three lanes were almost empty – it was two o'clock in the afternoon – but I held it at a Presbyterian sixty-five. Beside me on the passenger seat was a slim, buff cardboard folder and on top of that was a cling-filmed plate of muffins. This was what you did in New Zealand, Mari told me, for illnesses, bereavements, any kind of mishap. No species of pain that a traybake couldn't as-suage. There's a book she has at home called *Ladies, A Plate*, which is what it used to say on party invites in Fifties New Zealand: 'Gentlemen, a bottle; Ladies, a plate.' I should have brought a bottle, I reflected, as a truck shuddered past on the outside lane.

In the fortnight since Moir's funeral it had snowed without a break. By the time it all thawed out and a thin white sun lit up the smoking streets, Moir's death seemed like something from a previous era. You like to think that you'd leave a hole, that your talents would be missed, but it doesn't always work like that. Like a river closing over a dead dog: that's how a paper like the *Tribune* meets your absence.

I learned that four years ago when they fired me over

the Peter Lyons story. The *Trib* came out on Sunday, people bought it just the same. No one complained that my byline was missing, or took their copy back to the shop: *What happened to Gerry Conway?*

For two days after Moir's death the newsroom was muted. The little groups at the fax machine and photocopier barely spoke. People pausing at desks were murmurous and cowed. But on day three laughter no longer seemed out of place and when someone upped the volume for the sports report on the lunchtime news, and someone else made a noisy joke about the Celtic result, we were back to normal.

After all, we had a paper to write. The stories didn't stop. Death went on. The missing pro turned up murdered in woodland near Duntocher. The dead squaddies turned out to be Jocks – a Black Watch sergeant from the East Neuk of Fife and a private from Dundee – so now they would merit six hundred words, with quotes from the parents, tributes from the Secretary of State. A fatal stabbing at a flat in Cumbernauld held the front page for a couple of days when it was mistakenly reported as sectarian.

I had my own distractions, too. Angus caught a vomiting bug – it was diagnosed as rotavirus – and spent a week in the Southern General. He wasn't in danger but we took it in turns to sit beside his steel-barred cot, Mari and I, stroking his hair and soothing his cries when the nurses changing his IV drip struggled to find a vein.

It was two weeks after the funeral before I thought about visiting Clare. What prompted me were the tributes.

In the days following Moir's death, an impromptu shrine grew up around his workstation. Photos, snatches of poetry, handwritten notes. The foliage of mourning. It looked like a 9/11 wall in New York. On the morning we heard of the death, someone pinned Moir's byline picture on his partition. Someone else added a snap of Moir at last year's Christmas lunch. Soon the dark-blue felt was buried under photos: Moir at the Scottish Press Awards; Moir holing out at a charity fourball; Moir in the Cope on the night of Rix's send-off; Moir at a City Council bash, his arm round Gavin Haining's shoulders. There were clippings, too, and a smattering of Mass cards.

I took them all down and put them in a folder for Clare. It looked bare and somehow abandoned now, Moir's workstation. The cops had taken his computer away and somebody had commandeered his chair. A key ring hung on a hook Velcroed onto Moir's partition, a purple hunk of plastic in the shape of a fish. I took it as a keepsake. Among the photos and clippings was a white postcard with a typed line of text:

Woe unto you, when all men shall speak well of you.

Luke 6: 26

I pinned it up on my own partition. I liked the sentiment. It wasn't the kind of admonition I was ever likely to need, but I liked it anyway. There was another postcard, an old Victorian photograph: two lines of men,

104

barefoot and bearded, on either side of a dirty street with a big hill looming in the background. I took it too and pinned it next to the first one.

The Mureton turn-off appeared and I flicked the indicator. 'Welcome to Mureton': every time I came back the sign was closer to the city. By now there was a good three miles of crescents and cul-de-sacs, semis of cheese-coloured brick, strings of matchbox front gardens and security-lit double garages that I refused to recognise as Mureton, and it wasn't until the squat grey bulk of the Goldberry Hotel loomed on my right that I counted myself home.

I was early – the new motorway had shaved ten minutes off the journey – so I drove on down to the town centre and turned into my old street. A short terrace of red sandstone villas confronted a short terrace of blonde sandstone villas. When I lived here each house had a square plot of flinty sandstone chips or small white quartzy pebbles out front. As boys we chased each other through these gardens, the chips shelving and mashing under our plunging feet. We sounded like the sea pounding a shingle beach. But now all the gardens were gone. The low retaining walls we tightroped along were gone and where the pebbles had been there were slick black flats of tarmac where angled cars were beached like boats.

I stopped in front of our old house, garden gone. The paint on the windows and eaves was wrong – it was white now, not blue. But there was my bedroom window, thin as a sentry box above the glass front door. I thought of walking up the path and ringing the bell, asking to see round the place, but what was the point? A tortoiseshell cat padded out from somewhere and wound in and out of my legs.

By the time I pulled up at Clare's front door I was late. The Moirs lived in one of the new estates and I lost my way in the yellowbrick crescents. I parked in the driveway behind a muddy silver Lexus, two years old. The house was detached – you could have ridden a bike between it and the house next door, if you tucked your elbows in and didn't waver – and not much older than the car in the drive.

No one was home. I thumbed the bell a third time and was bending to lay the muffins on top of the folder when the snib clicked.

'Gerry Conway.'

I gathered the stuff and rose from the step, knee cracking. When I went to hug her with my free arm Clare turned aside and I kissed her cheek instead.

That morning on the phone she had sounded woozy. Tranquillisers, I thought, but now I could smell it, the rank tang of whisky and something else behind the booze, a stale, sweetly sexual reek.

I followed her down the hall. The living room was humid and dark and here they were, shining in the gloom, white orchids, their horns jutting out from a vase on the table. That fleshy smell, like something's crawled into the floor space and died. I started at a movement in the gloom, something stirring on the room's far side, but it was only us, our awkward shapes in the streaky mirror.

She didn't offer a seat. Her hand rose vaguely, pushed the hair from her eyes. We stood there for a moment as if listening out for something, straining to hear. When I mentioned coffee she waved her hand distractedly and drifted off to stage a decorous riot, yanking drawers and banging cupboard doors like somebody rifling the kitchen for drugs.

I threw back the curtains. Two white sofas faced each other across a coffee table and a slippy strip of laminate flooring. There were toys and clothes on the floor, a bunched yellow towel. I gathered the towel and a stripy kid's T-shirt and a pink cloth that became, as I lifted it into the light, a pair of women's knickers. I bunched the lot together and pushed them under the sofa.

The mantelpiece was crowded: sympathy cards with swirly golden copperplate, the smaller Mass cards like holy football stickers with their robed, androgynous saints. The room was too hot. I shrugged out of my jacket and dropped it on a couch, drifted over to the bookcase. Major, Blair, Mandela, Clinton: a sheaf of political bios, none of which I had read. That was the difference: Moir believed in politics. The things that were just words to the rest of us – democracy, the rule of law, the parliamentary process – meant something to him. He'd seen the alternative, I suppose; what happened when you swept those off the table and went to work with guns and bombs. But we laughed at him a little, around the office, down the Cope, teacher's pet, the Ulster anorak, the boy who said his prayers.

The riot in the kitchen had stopped. Brittle plinking sounds were coming from behind me, guitar strings at a barely audible volume. The hi-fi in the corner. Between the tall, thin speakers was a flat slab of silver, its surface flawed by sticky rings of red. I ran my finger along the dusty edge and bent to read the tiny lettering: LINN KLIMAX DS. The CD case was open on one of the speakers: Andrés Segovia, Picasso's *Still Life with Guitar* on the cover.

'Here you go.' She passed me an over-full mug, scalding, I practically dropped it onto the coffee table.

We sat on opposite sofas. I could feel the heat at my back and my palm leaped like a cat when I slipped it behind the sofa to check the radiator. I sipped my scalding coffee, shallow-breathing to mask the scent of the orchids. The ball of my thumb was throbbing from the radiator. Clare looked at a spot on the floor just in front of my shoes. She was waiting it out. I was just another well-meaning, irrelevant distraction.

'Anyway, there it is,' I said. I had laid the slim folder of tributes on the smeared glass top of the coffee table, beside the muffins. She barely glanced at it, sat with her hands between her knees. The stink of the orchids was making me heave. Say something. The girls.

'How are the girls?'

She shrugged. 'They're at my sister's just now.'

I nodded.

'Just till I get things together,' she said.

'No, that's good. That makes sense.'

There was a pinkish smear on the rim of my cup, a lipstick trace.

'They still don't know.' She was staring at the floor again. 'I've told them more than once but they don't take it in. They think he's coming back. They bring his shoes through from the porch and walk around the house in them.' She shrugged, put her hand to her face, I could see the features crumple.

There was nothing to say. I rubbed the pink smear with my thumb but it wouldn't shift. I wanted to cross and comfort her but the slope of her shoulders, the jut of her elbows, the tight quivering ball of fist pressed to her mouth made me pause.

'I'm here for you Clare.'

'Yeah.' She spoke to her mug. 'You're here now.'

Suddenly it was chillier, even in that hothouse. Okay, I thought. Let's hear it.

'He used to admire you,' she said. She was looking at me now and I winced at the raw blue eyes in their reddened rims. 'Gerry Conway. He wanted to *be* you. The big reporter.'

'He was twice the journalist I'll ever be.'

'He was, though, wasn't he? And do you know why? Because he meant it.' Her ponytail tossed as she shook her head. 'The stupid fucker. He meant it. He believed all the shit you're supposed to believe.'

It was true. I set my cup down on the table. 'You're right. Clare. I'm sorry.' I stood up. My keys hissed as I lifted my jacket. 'I'm sorry. I shouldn't have come. I'll get out your road.'

She seemed to see me then for the first time, reached out as I passed, gripped the hem of my jacket.

'Don't go, Gerry.' She tugged on my jacket. 'I'm sorry. It's not you. Stay, for God's sake. Finish your coffee.'

'Is that what you call it?'

She looked up. 'What?'

'Coffee? Jesus, I've tasted nicer engine oil.' I sat back down. 'I was trying to make my escape before I had to drink the stuff. Or find a pot plant to pour it into.'

She was laughing now, it might have been a laugh, wiping her eyes with the heel of her hand. 'Cheeky bugger. Hey, you want me to fix it? Wait here.'

She came back from the kitchen with a half-bottle of White Horse. It wasn't the best whisky but it could hardly make the coffee any worse. She tipped a good half-inch into each of the mugs.

'It's good to see you, Gerry.' She tucked her legs underneath her, raised the mug in a silent toast.

'And you.'

'I must look fantastic.' She dabbed at her eyes, choked out a laugh. Her eyes and the tip of her nose had turned pink and her lipstick was smeary.

'You look fine.'

'Jesus, that's your idea of a compliment? No wonder you turned me down.' She shook her head. 'I'm sorry, Gerry, I don't know why I said that.'

'Don't apologise, Clare. It's fine. You've had a shock.'

'It isn't that.'

She looked away across the room and her lips tightened and her eyes filmed over again.

'What, then?'

'It's something else. Money.'

She nodded meaningfully.

'You mean they won't pay?'

'Pay what? Who won't?'

'The insurance company. They won't pay out for, you know, how Martin died.'

'No, they won't. But that doesn't matter.' She rose from her chair. 'That's not what I meant.'

The little drawer in the sideboard rattled as she yanked it open. She sorted noisily through some papers and when she found the one she wanted she flourished it fiercely and thrust it at my chest.

A woman, I thought; *Moir had a woman. She wants money. She's written a letter.*

But it wasn't a letter. It was an official document, on thin A5 paper. A building-society statement.

She stood over me as I read.

The account holder was Martin Ronald Moir. The current balance, in bold black numbers in the bottom right-hand corner, was £26,420.

Chapter Nine

'A relative?' I said. 'Someone died and left it in their will?'

She shook her head.

'Uh-uh. I checked with his parents. Nothing like that.'

I looked again at the statement.

'Horses?'

'Sorry?'

'Did he gamble?'

She gave a short laugh. 'What you asking me for? I'm just the wife. You know more than I do. Did he gamble?'

'Come on, Clare.'

'You asked the question. What do you think?'

'I've barely seen him since I came back. He was never in the building. He worked his own stories, half the time he didn't even come in to write them up. He stopped coming to conference. I've barely seen him, these last six months.'

I could see what was coming next, see it in her eyes as clear as if she'd spoken. I slapped the statement with the back of my hand.

'Well, look, it's not that much, is it?' I waved the piece of paper at her. 'It's not like we're dealing with a lottery win here. It'll be something obvious.' I sighed, held the paper by a corner. 'Look. This doesn't mean he didn't kill himself, Clare.'

She was shaking her head, her eyebrows arching.

'The week before his daughter's birthday?'

'Look, I don't think—his priorities aren't—'

'We were going to Gleneagles for Hogmanay. Three nights.'

'Oh, Clare.'

'No.' She backed away, her hands up to ward off my scepticism. 'No. I don't just mean a holiday. It was our anniversary. He was taking me to Gleneagles for our anniversary.' They'd been married on the weekend between Christmas and New Year. Eight years ago, or maybe nine. Rod was still a toddler, skidding around the dance floor in his waistcoat and trousers. We stayed the night. Bathrobes. Dark wood. Tartan bedspread. Jamie was conceived around then, or soon after.

I stepped towards her. This time I did reach out, I gripped her by the shoulders and held her at arm's length but the words I needed wouldn't come. Give it up, Clare, I wanted to tell her; people don't clear their diary once they decide to kill themselves. They don't need to. Driving into a flooded quarry with your wrists lashed to the wheel tends to do the job for you.

But I didn't. I released my pointless grip on her shoulders. I stood there for a minute and then dropped back onto the sofa and let the radiator slowly singe my shoulder.

'He'd booked it all up. He only told me about it the week before he died. Why would he do that, Gerry? Why would he tell me if he knew he was going to kill himself?'

'Clare, he wrote a note.'

'Right.' She laughed. 'They showed me that. Let's see your phone, Gerry.' She had her palm out, four fingers flexing back and forth. 'Give us it.'

'The police took it. It's still with the police.'

'When you get it back, then. Check your old messages. Gerry, he spelled everything out. In full. All the time. He had a thing about it. He was a bloody *bore* about it. He thought text language was the end of civilisation, the first step to Armageddon. Thin end of the wedge.'

Was this true? Did I remember this? I tried to think back, picture one of Moir's texts on the Nokia screen but nothing came.

'Do you not remember, Gerry?'

'Yeah. I don't know. He usually phoned me, Clare. I don't know what his texts were like.'

'Well look then.' She strode over to the mantelpiece, snatched up her mobile, marched back, thumbs working. 'Here!' She held it under my nose. 'Take it!'

The screen showed a zigzag of speech bubbles, hers in green, Moir's in grey. I scrolled up, read one of the greys: *Another late one, Clarabelle. Sorry, babe. Will try to make in before twelve. xx*

'Okay?' Her voice was fierce now, eyes flashing.

'Aye. I suppose.' I handed back the phone.

It occurred to me that a man's hang-ups about text abbreviations were liable to seem less pressing under certain conditions. Like when you're lashing your wrists to a steering wheel and about to drive to your death. Or maybe she was right and Moir never wrote

114

the text. Or maybe he wrote it with a gun to his head or a blade at his throat, and this was his way of conveying the message, telling us he didn't kill himself.

I remembered Hamish Neil in the Goldberry car park. *Take him off the streets while the tally's at two.* Did he mean that the two deaths were murders? Walsh had killed Swan: he hit Billy Swan to get at Neil; that was clear. But did Walsh kill Moir, too? Was that what Neil meant?

'But the cops, Clare. The post-mortem.'

'It's on its way. I've asked for a copy, we'll see what it says. And the police thought it was murder, too – remember that, Gerry. That was their first response. It was just your text message changed their mind.'

A shadow fell on the window, a dog-walker, pausing for the dog to sniff, do its business. The last rays of sun showed up the smears on the glass, dozens of handprints, kiddie-sized hands.

'Have you spoken to the cops, have you told them?'

'They're not interested. I spoke to the woman, Gunn, her mind's made up. They won't even see me now, the proper police. They send round a "liaison officer". I have to make her tea and biscuits while she tells me how she's here for me.'

I reached for my cup, three-quarters full, took a big burny gulp. I needed to get out before she asked me.

'I'm not asking much, Gerry.' She was sitting back down now and she leaned across to grip my wrist. 'I don't expect miracles. Just look into it. Dig around. Do what you're good at.'

I smiled, despite myself, at her naivety, the gauche stab

at flattery.

'Topping and tailing press releases, Clare. That's what I'm good at. Transcribing interviews with bored front-benchers. I'm not a proper reporter any more. If I ever was. It's why we had Martin.'

She watched me over her cup, said nothing. Behind her in the window the light was dwindling, grey clouds massing on a luminous white horizon. Across the street the seedlings in their tubes of mesh were lashing in the wind.

'Look, even if I could, Clare, I'm up to my neck. This referendum stuff, Martin's crime beat. I'm doing two jobs as it is.'

Silence. The red eyes over the mug's chipped rim, the tousled hair, the sad, uncared-for room. I couldn't hold out. I shook my head, took another pull on the fortified coffee.

'No promises,' I told her. 'I'll do what I can.'

*

I drove back to the city, windows down, cold air stinging my cheeks, the sense of regret filling the car. I wasn't even sure what I'd offered to do. Look into Martin's death. Do what I can. What did that mean? Where would I start? Away from the feverish heat of Clare's living room, the evidence looked thin. A text message? Two dozen characters on a screen? And the money? Twenty-six grand, not the stuff of heists and coke deals. I passed the Covenanters' Memorial, a Celtic cross in a patch of purple moorland, the long grass switching in the wind.

Let it lie, I thought; don't dig it all up again, but then Clare's words came back to me, the words she'd spoken as I stood on the threshold.

'I want to know that the man I wake up crying about is the man I shared a bed with for nine years. I want to know that the man I loved was the man I loved.'

I crested the rise at Priesthill and the lights of the city rose out of the dark. Somewhere in that vast illumination was the truth about Martin Moir's death, if the truth hadn't already been established by DS Gunn, chapter-and-versed in the PM report. Was there another story here, a different version of events? And if there was, how did I aim to find it? I had a building-society statement in my pocket. That this slip of paper might refute the approved conclusions of Strathclyde Police, the Procurator Fiscal and the state pathologist seemed a lot to ask. It was a fool's errand and I was already looking for a way to shelve it. Anyway, I'd told Clare I would need to square it with Maguire. That was my out. Maguire would stamp on it. I flicked the indicator, pulled out to overtake.

Chapter Ten

It was after four when I left Clare's. The city-bound traffic was light, all the headlights streaming south to the coast, the dormitory towns of Ayrshire. I stopped at Shawlands and ate dumpling soup in a Taiwanese restaurant and then drove on up to the Quay. Maguire was in her office but I couldn't face her just then. Tomorrow would do. I worked hard on Sunday's piece and it was half past ten when I raised my head, just the night ed and a smattering of diehards at their desks.

I was checking my Twitter feed when a shadow fell on the screen.

'Hard at it, as ever. Is there no stopping this man?'

It was Neve McDonald, coat buttoned up, bag on her shoulder.

'Matter of fact, no, there isn't.' I swivelled round to face her. 'Just filed Sunday's copy.'

'Woo! Put out the bunting. I'm heading over the road for a swift one. Fancy it?'

'This is a drink we're talking about, right?'

She hitched her shoulder-bag, raised her plucked brows in mock outrage.

'They've got laws against that sort of thing now. Did nobody tell you?'

'Laws against propositioning newspapermen? I'm glad

to hear it. I won't press charges if you buy me a drink.'

The Cope was empty. Couple of subs at the bar. Joe had switched off the gantry lights and seemed less than thrilled to see us.

'My shout, then.' Neve was reaching into her bag. 'You find a seat.'

'I'll see what I can do.'

Every seat in the place was free. I walked along the line of booths, slid without thinking into 'our' one, second from the end. We'd spent a few drunken evenings parked on this red leatherette. This booth was also – I belatedly remembered – where I'd finished things with Neve, though she'd taken the news disturbingly well. I was wondering whether to move somewhere else when Neve came up with a drink in each hand. She set them down on the table, a White Russian, a Lagavulin, went back to fetch the little water jug. When she slid in across from me she raised her drink in a silent toast, took a greedy gulp.

'Better?'

She smacked her lips, breathed a long slow sigh through a bright red 'O'. 'Getting there.'

She unlooped her scarf and shrugged out of her jacket and I did my best not to notice her breasts in the mint-green sweater.

We sat there sipping our drinks, like we did this all the time, like this was just a normal week-night in the Cope. In fact, I hadn't talked properly to Neve for three or four years. It was only now, half-listening to Sky News, Joe stacking glasses, that I started to wonder what this was about. I looked around the pub. One of the subs was zipping his jacket, patting his pockets. Cammy Bell, the other sub, was emerging from the gents. He winked and gave me the thumbs-up as he passed. Was that what this looked like? Were we two colleagues enjoying a drink after work, or did it look like something else?

I shifted in my seat. 'How's . . . Ronnie? Arnie? Shit, I can't even remember his name.'

'Ruaridh!' Neve laughed. 'Oh, Ruaridh's finished. He was more of a friend, anyway. Don't worry, Gerry. I'm not going to jump you! Not tonight, anyway.'

I sipped my whisky. 'You never know your luck.'

'No, but there *was* someone.' The grin was gone now. She tilted her head, looked up through the shadow of her fringe. 'For the past year or so.'

I felt the atmosphere shift, a tightening of the air pressure. I gripped my glass.

'So what happened?'

'You know what happened.' She held my gaze. The answer was there in her eyes but I couldn't read it. Then her eyes filled up and she was rooting in her bag for her paper tissues. I should have reached across and gripped her hand but her words had spooked me and I froze. She looked so unlike herself. The Neve McDonald I knew didn't cry. The hardest of tickets, the patented nippy sweetie. I had never seen her cry, none of us had, except – I now remembered, watching her press a tissue to her upper lip – at the funeral.

'*Moir*? It was Martin Moir?'

'I miss him, Gerry. I miss him so much.'

Jesus. I caught Joe's eye and waggled my finger: two more.

120

'Did people know?'

She shook her head. 'My pals, some of them. But no one at the paper.'

'Clare?'

'Jesus! No.'

I went to the bar to pay for the drinks. 'That's your lot,' Joe told me. 'Bar's closed. *I wish I was, ho-omeward bound,*' he crooned softly. I nodded. Was this another motive, another reason why Moir might have killed himself? His marriage was failing, he'd let them down, Clare, the girls?

I carried the drinks to our table, slid into the booth.

Neve was putting her compact away, snapping her bag. 'Are you shocked, Gerry? Have I scandalised you?'

'Ach I'm sorry, Neve. I'm sorry for your loss. It's a hellish situation.'

'Yeah.' She gave a clenched little smile. 'The other woman. The home-breaker. That fucking funeral. Jesus, you ever felt invisible?'

Joe was putting the chairs up on tables, making plenty of noise.

'So why are you telling me now?'

She started on her second drink. 'Can I ask you something, Gerry? You think he did it?'

Christ. Not her too. I glanced at the bar where Joe was bringing the shutters down. I put a hand on top of hers. 'Neve, people do things.' Mari's line came back to me. 'It's not a reflection on you.'

She took her hand away. 'See, I just don't buy it. I know, I know. Times like this, people believe what they want to believe. That's not me, Gerry. I was under no illusions. I knew he was never going to leave Clare, the kids. I accepted that. I'm not sure we even loved each other, if you come right down to it. But I liked him. And Jesus I miss him. And when I saw him on the Friday night, the night before it happened – I can't explain it, Gerry. It's just something you know. He wasn't getting ready to kill himself.'

'Okay. Say you're right. Why are you telling me?'

She finished her drink, shook the ice against her teeth, let the last milky drops slide through.

'I've got his laptop.'

'The police have got his laptop, Neve. They came into the office and took it.'

'I mean it's my laptop. An old one. Martin used it when he came round. He'd upload stuff from a memory stick. I think there might be something on it.'

'You haven't looked?'

'What can I do? I interview soap actors, Gerry. TV comedians. Dickheads. You're the reporter. You have a look.'

The fresh-foul smell of the Clyde gusted up as we crossed the road to the *Tribune* car park. I followed Neve's Mazda across the river, along the Clyde Expressway. She lived in Yoker – it was on my way home, or near enough. A new-build brick tenement with smart steel balconies, little tables with folded parasols. If an earthquake should ever pitch Glasgow up in the South of France she'd be sorted. I parked behind her MX-5, hung back when she opened the communal door.

'Oh for Christ's sake come up, Gerry. Nothing's going to happen.'

Inside the flat she tossed her keys in a dish by the door. 'Through here.'

The flat was spare and tasteful. Bare floors. Original art. A little workstation was set up in a corner of the living room, a lacquered black computer table and a three-shelf bookcase. A dartboard was mounted to the wall above the computer; she was using it as a corkboard. Photos and leaflets were pinned to the felt.

She unplugged the laptop. It was a fat old Toshiba, with keys like Scrabble letters. It weighed about as much as her MX-5 probably did.

'These are his, too.' There were six or seven Post-its round the dartboard's edge. She plucked them off, passed them to me in a pastel-coloured wodge. 'Might mean nothing, I don't know.'

I nodded. I made no promises. I stuck the Post-its in my hip pocket, wedged the Toshiba under my arm, set off down the stairs.

Chapter Eleven

'Nice work, Gerry. Tight, clean, sharp.' Maguire was nodding. 'It's all coming back to you now. You're back in the game.' She handed back my copy. I had written up the prostitute, the dead woman, Helen Friel. I was back on crime.

I wasn't happy with this but Maguire didn't care. With Moir gone my chance to handball the crime brief to some likely newsdesk sap had passed. The Friel story was mine. The Billy Swan story and its bloody repercussions would be mine. This on top of my politics brief, the referendum, the march to independence. It was too much. It made a hard job impossible. I put this to Maguire and she shrugged her folded arms. Exceptional times, she said. We were under the cosh, the Yanks slashing budgets left and right, it was up to senior staff to come to the mark. I was the top reporter – she didn't add, 'now that Martin's gone', but we both understood that rider – and my business now was to lead from the front. I would be covering politics and crime, the big stories in either field, though I could draw on the assistance – I detected a flicker of irony here – of the newsdesk's unpaid interns.

'You alright with this?' Wide eyes, tight lips, Maguire had her game face on, she was spoiling for a fight. I glanced through the glass at the bent, hushed figures in the newsroom, the smatter of empty desks.

'I'm your man.'

On my way out I paused in the doorway.

'Something else?'

'Actually, yeah.'

I told her my idea. I wanted to spend some time look-ing into Martin's death, try to figure out what happened, follow up some of his stories. Maguire frowned.

'We know what happened, Gerry.'

'Do we?'

'You're saying it wasn't suicide?'

'No. I don't know. I'm saying it's a bloody shame, Fiona. And we should find out why he did it, if we can. We owe him that much.'

She looked at me sharply.

'Everything isn't a story. You don't have enough on your plate? You've just said it. The job's big enough. Don't make it more than it is. We tell people what happened, we explain things as far as we can. That's the job. There's things you can't explain in seven hundred words.' She ran her tongue across her teeth. 'Why a man kills himself. You want to explain that in seven hundred words?'

'Explain it in two.' I said. 'If you get the right words.'

'Oh for Christ's sake.' Maguire's lips had tightened. 'Bit late in the day, no?'

She kept one hand on her laptop, the red nails splayed on the keys. Her glasses were clutched in the other fist, one black shellac leg poking out like a blade.

'For what?' I was still hovering just inside the door,

hoping that the sportsdesk wasn't within earshot.

'Turning back the clock. Reliving your hot youth. When's the last time you broke a story?'

'I don't see what that . . .'

'Proper story. Something you dug out and stood up. Five years ago? Six? And now you want to get back into the swing of things by establishing, what exactly? That our Investigations Editor didn't kill himself, as the post-mortem indicated, as Strathclyde Police believe, but was murdered? By persons unknown?'

'There was money,' I said. 'Twenty-six grand in an account Clare knew nothing about.'

Nothing changed in Maguire's face. 'Meaning what?'

'Meaning who knows. Meaning I want to look into it.'

The red lips split in a scoffing grin.

'We're not the fucking civil service. You're not the ombudsman. We don't "look into things". We find stories and stand them up.'

I could sense someone at my back.

'Knock knock.' Jimmy Driscoll was behind me in the doorway, nosing some conspiracy. He gave a gulped little laugh and his eyes bounced from Maguire to me and back. He wore his feckless half-smile, cocked his head like a dog, a happy spaniel.

Maguire held my gaze and then faced slowly round to Driscoll; waited. He shrugged one shoulder.

'This a bad time?'

'What do you want, Jimmy?'

The shoulder slumped. 'It's Donald Kerr,' he said glumly. 'He's in the lobby.'

126

'I'll be right out.'

When Driscoll withdrew, sliding a querulous look my way, Maguire tossed her glasses on the desk.

'Oh for Christ's sake Gerry sit down.'

She motioned me to close the door, kicked a swivel chair towards me.

'How is she anyway?'

'Clare? She's not good, Fiona. I took the cards to her yesterday, the stuff from Moir's partition. She's upset. She doesn't think he killed himself.'

'The text message.'

'She told you?'

'The police told me. The woman, Gunn.' Maguire rubbed both hands down her face, put her glasses back on. 'What did you say to her?'

'I said I'd talk to you, I said we'd talk. Even if it was suicide, we need to know why he did it.'

She leaned back, folded her arms. She nodded slowly as if in reluctant agreement. 'I get it, Gerry. You were his friend. You feel bad. We all do. But who does it help? You find the truth, it was drugs, it was another woman. Clare's going to thank you for digging that up? His girls? This can only hurt them. The truth can't help.'

'Can't help the paper, you mean.'

'That too.' She glared at me over her folded arms. 'He's on a roll.' She jerked her chin at the ceiling. 'Niven. Wants to start an award in Martin's name. The Martin Moir Award for Investigative Reporting. An internship too. You start looking for dirt, it helps no one.'

'Unless he was killed. It might help then. Just a little.'

127

'Well that's what I wonder. See, I've heard this song before. The Fiscal's wrong. The pathologist's wrong. The DI from Stewart Street; everyone's wrong except Gerry Conway.'

'DS.'

'What?'

'She's a sergeant not an inspector. The giant's fingers, Fiona. And it's not just me. Neve doesn't think it was suicide either.'

'Neve McDonald? The fuck's Neve got to do with this?'

So she didn't know about Moir and Neve.

'She's a colleague, Fiona. She cares about Martin. She wants to know what happened. We all do.'

Maguire spoke slowly, as if to a child, young child, a slow learner. 'A note, Gerry. An actual note. There's a fucking suicide note.'

'Not his, there isn't. A suicide *text*, Fiona. A text. Using text language, which Moir fucking hated.'

'You're worried about the prose style? The prose style of a suicide note?'

'What else is there? He was a writer, prose style's his fucking DNA. You at least should appreciate that.' The wind was up now, I got to my feet, the chair toppled, hit the carpet. 'Anyway, fuck it. You're probably right. It's just bad timing. He was going after Packy Walsh and next thing he's dead. Nothing to see here.'

'Gerry!' The light caught her talons as she raised her hands. 'Gerry, he'd been writing crime for the past five years. He was going after half of Glasgow. You know how many people had a reason for wanting him dead?'

128

I let that question hang in the air.

Her phone rang and she snatched it up. Her eyes locked on mine as she spoke, five or six words, yes, yes, no, alright, put the phone down.

'You've got a plan, I take it? If I say yes?'

I righted the chair, stood behind it, hands on the seat-back, shrugged. 'Look at his stories, follow them up. Dig around.'

'OK, Gerry.' She held her hands up, palms out. 'Go for your life. But you do it in your spare time, once you've finished your real stories. Alright? You're not on holiday. And I'm not subsidising this. You bring a splash within two weeks or you drop the whole thing. Agreed?'

A gust of sleet smashed against the window, a sound like a wrecking ball. Maguire didn't flinch, didn't turn her head.

'Appreciate it, Fiona.'

She stretched her arms, took in the view across the Clyde, the darkening sky, the dirty river. 'It's handy anyway,' she said.

'What is?'

'Govanhill.'

'You want me to go to Govanhill?'

Govanhell. Square Mile of Murder. Martin Moir country.

She frowned. 'You think it's played out?'

'Played out?'

'I know what you mean.' She nodded. 'Still, should get another splash or two out of it. Do some follow-ups, Gerry. Find a story. But keep the head. No Deep Throats.

No grassy knolls. Happy?'

She was frowning at the screen now, keyboard clicking. I stood up. She was right. Already the blogs and discussion threads were loud with lurid guesswork. Everyone had a theory about Moir's demise. Five different Glasgow gangsters had been named as the assassin. Some of the posters fingered a drugs mule. Others favoured the UVF – Loyalists from Moir's Ulster past reappearing to settle old scores. The cybernats leaned towards MI5: Moir had uncovered some deadly secret that would rock the tottering bulwarks of Union. There was speculation on the stories Moir was working on when he died. He'd cracked a paedophile ring involving top cops and cabinet ministers. He'd found the real dope on the World's End murders. Bible John. The Lockerbie bombing. The wilder the claim, the more boldly it was pressed. I agreed with Maguire. The last thing we needed was more of the same.

But still. The best way to end the speculation was to find the truth.

Back at my desk, I filed my copy to Driscoll. Sat back, fingers laced behind my head. Sleet-streaked windows, the blurred city streets. The clouds had closed in, obscuring the hills and their dark wooded flanks. I thought of the dead woman, dumped in the woods. The dead prostitute, the redtops called her, as if the way she earned a living engrossed her whole identity. I thought of how Moir would have tackled the story, his line of approach. If he hadn't died he'd have written the piece – *The body of missing Airdrie woman Helen Friel was discovered last night in Lanarkshire woods*. I felt sorry for her then, as if she was lonely in death, as if she'd been denied some last important rite. As if her death was not yet finished. They were equal now. Martin Moir. Helen Friel. Waiting mutely for their stories to be told.

Chapter Twelve

For the next few days I played at being Moir. I wrote the stories Moir would have written. They were stark and shocking and violent and true. After years of commentary and cleverness, after half a million words of 'expert analysis' and worthless insider opinion, it was nice to tell a story. As a Sunday commentator you were last to the party, all your facts had been chewed over by the daily hacks, you were sucking old bones that had lost their savour. As a political journalist, the people you wrote about were chewed over, too, with their tweets and blogs and podcasts, their suits and corrected smiles, their approved colour-schemes. Gangsters were different. Gangsters were mythical figures, rarely sighted, known by word of mouth and half-legendary acts. The photos that appeared in the papers – always the same ones; grainy, fuzzy, out of date – had a doctored, unconvincing look, like the long-shots of Sasquatch or Yeti. Gangsters were figments, bedtime bogeymen. In bringing news of their crimes you were the messenger on horseback, riding into the marketplace, standing in your stirrups to address the eager crowd.

An honest tiredness buoyed me up each evening, hanging on the oily chrome rail in the rattling car, stamping onto the great meshing teeth of the escalator, emerging onto Christmassy Byres Road with its puddled lights, its shuddering buses, its scarved and hatted homegoing crowds. At Clouston Street we drank Rioja and speared pesto-coated penne, listening to Steve Lamacq on 6 Music, taking turns to spoon Angus's food or stoop to retrieve his dropped or slingshot plastic forks and spoons, his overturned beakers. With Angus down we often finished the wine and turned in early ourselves.

But pretending to be Martin Moir didn't get me any closer to the nature of his death. The phone rang one evening as I lolled on the couch with my stockinged feet in Mari's lap, Angus asleep on my chest and a broad-bottomed glass of Montecillo in my grasp. It was Clare. She was crying, drunk. Couldn't we press for an inquest into Martin's death? I told her it was a waste of time. This wasn't England. Down south, almost every unnatural death, every suicide and accident, triggered an inquest. We didn't do that here. A Fatal Accident Inquiry was a rare beast, it was ordered for deaths that occasioned 'serious public concern'. Other than Clare, me and – though Clare didn't know it – Neve McDonald, was anyone seriously concerned about Martin's death? If we wanted answers we'd have to find them ourselves.

Later that evening I sat before the screen. *Can't believe you're gone, Big Man. Sleep tight, Marty. You're in a better place. Taken too soon.* I scrolled through a dozen of the eighty-seven comments on Moir's last status update, every 'friend' giving their own maudlin twist on his demise. A better place? The minister at the funeral had spoken of Martin going 'home'. A hole in the ground?

Six sodden feet of Glasgow mud? Some fucking home. I resisted the temptation to add to the comments or to 'like' any of these Facebook aperçus but I did take Moir's old Toshiba down from the airing cupboard where I'd stowed it, plugged it in and booted up, entered the password Neve had scribbled on one of my business cards.

I was looking for the final piece, the story Moir was working at the time of his death. For years I had envied the stories Moir told, the tales of mayhem and death that seemed to land in his lap. People would come to him with tip-offs, titbits, overheard snippets. Even gangsters would seek him out; being written up by Moir became a hoods' badge of honour. I remember one story, shortly after I came back to the *Trib*. A rumour got out that Frank McGreevy, Packy Walsh's right-hand man, had been assassinated. McGreevy's big rival was Jamesie 'Front Man' Leonard, a Neil family associate who had once dated McGreevy's sister. Leonard was fresh out of Saughton, having served four years for aggravated assault. All the reporters were getting texts saying the same thing: McGreevy's been topped; Jamesie's chibbed him. One of the junior reporters jumped in a cab and headed south to McGreevy's house.

Then a call came through to the newsroom: it's Francis Xavier McGreevy, sounding a little put out. He wants to speak to Martin Moir. As Moir takes the call we're all gathered round his desk, but he just nods and uh-huhs and then he snatches his coat from the back of his chair. An hour later, he saunters back, Starbucks in hand, and plumps down at his desk. He starts tapping out the piece, an exclusive interview, quashing the rumours of Frankie's demise.

That evening in the Cope we got the full story.

'I get to the house,' said Moir. A large Talisker was slopping up the sides of the tumbler as he waved it around. We'd been buying him drinks all night and his face was slick with whisky sweat. 'I know it's the right house because the Beeb van's parked outside and a Strath-clyde chopper's nearly sitting on the roof. Jesus, the noise these things make – you've no conception. There's two heavies at McGreevy's gate and they huckle me into the house, past the hacks and the cameras. Frank's in his living room, large as life, watching the snooker. "Right," he says when he sees me. "Keep your fucking eyes open." Then he stands up and whips off his T-shirt, and twirls right around with his arms above his head. Like a fucking ballet dancer. "Do I look like I've been fucking chibbed?" *Then* – I'm not making this up, it's the God's honest – he drops the trousers and touches his toes. "Okay?" he asks me, his head at his ankles. "Fine," I tell him; "that's great." "Okay then." He straightens up and fastens his belt: "Now go and fucking write it."'

Moir called it the shortest interview he'd ever done but McGreevy had got his message across. The rumour was he'd been stabbed in the arse and McGreevy was having none of it. After the story appeared, a parcel was cour-iered to Moir's desk: twenty-five Juan Lopez No. 2s. He handed them round in the Cope the following Saturday.

That was classic Moir, but the piece he was writing when he died was a squib, nothing, a piece of shit. According

135

to Driscoll, Moir had been probing a spike in sectarian crimes. The copy was on his laptop, in a file labelled 'Sectarian'. He'd written the first five pars. He gave the stats – *Hate crimes defined as 'sectarian' jumped by ten per cent to almost 700 last year* – and he marshalled the quotes. A spokesman for the Catholic Church expressed alarm at the increase and called on the government to do more to tackle the problem. A spokesman for the government welcomed the figures as evidence that victims were coming forward and that the police were doing their job. It was bromide stuff – page six or seven at best, a flimsy wing under 'Home News' – and not even Moir's metallic prose style could redeem it.

But this wasn't the story. Like most Sunday journos, Moir kept the real stories back, held them in check till the very last minute. He'd feed Driscoll a bullshit schedule – stories he was supposedly working on, stories he might even start to write but would ditch when the deadline loomed. The hate crimes piece would be one of those. Moir had been working on something else.

Probably he kept them on a memory stick, the real stories. His laptop – the old Toshiba he'd used at Neve McDonald's – wasn't much help. As far as I could see, Moir's stuff was in two folders, one that carried a few files of notes and a dozen archived stories. The other folder, called 'Streets of Stone', contained a few drafted chapters of Moir's book. Moir had been writing a history of the Glasgow street gangs. The Billy Boys and the Baltic Fleet. The Toi and the Cumbie. The Penny Mob. The Parlour Boys. True crime was the city's favourite genre.

The bookshops on Buchanan Street and Sauchiehall Street have designated sections on hardmen and neds, intimate histories of neighbourly mayhem with titles like *Fly Boy* and *Tongland* and *Square Go*. The books have a redtop feel, embossed titles in scarlet and black above coarse-grained, monochrome headshots of hoods. Most of the city's crime corrs have tried their hand at the genre, but Moir was more ambitious than most. *Streets of Stone* would have taken the story back to the nineteenth century, to the immigrant Irish brotherhoods and oath-bound secret societies, the Tim Malloy, the Village Boys.

But the story he was writing, the one that may have got him killed – that story wasn't here.

The next night I stood on the yellow tiles on the Outer Circle platform at Ibrox station, hot wind on my face as the train thudded in. I counted off the carriages, took the third, found a seat at the far end, placed my bag on the seat beside me. Across from me was a girl of twenty in a green suede jacket with tasselled sleeves, the strap of a satchel across her chest.

At Kelvinhall the doors shushed open and I moved my bag from the seat. Lewicki sat down.

'Twenty-six grand,' he said. 'Lot of money for a man in Moir's line of work. You got something similar, Gerry, nice nest-egg of twenty-six grand?'

'I've got a 2002 Subaru and a lottery scratchcard.'

Lewicki hissed, the sound he made in lieu of laughter. 'What was he writing? You looked at what he'd done before he died?'

'Nothing. Two-bob stories. Nothing to get you killed,

let's put it like that.'

'What were they?'

I blew out some air. 'From memory? Incidence of sectarian crimes, alarming rise thereof. Firebomb attack on the athletes' village. I'm starting to wonder what the fuss was about, why we all thought Moir was the talent.'

'That's not a two-bob story.'

I caught the girl's eyes, flicked up to the ads above her head.

'The firebomb? It's an act of vandalism, Jan. Zero-tolerance policing, very commendable, but this is not a front-page lead. They knocked the wheels off an earth-moving vehicle.'

Lewicki tugged at the knees of his trousers, fixing the creases. 'Hard to move earth without wheels. Hard to prepare a site for construction.'

'Knock-on effects, Jan, yes. Big news: no.'

We swayed in silence for a minute, bumping shoulders as the train took the corners and then the light of a station filled the carriage, Hillhead, the students packed together on the platform. When we moved off a row of straphangers stood in front of us, their backpacks and satchels swinging back and forward with the movement of the train. Lewicki leaned back, spoke out of the side of his mouth.

'You heard of Bellrock?'

'The lighthouse?'

'The security firm.'

A hoarding came to mind, picture of a lighthouse, blue on a white background, lettering along the beam of light, the big 'B' tapering down to the 'K': Bellrock.

'I've seen it,' I said. 'On signs. Hoardings.'

'It's one of Neil's. It's a Neil front.'

Neil had any number of fronts. So did the Walshes. Places they could rinse the dirty money, the drug money. Security was a favourite. Likewise construction.

'There's some buildings coming down on the athletes' village site. They came to see us, the demolition firm. Manchester company. They hired an Edinburgh outfit to do the security. First day on the job, six guys in Bellrock vests march onto the site: *We do the security here.* Site manager comes out his office: *Actually, no, you don't. We gave the contract to this other firm.* Bellrock guy shakes his head. *Missing the point,* he tells him: *we do the security here* – meaning here, in this part of the city, like it's a hereditary right, passed down through the generations. Site manager's a busy man, tells them to fuck off, he's calling the police.'

Kelvinbridge. More students. The straphangers shuffled closer, squeezing together like the pleats of an accordion.

'So they firebomb the digger,' I said.

'That's the first night. Second night they waylay one of the guards on his way to work. Persuade him not to report for duty. Someone sets off a distress flare beside the site office. On it goes. The local cops pay a visit to Bellrock, warn them off. Next night it's kids, wee boys of nine or ten. Climbing the fence, stoning the guards, lobbing bricks onto Portakabin roofs.'

'But the contract's been signed. They're not going to tear it up and give it to Bellrock.'

'*This* contract's been signed. But this is just the demolition phase. There's clearing and then construction to come. More contracts up for grabs.'

'They'll go to Bellrock?'

'What do you think?'

The girl in the tasselled jacket caught my eye again as she stood up to leave.

'But there's no gangland angle in Moir's piece.'

'Gangland angle to everything, Gerry. It just hadn't developed yet.'

We sat in silence for the next few stops. The train rattled into the station: the yellow walls of Ibrox. We'd come full circle. I shouldered my holdall.

Chapter Thirteen

I sat at my desk staring at my screensaver, a snap of Rod and James in Arran, milk-teeth grins, dunes in the background. Beyond the monitor's rim I could see upriver to the Kingston Bridge, cars and buses zipping across it. I was waiting for Lewicki's comments to make sense. If the athletes' village story had a gangland angle, how had Moir missed it? Or if he knew about the Neil connection, why had he suppressed it? There were all sorts of questions to ask but they all seemed to circle round the big one, the question I'd been asking since Maguire called me to break the news. Asking and not asking.

Did Moir kill himself? Could he have done it?

I remembered something he told me more than a decade ago, not long after he started at the *Trib*. He was talking about growing up in Ulster, his dad a sergeant in the RUC. Every morning his dad lay down on the pavement to check beneath the car. He drove Moir to school along a different route each day. The threat of violent death was always with them, like the colour of the living-room wallpaper or the smell of his mother's cooking. There were people who would kill his father for the job he did, the church he attended, for who he was. You might react to that experience in various ways, but I thought I knew how Moir would react. Moir would

141

live, he would walk tall in the world, he would perform a useful job to the best of his abilities. That would be his rebuke to the would-be killers, the cowards in the shadows with their bombs and their guns. To take his own life would have been, for Moir, an act of ingratitude, an act of civic dereliction. He could no more have killed himself than he could have failed to exercise his vote at an election.

I roused myself and clicked on Google Maps. The USA filled the screen, green and brown and sectioned into clear-edged boxes. I pulled back, scrolled across the Atlantic and dropped down onto Scotland, homing in on Glasgow. Now the screen was a soiled, slushy grey, split by the black gash of the Clyde. I pulled back till some green appeared and then pushed north and east. It took a few attempts, swooping in and out, but here it was. A black hole, fringed with trees. Cars in the car park, paths round the edge. I zoomed in, closer and closer, as if I might drop straight through the glinting surface and root around in the murky depths but the screen came to rest on a square of inky blue. At this level, the glints of sunlight on the water looked like swirls of stars, an undiscovered galaxy. Moir had been down there in the blackness, in the interstellar cold.

I moved the focus out again and something struck me. Lewicki answered after eight or nine rings.

'The locus,' I said, 'tracks? Footprints? What did they find?'

'Nothing. It snowed overnight. Three inches. When the uniforms arrived there were no tracks at all, just their own and the climber's. Blanket of white over everything else.'

'They couldn't wait till it melted?'

'It didn't melt, it rained. Pissed down all afternoon, churned it to mush. No way to tell if it was one car or three, how many sets of footprints round the car. Nothing. Fuck all. A blank page.'

I thanked him and went back to staring at the screen, the shirred surface of the water. What did this mean? Assume it wasn't suicide. Assume someone – two or three someones – held a gun to Moir's head and lashed him to the wheel? They couldn't have counted on snow. They couldn't have known that the snow would lie, that enough snow would fall to cover the tracks, that the rain would turn it to slush before it could melt. So was it suicide after all? Or were the killers just careless and lucky?

I opened my drawer and took out the wad of Post-its from Neve's corkboard, the ones Moir had left. I unstuck them from each other and laid them out on my desk. There were six of them. The first three were lists of figures – they might have been prices or times – but there were two yellow squares with telephone numbers. Neither number meant anything to me. On the final Post-it was the single letter 'S' and an exclamation mark, and then 'FC, 7.30' underlined twice.

I put the two telephone numbers side by side and dialled the first one. Disconnected number. The second number didn't even ring before a voice answered, foreign.

'Speak.'

Just the one word. Blunt, dark, guttural. A thickness

to the syllable, a suggestion of phlegm.

'This is Martin.'

A pause.

'Who is this?'

Not foreign, exactly. Not Scottish, but close.

'This is Martin Moir. From the *Tribune*'.

'You fuck yourself.'

End of call.

Fock. The voice was Ulster, maybe Belfast.

I phoned Lewicki, asked him to trace the number. I had just replaced the handset when the phone rang. I snatched it up.

'I've got the President for you.'

Kathy from Reception. Then the lull: who speaks first?

'Hello?'

'Gerry. It's Gavin Haining.' The voice like its owner: hearty, overbearing, smooth. Now dropping to a sympathetic bass: 'I was sorry to hear about Martin. I truly was. I know you were close. Just a terrible waste.'

Was he in his office, I wondered? Standing at his desk in the chalk-stripe suit, looking out on the twin stone lions?

'Yeah. Thanks, Councillor.'

'I'd been meaning to call, Gerry. Partly to tell you how glad I am you're back.'

'Well that's nice of you to say so, Councillor.'

'No, I always looked out for your stuff. The city needs good journalists. Top professionals. Sunday's piece on the Homecoming? Excellent. I said to myself: I should know this guy better. How're you fixed for Friday?'

144

'I'm not sure.'

'Are you free for lunch? I meet up with some guys on a Friday. Good clean fun. You'll like it. You know the Jarvie Club.'

'By reputation.'

'There's an upstairs function suite: the Glasgow Room. I'll look for you around one o'clock. You'll enjoy it.'

Haining was ambitious. Fat man in a hurry, as Driscoll unkindly put it. Big things in the offing. The National Stage – only in his case, this meant Edinburgh, not London. Even a decade back, Haining would have aimed for the green-ribbed benches and the posh *rhubarb-rhubarb* of PMQs. Now, though, the up-and-comers saw Holyrood as the big gig. Haining was bound for glory, Labour-style. He would win the party leadership next year. The following year he would stand for parliament, hammer the Nats and take his place as Scotland's First Minister.

*

Haining's Friday Club. It was a city institution, a kind of weekly freemasonry of the great and good, a bun-fight for Haining's favourites. The *Trib*'s diary pages often ran items on the quantities of claret or Loch Fyne oysters or Carradale lobsters shifted at each of these sessions. Moir had been part of it. Now with Moir dead there was a vacancy, a berth for a tame hack, and I was the beneficiary.

Cui bono. Who else would benefit from Martin Moir's death? Moir's enemies – or at least the people who wanted him stopped – were everywhere. The people he exposed were the hoods and gangsters, but in some people's eyes he exposed us all. They were lining up to complain: the councillors, the CEOs, the tourist chiefs. Moir was letting the side down, blackening the city's name. Every other Sunday some civic patriot would be shaking his head in our letters page, dismayed that the efforts of so many dedicated, hard-working people to restore the city's image were being thwarted by the antics of slipshod hacks. The implication was always that the *Tribune* – venerable, staid, the journal of record – needn't stoop to such tactics, though the truth was that Moir was the paper's last chance.

For a time the letters had a certain plausibility. You couldn't live in Glasgow through the Nineties and not feel that the place had changed, that the city had shed its skin of soot and been born anew in a blaze of yellow sandstone. The glassy towers round Charing Cross, the Concert Hall on Buchanan Street, the Versace store in the Italian Centre: they hoisted us clear of the past. Riding upwards on the escalator in Princes Square you could feel that you had left it all behind, the gangs and the grime, the ice-cream wars, the maudlin squalor.

Then Walter Maitland went to jail. The papers had half-forgotten his existence, but Maitland controlled the supply and distribution of heroin and coke to the city's northside and the East End. The gangs hadn't disappeared; it just looked that way because Walter Maitland's grip was so tight. But with Maitland gone, it fell apart. His weak sons floundered. His successor, Hamish Neil, couldn't boss his troops. The bested rivals, the skulking outfits on the edge of Maitland's empire saw their chance. The Walshes came out swinging. It was a free-for-all. There were shootings in pub car parks. Bodies dumped in the Forth-and-Clyde, firebombs in tanning salons. Over a single summer seven murders landed on the desks of the Strathclyde CID, all of them involving persons of interest to the Scottish Crime and Drugs Enforcement Agency.

The chaos didn't last. Once Neil found his grip, purging his dissidents and crossing the river to hit at the Walshes, then the city settled down to a simmering feud. And while no one mistook this for peace, the boosters and the image-makers, the tourist chiefs and city councilors crawled out from their holes to have a go at Moir. Still, it was hard to envisage the Hoteliers' Association or the City of Glasgow Marketing Bureau putting a contract out on Martin Moir. If Moir was killed, there was a shopping list of hoods who might have done the deed. *If* he was killed.

Chapter Fourteen

'Legs. I never understood that expression. "It's got great legs." You hear it on the food shows. But this one does. Look, you can see it.' He swirled the glass, held it to the light: viscous drips in a string round the rim. 'Beautiful.'

'The French call it tears,' I said. 'The tears of the wine.'

'Is that right?'

He took a healthy pull and set down his glass. He smiled. I had my notebook on the table, my Sony UX.

'Thanks for meeting me.'

'Thanks for buying me lunch.'

We were in the courtyard restaurant at the Ubiquitous Chip. Cobbled floors and foliage; vines and tendrils trailing from the latticework. Behind Drew Cruickshank was a roughstone water-feature, swathed in ferns and verdure, great waxy leaves. It looked like he'd just stepped out of the rainforest in a Jaeger sports jacket, toting a glass of Australian red.

Drew Cruickshank was a forensic pathologist, recently retired from the Scottish Police Services Authority. I got his number from Lewicki. I'd told him some of the details on the phone, and of course he'd read the papers. But now, amid the napery and marble-topped tables and hum of lunchtime gossip, with the waiter tipping another half-inch of shiraz into Cruickshank's glass, the idea that a

Glasgow Tribune journalist had been murdered by gangsters began to seem like a preposterous fantasy. I could feel my skin pinken at the prospect of having to talk this through and I was glad when our conversation meandered from Saturday's football results to the likelihood of a 'Yes' vote in the referendum. But when the waiter collected the soup plates Cruickshank resettled his napkin and planted his elbows on the table.

'There are easier ways to do it,' he was saying. 'Your faked suicide. A fall. A hanging. Much easier ways to fake a suicide.'

I nodded. He was right. It wasn't faked, just a suicide, it was stupid to have thought otherwise. I sipped my wine. Cruickshank frowned.

'Suicide's the pathologist's finding?'

'It is,' I said. 'We haven't seen the report yet but Clare – the widow – has requested a copy. The pathologist thinks it's suicide. The Fiscal's happy, cops are happy.'

'But you're not.'

I shrugged. 'I don't know. I don't think he was planning to kill himself.'

He nodded, weighing this up. 'Ask you something, Gerry?' Cruickshank steepled his fingers, tapped them against his lips. 'What does he look like, a man who is planning to kill himself?'

I shrugged, took a sip, waited for enlightenment.

'He looks like you. He looks like me.' Cruickshank craned round, nodded at a white-shirted waiter squeezing between tables, 'He looks like him.'

The waiter caught the gesture, appeared at the table.

'Yes, gents?'

I pointed at Cruickshank. 'He was saying you look like you're about to kill yourself.'

The waiter looked at Cruickshank, back at me, eyes narrowed, waiting for the joke.

'Well,' he said, nodding slowly, 'could depend on your tip. You might want to factor that in. Man's life in the balance.'

'We'll bear that in mind.'

Cruickshank was smiling. He looked too spry and un-lined to be retired, late fifties at most. Maybe carving up cadavers kept you young.

'Had he spoken about suicide?'

'Not to me.'

'You're a journalist, you know the suicide rate in Scotland. Young males. Twice what it is in England. Occam's razor, Mr Conway. Are you making this more complex than it is? Oh, lovely.'

The waiter was here with the mains. We both ordered the lamb and it came with lightly browned dauphinoise and waxy cabbage, a bright ring of redcurrant jus.

'Humour me,' I said.

He sat up straight when the waiter leaned across to give the pepper-grinder three sharp twists then his elbows were back on the table. He shuffled in his seat.

'Okay. You're planning to murder someone,' he said, 'by tying them to their steering-wheel and submerging their vehicle. You want it to look like suicide. First question—' he jabbed his knife at me: 'how do you get them into the car, tie them to the wheel?'

150

'You drug them?'

'No you don't. The drugs will show up in the post-mortem.'

'You pull a gun on them.'

'Better.' He nodded, playing out the scenario. 'You could force the victim into the car at gunpoint, then apply the ligatures. This car was manual?'

'Automatic.'

'OK, then you have the car in drive with the handbrake on. Once the victim is secured you release the handbrake and close the doors. Naturally the victim will apply the footbrake but even if he keeps switching feet he can't do this forever. The muscle will eventually relax and then . . .' He put down his knife, slid his hand across the tablecloth and over the edge.

His glass was empty. I filled it.

'How would you do it?' I asked. 'Supposing it was you.'

'Hit them on the head,' he said simply. 'Stun them. If the post-mortem shows a head trauma, this could be explained by the impact when the car entered the water. No one knows if the victim died from the head-wound or drowned.'

Cruickshank seemed unduly pleased by this. He cubed his lamb with dainty strokes of the knife, speared one of the pink squares, puddled it in the pooling blood.

'But the seat-belt,' I said. 'You'd need to make sure he wasn't wearing his seat-belt so his head could hit the windscreen when the car hit the water.'

'Not so.' Cruickshank jerked his head sharply to the

side. 'Not hard to smack your skull on the driver's-side window in a sudden impact. Particularly if falling from a height.'

'But the autopsy would tell you anyway, wouldn't it? If he drowned or not?'

He shook his head, held up his hand while he finished chewing.

'The post-mortem. No.' He swallowed with some difficulty and slugged some red. 'Not necessarily. Not always easy to spot a drowning. You've got your body in the water. You're trying to establish, was the victim alive when he entered the drink? Or did someone bash him on the head before he went in? The problem you've got is that the signs are exactly similar. In a drowning, you'd look for froth in the airways, froth round the nose and mouth.' His finger-ends fluttered round his goatee beard. 'But you get that with a blow to the head. Or you might look for fluid on the lungs; again, that's a symptom of head trauma. Haemorrhage in the ears, it's the same story: you get it in drownings, you get it in head injuries.'

'So there's no way to tell them apart?'

Cruickshank frowned, tilted his glass in the light.

'I wouldn't say that. It's hard to be certain but you look for certain things. Like water in the stomach. Is there a large amount of water in the stomach? If so, they were alive when they hit the water. Very little water, then they've either drowned pretty quickly or, more likely, they were dead when they went in.'

'What else?'

He was chewing again. 'Sorry?'

'Water in the stomach. What else would you look for?'

He dabbed his beard with the napkin. 'In your example? The deceased's wrists are bound to the steering wheel?'

I nodded.

'Lacerations to the wrists where the cords bit in. Also, bruising around the shoulders, neck and chest. Ruptured muscles. He's thrashing around, tearing these muscles, it means he was breathing when he hit the water.'

'And if there's no bruising in those areas?'

'Then he's either very Zen about his predicament, or else he's unconscious when they put him in the car. This really is *very* good; you're sure you won't?'

'I'm fine. Thanks. You've been very helpful.'

I clicked off the UX, stowed it my pocket with the notebook. Cruickshank was leaning back, watching me with narrowed eyes, hint of a smile.

'You wrote that story,' he said. 'Last month. The football field.'

I nodded. He was waiting for the inside dope, the word on who might be next, where Neil would hit back. I drained my water, stood up to go.

'Will there be any – any developments, do you think?'

'Oh that story will run.' I looked at the glass he was holding by the bowl, its contents astir. 'That story's got legs.'

I left him nursing the last of the Bobbie Burns Shiraz. At the till, waiting to pay, I spotted the waiter standing at the serving hatch. He held his hand above his head, tugged on an invisible rope, dropped his chin onto his shoulder, tongue lolling. I took a twenty from my wallet, held it up, dropped it in the tips jar. The waiter patted his heart, smiled.

Ashton Lane. Snow falling in lazy flakes, edging the cobbles in white. A boy being towed along by his mum had his tongue out trying to catch a snowflake. Round the corner a busker with a banjo segued from 'Blue Christmas' into 'Fairytale of New York'. I texted Lewicki – *Inner Circle, 20 mins?* – and jouked into the Curler's for a pint of IPA. The text chimed back in a minute: *Done.*

At Hillhead station I bought a single, rode the escalator down to the platform, boarded the Inner Circle train. I texted Lewicki again: *middle carriage.* I wasn't sure what I'd learned from Cruickshank. If Moir was dead – or even unconscious – before the car hit the water then he'd probably been murdered. The proof would be an absence of bruising round his upper body, and a shortage of water in the stomach. But would the post-mortem even show this? Would an examiner bother recording an absence? And even if Moir did drown, it didn't mean he wasn't murdered. Someone pulls a gun. They threaten to kill his family if he doesn't get into the car. They stun him with a blow to the head. It wasn't hard to imagine.

Lewicki came on at Partick. I told him what Cruickshank had told me and then we got onto the police investigation.

'You don't think they dropped it a bit quick?'

Lewicki leaned into me as the train took the curve

154

before Govan. I felt him shrug.

'What's her name, the DS: Gunn?'

'Gunn, yeah. The sidekick's Lumsden. One minute it's a murder investigation. Next thing it's suicide. Done and dusted, no loose ends.'

We straightened up as the train came out of the bend and slowed for the station.

'It was never formally a murder investigation, Gerry.' Lewicki spoke low now that the train had stopped. A woman with a guitar case got on and sat across from us. 'Murder was one possibility. They couldn't rule it out. Not at that stage.'

'And a text is enough? They rule out murder on the basis of a single text message?'

The warning beeps sounded and the door closed again and the train hauled off into the dark.

'Well, what else do they go on? There's no sign of a struggle. He's got water in the lungs. There's no other footprints at the locus, no tyre-tracks. There's nothing to say that Moir wasn't alone.'

'But it snowed,' I said. 'Then it rained. You said it yourself.'

'Yeah, okay. It snowed and rained. But you go with the evidence that's there, Gerry. Not with the evidence that might have been there.'

There was no answer to that. The blackness smacked past the carriage windows and the woman with the guitar case studied the adverts over our heads. Lewicki shook his head. 'It happens, Gerry. It's happened before. Ninety-seven, ninety-eight, up in the North-East. A guy tied his hands to the wheel, a solicitor. Drove into Fraser-burgh harbour. Straightforward suicide.'

'Straightforward? You drive a car into a fucking harbour?'

Lewicki clicked his tongue. 'You know what I mean. Clear-cut. Unambiguous. Plus Gunn'll be under pressure to wrap it up, move on. There's new priorities.' He tugged at the cuff of one of his gloves, flexing the fingers. 'This Swan thing.'

'Billy Swan? Gangsters killing each other? I thought the principle there was let them get on with it.'

'It is. By and large. But in a public park, civilians around? Come on, Gerry. Plus there's other factors. *Panorama*'s doing a programme on Glasgow gangs. The scourge of the city, what are the cops doing about it? Network's showing it later this month. Brass are shitting themselves.'

'They want to look busy?'

'Expect to see press conferences. Expect the word "taskforce" to figure prominently. "Crackdown." "Taking the fight to the criminals." All that shit. There's the hoor, too, don't forget. Out in Duntocher.'

I turned to look at him. He held up a hand. 'The hooker. The fucking sex professional. It's still open's what I'm saying.'

The woman with the guitar stood up, moved to the exit.

'So's Moir,' I said. 'As far as I'm concerned.'

We sat in silence for a couple of stops. As we pulled out of Bridge Street Lewicki shifted in his seat.

'You're saying what – they've been told to drop the case? It's a conspiracy?'

'He didn't send the text, Jan.'

'It came from his phone.'

'He ever text you? He ever send you any texts?'

'Moir? Aye. Some.'

'He use those abbreviations? L8r. M8?' I drew the figure in the air. 'Like a twelve-year-old boy?'

'Not just twelve-year-olds.'

I looked at him. He shrugged. 'No,' he said. 'He didn't.'

'He never sent it, Jan. He never sent that text.'

*

That evening I read the first chunk of Moir's book, from the nineteenth century up to the Thirties, the Billy Boys and the Norman Conks, running battles in Cumberland Street, faces slashed with open razors. I wondered what he saw in it all, what drew him to spend his leisure time with the shades of long-dead hoodlums. Perhaps it was the honest criminality. There were Protestant gangs and Catholic gangs in Glasgow, but it wasn't like Belfast. Politics was kept to a minimum here. The gangs didn't have a cause beyond the next attempt on a wages van or a sub-post office. And maybe, too, it was distance. Eighty years down the pike it all seemed innocent fun. Cops and robbers. You could fall in love with the extravagant nicknames. You didn't have to think about the stink of shit in tenement rooms, the punched women, lice in the

157

walls, the shilpit weans in their soiled box-beds.

There was a soft crash behind me, then another. Angus was pulling books from the shelves, books with flaps and tabs, picture books, books with textured sections on their pages, the velvet of a horse's nose, the pink sponge rubber of a pig's snout, the tacky transparent gel of a beagle's tongue. The ones he didn't want were thudding onto the carpet. When he'd made his selection of five or six he carried them over one by one and slapped them down on the couch beside me. He hauled himself onto my knees and plunked himself down on my lap. I lifted a book.

Chapter Fifteen

I woke early, sweating, a sense of having overslept. Angus and Mari beside me, breathing in unison, heads canted at the same degree, their lips parted in a uniform pout. Even in sleep I spoiled the symmetry of things.

I slid out of bed, lifting my jeans from the chest of drawers, holding the buckle to keep it from rattling, eased shut the door. There was a shake of orange juice in the carton in the fridge. I left a note on the kitchen table.

Down to Charing Cross. It was barely light, the traffic sparse. The M8, then signs for Stirling. I spun the wheel and whistled along to the harmonica on 'Don't Think Twice, It's Alright'.

Maguire was right. What was I doing? There wasn't enough crime to report on, I had to go out and find more?

'We don't report crime. That's the first thing to get straight. We report *some* crime, and some *types* of crime.'

That was MacCrimmon, my first week at the *Trib*. Lunchtime in the Cope. The newsdesk grinning into their pints, watching the Crimmer school the rookie.

'You know how many crimes are committed in the Strathclyde police area in a single month? I'm talking about crimes made known to the police and cases coming to court. Everything, the whole jing-bang. Rapes, murders, traffic offences. What's the figure?'

The others smiled. They'd heard it before. I took a sup of McEwan's and pictured the city, spread out below the Campsies, the spire of the Uni, the high flats on the northern edge, the packed tracts of housing in the outlying schemes. The acts of malfeasance that seven hundred thousand souls could get through in a calendar month. I hadn't a clue.

'Couple of thousand?'

He looked at the others, shaking his head, stilled the glass at his lips. '*Fifty* thousand, son. *Fifty* thousand. How many crimes does the *Trib* report in a month? Eighty. A hundred if you're lucky. It's not even one per cent. We don't report crime.' He drained most of his beer, left a half-inch of dregs, swirled it, held the glass to the light.

'Drop in a barrel, son. That's what we report. Crimes of violence, sex crimes. *Some* of those, almost none of the rest.'

A fresh pint appeared on the bar-top and he tipped the dregs of the old one into it.

'It's just numbers, son. That's all they care about, the politicians, the coppers.' He brought his face close to mine. '*Fuck* the numbers. Fuck the numbers, son. It's your job to tell the story, make it real. Make them feel what the victim felt. It's all you can do.'

The window dropped as I held the button. Cold air bumping my forehead and cheeks. I drove through Moodiesburn and Mollinsburn, the streets looking scoured and penitent, small towns shuttered against the winter cold. I felt like an absconder, entertained a momentary urge to keep on driving, to motor clear to the Highlands, board a ferry to one of the isles, hole up in some hotel bar with a tumbler of malt, in earshot of the booming surf.

At Croy I stopped to look at the map. Up ahead was the Forth & Clyde. The canal had been widened here and the boats were tethered in rows, their glossy black hulls reflecting the water. Their cabins were painted in deep greens and yellows and smoky bright reds: they had the sombre gaiety of gypsy caravans. An ugly new hotel stood by the roadside. A weatherproof banner with a loose, flapping corner advertised Happy Hour and all-day breakfasts. He'd stopped for a drink here, Moir had. A *deoch an doris*, one for the road. The bar staff remembered him.

I parked the Forester and pushed through the double doors. The reception desk was empty. Beyond it was a bar area and off to the left a big wilderness of yellow pine tables and chairs.

'We don't open till eight.' A man was crossing towards me with a J-cloth in one hand and a spray-gun in the other. 'But I'll get you a coffee if you want to wait. Have a seat.' He gestured at the empty tables.

'Great,' I said. 'Good man.'

When he brought the coffee I had my business card ready for him. He fished his reading glasses from the V of his polo shirt.

'*Tribune on Sunday*,' he read. 'It's about the journalist, isn't it? The guy who died.'

'It is. Martin Moir was his name. Was it you who saw him?'

He shook his head. 'I was off on a golfing weekend,

161

over in Islay. Izzie served him. My wife.'

'Is she here? Can I speak to her?'

'Wait there.'

He was back in five minutes with a short plump woman in sweatshirt and jeans. She had one of those pork-pie hat-style hairnets on her head.

'I'd shake your hand but . . .' She held her hands before her in their latex gloves, a surgeon on his way to theatre. 'I'm prepping the turkeys for lunch. And dinner. Turkey turkey turkey.' She rolled her eyes and gave a bright little laugh.

'It's that time of year,' I said. 'Gerry Conway.'

'Isobel Tweedie.'

'I'll spell you with the turkeys,' said the husband, setting his cleaning stuff down on a table and heading off to the kitchen.

'Can you tell me about Martin, the guy who died? How come you remembered him?'

She rested a forearm on the back of a chair, keeping the glove free from contact. 'I remembered him fine. Still do. It was early, maybe 7.30 when he came in. We don't get busy till around nine. That's when the band starts. He was wearing a beautiful suit, dark grey, that shiny shark-skin stuff. He ordered a fresh orange and lemonade and sat over there.' She waved her arm at the tables near the reception area. She leaned down towards me, spoke in a raspy stage whisper. 'You wouldnae have kicked him out of bed, either. That's how I remember him.'

'Right. He didn't seem, I don't know, distressed? Upset?'

162

'He was fine. A bit maybe distracted, you'd say, but he didn't look, you know, suicidal, if that's what you're asking.'

I nodded, took a sip of the coffee, put my cup down. 'That's lovely. Italian roast?' She nodded. 'So. Was he drunk?'

Her eyes narrowed. She straightened up, holding her hands primly away from her body. 'We're not in the habit of serving customers who are intoxicated.'

'Even if they're drinking fresh orange and lemonade? Look, I'm not the cops,' I told her. 'I don't care who you serve. I'm just trying to find out about my friend.'

'Trust me,' she said. 'I know a drunk man when I see one. This guy, your friend? He was stone cold.'

'Okay. Point taken. He speak to anyone? Anyone speak to him?

'Not that I noticed. He was waiting for someone, though.' She caught my look. 'Oh aye. He was waiting.'

'How do you know?'

'He hardly touched his drink. Kept looking at his watch, looking at the door.'

'Did he meet them outside, maybe? You got CCTV in the car park?'

She smiled. 'That's what the cops asked. No. We've got the entrance, the back door. But the car park's blind. Anyway, he got fed up waiting. He gave it half an hour and then left. Left most of his drink.'

I pictured it. Moir walking into the cold dark night, making for his car. Someone waiting in the car park, two guys, maybe more. Moir opening the driver's door, the point of a gun in the small of his back. The short drive up to the quarry.

It wasn't hard to imagine.

'Listen, that's brilliant. Thanks for your help. Thanks for the coffee.'

'Hurry back.' She waved both gloved hands, turned on her heel, ambled back to the kitchen.

Back in the Forester I turned right at the exit, followed the last half-mile of Moir's journey. At the quarry turn-off the road climbed on but I turned into the empty car park. The wind was worse up here and I zipped my Swanndri against the cold, shaded my eyes against the white winter sun. There were mounted signs on the grassy verge: NO SWIMMING and DANGER: RISK OF DROWNING, with a stylised image of a swimmer in distress, a stick man with upraised arms, disappearing into wavy lines of water.

The ground beside the bushes was churned to hell, a mess of pits and ridges. Massive tyre-tracks – the recovery vehicle, presumably – had gouged deep diagonals in the brown earth. The treads of various work-boots criss-crossed the verge. Whatever clues the snow might have covered had long since gone.

I stepped towards the edge. The dark water swung into view. I felt a tremor in my knees, my toes curled in my training shoes the way they curled on the high board at Mureton Baths. It all came back, the echoey shouts of my friends, the wavering oblong of blue, the white Speedo wall-clock, the curious sleepiness that always seemed to grip me as I swayed above the pool.

Easier to fall than to jump.

Then a hand grabbed the back of my shirt and yanked me back.

'Jesus, mate.' He put his hand on my chest. 'You were nearly away there.' A bearded face peered into my mine. 'Are you alright?'

A dog was pawing my thighs, a wolfish grey mongrel, pink tongue and shiny black eyes, I could feel its nails through my jeans. I knelt down beside it, ruffled its throat, dodged the pink tongue, ran its ears through my hands.

'I'm fine,' I said. A smile spread over my face. 'I'm absolutely fine.' I stood up and put out my hand and the man took it warily, shook it limply as if agreeing to something he would later regret.

Back in the car I dug around in my CDs, found Otis Rush, *The Cobra Recordings*, and cranked it up. I drove off fast for Glasgow with 'I Can't Quit You Baby' slicing the air. I stopped for rolls, a packet of square sausage and half a dozen eggs at the minimart on Queen Margaret Drive. Back in the flat, I knew by the silence that Mari and Angus were still asleep. I stepped out of my shoes, hung my jacket on the hook, stuck the sausage and eggs in the fridge, kicked off my jeans and slipped back into bed, snuggling up behind her. She groaned and stirred and reached back a hand to pat my leg. The nape of her neck was damp with sweat. I hooked my chin over her shoulder, smelling her stale-sweet sleepy breath. On the bedside cabinet was a photo of Mari's old dog, her childhood pet, a dozy golden lab with a brown shoe in its mouth.

165

Chapter Sixteen

That morning, after sausage-and-egg rolls with brown sauce and hot sweet milky tea, I sat at the kitchen table with the folder of Moir's cuts. I spread the pages out on the scrubbed wood, stared at the headlines, scanned the opening pars. Behind me, Angus was standing on a kitchen chair, splashing at the sink. *Skiddling*, was the word we used when I was wee; *he's skiddling at the sink*. Mari had filled a basin with lukewarm water and dropped in some plastic cups and bowls. I could hear the scuffed cups knocking together, the spattered drumroll as the water spouted out, the bloop of a cup plunging under. I thought of the reservoir, the car smacking the surface, the inrush of water, the languid gulp as the blackness swallowed.

The printer had deepened the shadows in Moir's byline photo. He looked menacing, fierce, like one of the villains in his stories. 'Journalist of the Year' in bold font beneath his byline. I could hear his voice as I read the cuts, that indignant Ulster whine. I remembered the day he started at the *Trib*, Maguire emerging from the lift with a lanky, crew-cut teen, a nervous copy-boy.

'Gerry, this is Martin Moir.'

He was twenty-two, though he looked eighteen. Not straight out of uni – he'd cubbed for a year at the *Belfast*

Tele – but the bland, open face above the smart blue suit made him look like a prefect, a kid on a placement.

'He'll be helping you out for the next few weeks.'

I took him to the canteen, stood him a greasy bridie and a cup of orange tea. This was 1997 when you could still smoke in public buildings and I offered my Regals. Moir didn't smoke. Didn't drink either, at that stage. He was serious and eager to learn. He reminded me of guys I'd known at uni, long-vowelled Ulster Prods, grammar-school boys from Crawfordsburn or Bangor. They intrigued me, with their complacent out-of-dateness, their neat side-partings, their schoolbook Britishness. They'd grown up amid bombs and political murder, but they seemed – to the rest of us – innocent and unworldly. Balefully square, they wore rugby shirts and stonewashed jeans. Their barbered heads were there in your line of vision, always in the self-same spots, when you eased in late to a lecture. Their assignments, spell-checked and double-spaced, landed in the tutor's pigeonhole with a day or two's grace. They joined the Glasgow University Union and drank in the Beer Bar, while we holed up in the QMU, necking cider-and-blacks in the Steve Biko Lounge.

Here we go, I thought, when Maguire left Martin Moir at my side. Another grammar-school boy. Another Ulster Prod determined to feel at home on this side of the sheuch. Moir had been hired to beef up the political staff for the devolution referendum.

He was good, though. This was quickly clear. He impressed us all with his contacts, his blue suits, his intimate knowledge of the Scotland Act. For the next few days I'd

167

see colleagues standing impassively in front of Moir, as he spoke to them in earnest advocacy, his hands making balancing gestures like a man choosing fruit. He was explaining the new voting system, its German-style fusion of party list and first-past-the-post. He was enthusiastic. We went to the same press conferences; did some vox pops together. I started to like him.

And then, with less than a fortnight till the poll: the smash-up in the underpass. The mashed black Merc. It was Sunday morning, naturally, so that was the paper fucked, our splash – whatever it was – now as trivial and tinny as a radio jingle. I spent the day in boxers and T-shirt, flicking through the channels. All the channels carried the same live footage, only the grain of the picture varied slightly. You kept thumbing through the channels, as if the granular variations were significant, as if some hidden message would emerge from the matrix. The newscasters looked hyped, buzzed. You felt they'd been preparing for this. Everything looked rehearsed: the tight, Churchillian tones; the black ties; the portentous pauses, the funereal punctiliousness between anchor and correspondent, who bowed like duellists after every exchange. And always, every few minutes, the fresh declaration; the need to keep saying it, to state the fact, keep telling the news, the anchor's head sinking reverently to his papers at the end of each sombre announcement.

'Fuck!'

Fiona Maguire was on the phone.

'I know.'

'Fuck! Bastarding fuck!'

'I know, Fiona.'

'You couldn't script it. Jesus. You know what's gonnae happen.'

'What?'

'Come on, Gerry. Union flags at half-mast. Yards of floral tributes. Have you seen the telly? It's the 1950s already, bring on the Dimblebys. It's a fucking nightmare.'

'It won't matter, Fiona. It won't make that big a difference.'

Maguire laughed, a mirthless bark.

'Right. Okay. Hold that thought, Gerry.'

Over the next few hours I began to wonder if she wasn't right. Maguire was paid to read these things, to decipher trends, divine the hidden consequences, the ramifying ambit of catastrophe.

I sat on in front of the screen, a bolus of dread collecting in my chest.

Campaigning was suspended for a week. Until after the funeral. Dewar, the Scottish Secretary, was reportedly livid; he wanted a shorter moratorium, but the word had come down from London. A full week.

For the rest of that week, Moir and I were redundant. It was like burst pipes at school: you turned up every day and they told you to go home. There was nothing to do. We couldn't even help with the Diana stuff – the news guys were all over it. We ended up going to the Cope at lunchtime, the afternoon passing in a sun-shot daze. The three-fifteen from Goodwood on the box above the bar. The winking of daylight through a last half-inch of lager. The ominous rumble of pool balls being released. It was then, during one of these sessions, that Moir told me about home, about his father in the RUC, the daily routine of checking the car for suspect devices. I began to see that he wasn't as artless or green as I'd thought.

I saw it anew as I read through his cuts of the past few months. The stories were the usual blend of the banal and macabre. A man smothers his fifty-two-year-old neighbour with a cushion while they watch a football highlights show and the body is dumped in a wheelie bin. A baby found dead, wrapped in a football shirt and a pink woollen blanket, in the stairwell of a derelict tenement. A prisoner on remand hangs herself two hours after being taken off suicide watch. I'm not sure what the cuts told me, but they didn't tell me much about Moir's death.

'Wet!'

The voice rose behind me, a tragic keen: 'We-e-et! We-e-et!'

He had sluiced the water all down his front, a black, damp V on his long-sleeved T-shirt. It had gone cold now and he was sobbing with abject abandon. I lifted him down from the chair and took his T-shirt over his head, the little arms rising. I popped the poppers on his vest and took that off too. Then I wrapped him in a towel and took him through to get changed.

It was late afternoon before I sat at the table again, bottle of Sol at my elbow. It was pointless. I was looking through Moir's cuts for the key to his life, his death. What if someone did this to me? Would my own cuts tell them anything worth knowing? So little of life, so little that is vivid or true, gets into a news story. Even things you've witnessed for yourself, they get warped, translated, standardised in the telling. The fixed format, the set phrases. The news is a kind of liturgy; names and places vary but the shape of the story stays the same.

On their own, the cuts were useless. What I needed was someone to sift them, someone to pick out the story that mattered. I could start with the other guys in the Hey You, the flagship three-man Investigations Unit ('IU') Moir headed up under Rix's regime. They were friends, I figured, not just colleagues. They were close to Moir. I remembered them swaggering up to the stage at the Scottish Press Awards, three amigos in their leather jackets and ties, sharing the mike, waggling their trophies as they trooped back down. These guys might have their own theories about Moir's death. If nothing else, they'd want to share their sense of Moir, talk out their grief. But when I reached Ian Ramage that afternoon – the third member, Dominic Young, had emigrated to Melbourne last year and was apparently beyond the reach of Google – he was curt to the point of rudeness. He was busy, he said. Work was hectic. He didn't see what good it would do. He'd be doing me a favour, I told him, and when I rode out the hostile silence that followed this remark he sighed and arranged to meet me in his lunch hour on Monday.

Meantime, there was one piece in the sheaf of cuts on the table, one story that stood out. Its heat seemed to waver up from the varnished wood. I flipped through the pile and found it. Six months old. Page six lead. 'Child Sex Probe at Southside Flats', by Investigations Editor Martin Moir:

A child prostitution ring is operating on the south side of Glasgow, the *Tribune on Sunday* can reveal.

Police have confirmed that several addresses in the Govanhill area of the city are under surveillance as part of an ongoing investigation into child sexual abuse. Children as young as nine are believed to be involved.

The abuse came to light when a local father-of-two stumbled on a man having full sex with a girl in a tenement close.

Grant McClymont, 41, was walking his dog on the morning of Tuesday 12 May when he made the shocking discovery.

'The dog was off the leash,' Mr McClymont told the *ToS*. 'He ran into a close on Temora Street. It's like a rubbish tip in there – bin-bags and what have you – so I went in after him. In the back close there's a man having sex with a young lassie. It stopped me in my tracks. They just looked at me.'

The girl, who appeared to be around ten years of age, was standing on an upturned crate.

'I couldn't believe it,' says Mr McClymont. 'This was ten o'clock in the morning, in broad daylight.'

Mr McClymont says he left the tenement to seek assistance and called the police on his mobile phone. However, when officers arrived the close was empty.

Both the man and his victim appeared to be of Roma origin.

Police say the incident was consistent with their intelligence.

'We have had persistent and credible reports of child prostitution at locations in the Govanhill area,' said a police spokesman. 'Our enquiries are ongoing. If we find any evidence of criminality we will come down on the perpetrators with all the force at our disposal. The abuse of children will not be tolerated.'

I slipped it back in the pile, took a pull of beer. The cuts lay in a square of sunlight. You couldn't not picture it. The girl in the dank close. Drugged eyes and thin limbs. Feet apart on the plastic crate. The frail frame jouncing as the man bucked and rose. The beer heaved in my gullet and I swallowed it back down.

But something else got me. A dog walker? An unnamed

police source? It was thin as piss. You could paraglide through the holes in this story. Moir had done something that Moir didn't do. He had taken a flyer. Why?

Lewicki answered on the sixth ring. The private number.

'Yeah, rings a bell. This was when, again?'

'March. The incident was 12 March. Story appeared on the sixteenth.'

'And no follow-ups?'

'Nothing. He never wrote about it again.'

I stood up from the table – the low sun was hurting my eyes – and wandered through to the living room, bottle swinging from my free hand's knuckles. Something big – a lorry or a van – was parking in the street.

'So what, then?' Lewicki was irritable. 'He couldn't stand it up. No big mystery.'

'You mean you don't believe it happened?'

I crossed to the window. A white van was parked across the street, next to the wasteground, its back doors ajar.

'Mate, I could believe anything happened in Govanhill. Not just Govanhill. But if there's no follow-up it was probably bullshit.'

A man backed out of the van, hugging the end of a sofa. He dropped it on the pavement and hauled on the arm until the other end bumped down from the van. The sofa was cheap velour, champagne-coloured, missing its cushions. The man – a lanky skinhead in jeans and a pale denim shirt, Timberland work-boots – shoved and kneed the sofa over to the railings, then stepped back into the interior.

174

'An unnamed police source,' I said.

'Mm. It happens.'

The guy backed out again, toting a floppy beige sausage of carpet. It buckled in the middle and the cheese-coloured boots kicked it to the railings. I could practically read it from the window – the 'No Fly Tipping' sign tacked to the railings. The window buzzed as I slapped it with my palm but the guy was back in the van.

'It couldn't be you?'

'What?'

'The police source. It wasn't you?'

A black TV. Bending at the knees he set it down beside the sofa. Rubbed his palms down his jeans.

'Why would it be me, Gerry?'

'I don't know, Jan. Just a thought.'

The guy was slamming the van's back doors.

'Right,' Lewicki said. 'I'll ask around. Be good.'

I battered the window again. The guy looked up, shielding his eyes from the sun, head bobbing as he pinpointed the window. Then the smile, the slow erection of the middle finger. The engine rasped as he drove away.

Chapter Seventeen

The school was tall, Victorian, a barracks in sandstone. High, square and cold; a building designed to terrorise kids. Carved in imperative capitals at one end of the façade was the word 'boys'. At the other end, as distant as symmetry would permit, 'girls'.

I locked the car. It was Sunday afternoon, a thin rain sweeping the playground. A trio of jacketless boys stroked a ball back and forth on the netball court. As I crossed the road, one of them sprang onto the railings and hung there grinning, thin brown fists and sparky black eyes, a patterned jumper with fraying cuffs.

The building I wanted was next to the school. I'd got the address from Doug Prentice, the snapper who'd worked on it with Moir, the Govanhill sex story. I stopped at the path. Two smashed windows on the ground floor, squares of cardboard taped to the glass. A big splotch of damp on the building's façade, a mossy green track where the downpipe had been.

The boy on the railings was watching. The front door gave at my push but slammed shut again. I shouldered it open and squeezed through. The big landing window was glassless and a gale was blowing through the close. But the cold wind couldn't mask the stench. Rubbish was piled at the foot of the stairwell, black bags burst and torn, their innards spilling on the dark concrete – glinting tin cans, buckled two-litre coke bottles, a streaked sanitary towel, a blue translucent nappy-sack. The paint in the hallway was flaking, there were holes in the ceiling, thin ribs of light-coloured wood where the plaster had fallen away.

I stood in the wind and the smell and half-closed my eyes. It came unbidden, the image, a grainy tableau. A girl on a crate amid strewn garbage, a man's shoulders rising, his breath short, trousers bunched at his ankles.

I picked my way through the rubbish to the back door and slid the bolt. The back green had a cold, abandoned look. A carousel stood like a broken tree, baby clothes limp in the rain, a line of white vests pinned by the shoulders. A black cat stepped from a washing machine that lay canted on its side, a foundered hulk in the uncut grass. A single mattress flopped against the back wall. The wall between the garden and the school had a yard-high metal fence along its top. One end had been worked loose and pulled back, so the schoolboys could squeeze through to get their ball back. Take a shit, too, by the looks of the grass.

'Hey!'

I turned and craned up. A man at a second-floor window, Asian, his hand raised. A woman at his back, flash of orange, baby on her arm. He stabbed his finger on the pane.

'You stay!'

Back in the close I could hear him rattling down the stairs. He caught me at the front door, grabbed my shoulder, hauled me round.

'You police?'

He was small, slim, his teeth bared under a thin moustache. He was wearing a tank-top over a white shirt. Stain at the shoulder, birdshit white.

'No.'

'No.' He was nodding. 'No. Why you come here?'

He was moving a lot, his head bobbing like a boxer's.

I shrugged, looked at the front door. He leaned across me to place his palm on the door, holding it shut. I could smell the stain now, not birdshit but curdled milk, a little splash of baby vomit.

'It finish.' He pointed at the floor. 'It finish here. All finish. No more here. OK?' His hand was on my shoulder again. A sort of anguished smile spreading as he stared into my eyes like a man scanning for signs of life.

'OK,' I said. I moved his hand from my shoulder. 'It's finished. Fine. I get it.'

'No come back,' he said. He took his hand off the door.

Back in the street I gulped the cold air. A passing car sprayed slush on my jeans. I crossed the road and leaned on the Forester, reaching for my keys.

'Big man.' The Glasgow accent. 'Mister.' A boy's footsteps crossing the road. 'Mister, I can help you.'

I turned. The boy from the railings. The refugee pullover. Dirty blue joggers. New white trainers.

'Help me with what?'

He smiled.

'What you want.'

'Yeah? What do I want?'

The smile broadened. The rain was beading his black hair. He was smiling at the trick question. I was a man, I had a cock, I wanted what everyone wanted.

He jerked his thumb at the tenement. 'They had to move. Too near the school. I know where it is.' He nodded. 'I'll take you.'

I looked across the street. The Asian man had gone back inside.

'Two minutes' walk, chief. No problem.'

I jerked my chin at the boy.

He held both hands up, fingers spread.

I nodded, dug into my jeans pocket for a tenner, watched him fold it into a tight tab and tuck it into a spotless trainer.

'Don't walk beside me. Stay on the other side of the street. The door when I stop to tie my laces? That's the close. Second floor left.'

I trailed him through the sandstone streets, keeping pace on the opposite pavement. When he stood up from tying his laces he turned and walked back, didn't glance in my direction.

Second floor left. The door had a spyhole, no nameplate.

'Yeah?'

A woman in her forties, heavy but holding it well, in a straight black skirt and a tight red sleeveless blouse. Her blonde hair hung in a shortish bob.

'The boy,' I said finally. 'The boy sent me.'

'What boy?'

The hallway behind her gave nothing away: a tasselled lamp, a mirror. What kind of hall would a brothel have?

'The boy at the school.' I gestured towards the stairs as if the boy was at my shoulder. 'I went to the old place. A boy in the playground brought me here.'

'Who told you?'

'What?'

'Who told you about the old place?'

'I don't know. A friend.'

She shook her head.

'I don't remember,' I said.

'Yeah, well when your memory comes back you can come and see us again, love. OK?'

The door was closing.

'I've got money.'

'That's handy. Have a good day.'

'Walsh!' I almost shouted as the door clicked shut.

'What's that?'

The door was open.

'It was Packy Walsh. OK?'

'You know Packy Walsh? Packy Walsh told you about this place?'

'Uh-huh.'

She stood aside and held the door but as I stepped through it she placed her hand on my chest. I looked down at the painted nails, the plump fingers puckered with rings.

'What's your name, sweetheart?'

A sour guff below her perfume, a spoor of meaty armpits.

'Gary.'

'Well it's nice to meet you, Gary. I'm Carol. No rough stuff, no excitement. We're through here.'

The living room was dark, the curtains closed. A yellow dancing glare from the telly. Three girls were on the sofa and they straightened as we entered, tossing their heads. I stood there, adjusting to the light, Carol at my elbow. The three girls smiled, heads up, backs straight. Carol snapped a lamp on and turned off the telly.

Two of them were veterans. Late thirties. Plucked and burnished, eyes like garnets. The third was trying to look hard but the eyes said something else. I nodded at her.

'Gina,' said Carol.

The girl rose awkwardly on her heels and I followed her down the hall.

The bedroom was cold. It smelled of damp, an earthy, underground musk. She crouched to flick the switch on a two-bar electric fire. She stood up and smiled.

'Sixty,' she said. The accent was thick, guttural. East European.

'Right. Sorry.' I dug out my wallet and took out three twenties.

'Thank you.' She put them in a box on the mantelpiece.

When she turned round she was already loosening the belt on her dress. There were buttons big as jam-jar lids all down the front and she snapped them open. I had the sense you have in dreams, of things moving out of your control, events proceeding at a pace of their own.

'There.'

181

The dress landed on the armchair.

'Brrr!'

She laughed, hugging herself and rubbing the backs of her arms. Her body in its flesh-tone underwear was skinny and pale, gooseflesh-grey. I noticed her collar-bones, the hollows at the pelvis where the fabric of her knickers stood away from the skin.

She stepped out of her heels and sort of skipped across the carpet and gripped the lapels of my jacket.

Her shoulders were stippled with cold. I ran my hands down the backs of her arms, traced with my thumb the little white hollow on her upper arm.

She pulled my jacket off my shoulders and tugged it down, pinioning my arms. I had to fight and wriggle to work it loose. It thumped onto the floor. She touched me then, cupping me lightly and I looked away.

'Don't worry. She smiled. 'Take your time.'

She pushed me onto the bed but when her hands started working on my belt I reached down and gripped them.

'No,' I said. 'It's not – I'm a journalist.'

I struggled up and stepped away, buckling my belt. She was kneeling by the bed like a child at prayer.

'I'm a journalist.'

She shook her head. I mimed fingers hitting a key-board. 'A reporter. For a paper.'

The girl shrugged, her breasts moving in the pallid bra. I sat on the bed.

'A man saw something. A few weeks ago. Not here but in the old place. On Temora Street. Temora Street?'

She nodded. She said the words, 'Temora Street.'

'He saw a young girl. Very young. A man was with her. There are young girls here?'

'Young.' She was nodding, she knew the word. 'You like young?'

'No! No. It was in the paper.' I mimed opening a newspaper. 'A news story. A man saw a girl. She is too young.' I pressed my palm down on the empty air, measuring the height of a child. 'A kid. A girl. With a man.' I pointed at the door. 'Is she here? Do you know her?'

I had lost her. She smiled uncertainly, waiting for me to go on, waiting for it to make sense. I could hear a door closing, movement in the hall. I had the ridiculous notion that the door would burst open and I'd be caught not fucking, caught with my pants up. The girl shrugged and smiled.

It was useless. I got her dress from the armchair and tossed it to her. She put it on slowly, still confused, rising from her knees, working the buttons. She was wary, now, something was wrong, she had failed, it was her fault.

I picked up my jacket. There were cards in the top pocket and I fished one out and passed it to the girl. She closed her fist round it.

'I'm sorry,' I said, though I couldn't have said what I was sorry about.

In the hallway the woman called Carol was waiting.

'Enjoy yourself, love?'

'Great,' I said, but she didn't buy it and I knew that the girl would be getting a hard time. Whatever I might have looked like walking down that hall, it wasn't like a man who'd just had sex.

'She works Tuesday to Saturday, afternoons. Friday nights too.'

'I'll bear it in mind.'

*

That evening I was flicking through the channels when Mari came through, pointing the phone at me like a TV remote, mouthing the word 'Lewicki'. He never gave his name when he called but she knew his voice by now. I killed the sound on the telly.

'Moir's story,' he said. 'Govanhill.' I'd emailed the cut to him. Lewicki had an email address in a bogus name; he checked it daily in an internet café.

'The lassie in the close. What about it?'

Angus was playing at my feet, moving his cars around on the carpet, running them up the leg of the coffee table.

'Well there's a reason it came to nothing.'

'Yeah?'

'The witness. Grant McClymont. Bit of history.'

'Not just a dog walker?'

'Assault. Couple of breaches. Intent to supply. Not a celebrity but he's done time.'

Angus looked up from his toys: 'Dog!'

'Doesn't mean he's lying, Jan. Doesn't mean he didn't see it.'

'No, but it means you ca' canny. Exercise a degree of caution. Plus, the dog – it's some fucking walker. It likes a walk that dog.'

184

'He's not local?'

'His *sister*'s local. She lives the other side of Queen's Park. He says he was visiting her. But McClymont's from Cranhill.'

A little stress on the last word, a rising inflection.

'Cranhill,' I repeated. Angus was running a car across my shoe, up my shin.

Lewicki sighed. 'Who's who in Cranhill, Gerry? You're the fucking journo.'

'You mean he's one of Neil's? He's working for Neil?'

'He *drives* for Hamish Neil.'

The guy at the Goldberry, standing at the fire door, the big bloke in the crombie.

'He's a person of interest, number of enquiries. We've interviewed him more than once. Blood from a stone. Suddenly he's down Aikenhead Road giving a statement. He's falling over himself to cooperate. He can name the pimp, he tells them. A Roma guy. Slovak. And the guy he names? He's a known associate of Packy Walsh.'

The old tactic. Grassing to settle scores.

'It could still be true,' I said. Angus had scrambled onto the couch and was running his car up my arm.

'It could still be true. Except the Slovak's got a decent alibi. He was in the Western on the morning in question. Recovering from stab wounds. Not discharged till the following day.'

The car was on my head now, catching hairs in its tiny wheels. I set Angus down on the carpet, passed him his car, leaned across to snatch a pen from my computer table.

'This Slovak.'

'Radislav Gombar.'

'Say it again.'

'Radislav Gombar. Just as it sounds.'

I wrote the name on the pad. The guy McClymont fingered for the incident in Govanhill was in hospital when it happened. Expect that was the point, wasn't it? The girl in the close, the milk crate, the child sex ring: it was bullshit. None of it happened. It was Neil's man setting up Walsh's man, a porky for the porkies, a fairytale Moir had reported as fact. I was suddenly angry, angry at Moir for writing the story, making me see what had never been, mad at myself for getting suckered.

'So Moir got stitched up.'

Lewicki sniffed. 'That's one way to put it.'

Chapter Eighteen

'She expecting you?'

The desk-sergeant had a boss eye. It gave him a bitter, incredulous look, as if life kept finding new ways to provoke him.

'She'll see me.' I pushed my card across the desk. 'Tell her it's to do with Martin Moir.'

I waited on the blue bench-seats, under the public-information posters in four languages, the Crimestoppers number, the announcement of a knife amnesty. There was a box of toys against the wall, a stunted Christmas tree in the corner under the telly. The desk-sergeant looked too old for his uniform. I didn't like him. The grin he kept for the bantering officers who passed in and out faded as soon as their backs were turned.

Twenty minutes passed. Half an hour. A buzzer sounded. Gunn came through the inner doors, shrugging into a grey pinstripe jacket. We didn't shake hands. She looked harassed. There were flakes of pastry on her black shiny blouse.

I signed in and followed her up the stairs. At the first-floor landing a thin man in a blue suit passed us on his way down and Gunn turned, spoke to him over my head.

'Derek! Can I use your room? Ten minutes.'

The man looked neutrally at me. 'Fine, Sheena.' He tossed a bunch of keys and she caught them right in front of my face.

The desk took up most of the cubicle. She squeezed behind it and frowned at me.

'Thanks,' I said. 'I appreciate this. Seeing me, taking the time.'

She nodded, said nothing.

'Look. He didn't do it.' I told her. 'He never killed himself.'

'Sit down, Mr Conway.' She rubbed her thumb and forefinger over her eyelids, looked at the wall beside her. A map of the city was tacked to a corkboard. Thick black lines carved the districts into unfamiliar wedges, operational divisions.

'I think he was murdered. You were right all along.'

She leaned back. A tiny skylight window threw its square of light in her face. She shielded her eyes.

'Slow news day?'

'Slow?' I snorted. 'Look in a mirror, you want to see slow. You've been sitting on this for bloody weeks.'

'Yeah. Okay. You're looking for a story, Mr Conway. Don't ask the police to help you.'

'Yeah, you're right. I've just dreamed this up in an idle moment. It never crossed anyone else's mind that Moir was murdered.'

Gunn's eyes closed briefly. When she opened them she was looking past me, sucking her top lip.

'We kept an open mind, Mr Conway. We considered

188

the possibility, yes. But it was your evidence. It was your phone that gave us the suicide note.'

'But you were right the first time. That's what I'm saying. He didn't send the text.'

She was looking at a spot on the wall beside my head.

I moved my head to catch her gaze. 'Look, it's simple, he always wrote things out in full. He never used text language. Never. He had a thing about it.'

She plumped her elbows on the desk, rested her chin on her clasped hands. She was tired and riled and unbelieving, and the set of her mouth drained all conviction from my words. We sat there in silence.

'Why don't you ask me who killed him?'

'Because I don't believe he was killed.'

'I think you do. I think you're scared of the answer.'

She looked down at the desk, brushed the pastry from her blouse. Folded her arms.

'You know what I ought to be doing right now?'

I shrugged. She was looking at me now.

'A wee girl's been attacked,' she said. 'Eight years old. I won't tell you what's been done to her. I'm working through the known offenders. That's what I should be doing right now. That's what you took me away from. So. Now that you've got my full attention, Mr Conway. Now that you've held up another investigation. Who killed Martin Moir?'

She gave it the sing-song lilt of a rote question. My answer sounded hollow, even to me.

'Packy Walsh killed him.' *'I' said the sparrow, with my bow and arrow.*

'That's good.' She nodded and tapped the desk twice as she got to her feet. 'Thanks for sharing that, Mr Conway. The clearance rate's going to look a lot healthier.'

'That's it?'

She held the door.

'Well unless you've got a slightly stronger card to play than the intuition of Gerard Conway I'd say we're finished here, wouldn't you?'

*

Back at the office an A4 envelope with an Ayrshire postmark was sitting on my desk: the PM report, with a note from Clare. It was nearly lunchtime so I took it to the Cope. It was a two-doctor autopsy. One doctor would mean they'd already decided it was suicide. Where the Fiscal suspects murder, where a prosecution is likely to follow, he stipulates two doctors. It's a question of corroboration.

I took a sup of Deuchars, started scanning through the pages. The report noted water in the lungs. There were abrasions on the wrists, consistent with the deceased thrashing around while drowning, and both wrists had been broken, possibly by the deployment of the air bag. The rope had been examined. The configuration of the knots was such that the deceased could readily have tied them himself. No indication of serious head trauma. Some bruising and contusions to the right temple, probably sustained at the moment of impact. No trace of controlled substances or toxins in the blood but very high levels of alcohol. The conclusion – suicide by drowning – had that air of judicious finality common to all PM reports. I folded it into my *Tribune* and finished my pint.

So that was that. As ever, it was the things that weren't mentioned that bothered you. No word of torn shoulder muscles or abrasions on the chest. And if Moir had been drinking, why had he seemed sober in the canalside hotel? The report hadn't settled anything. We knew in advance that it might have ruled out suicide, though in the event it hadn't. But despite the pathologists' conclusions, it hadn't ruled out murder either.

Back at my desk I was reading Moir's cuts when the phone rang loud, seemed to bounce at my elbow.

'Gerry, a word.'

'Fiona, give me five minutes. I'm onto—'

'Now.'

I looked up from my screen. She was framed in her doorway, a vengeful silhouette, then the doorway was clear. I got to my feet.

'Sit down, Gerry. Shut the door.' She went behind her desk and stood at the window. 'I give you a few days to get this out of your system. Now, what, you're visiting brothels?'

'What?'

The daylight haloed her. I couldn't see the expression on her face. I thought maybe that was a good thing.

'You're visiting brothels. On company time.'

'On a story, Fiona, I was on a story. Who told you this?'

'What story?'

'Moir. Govanhill.'

I told her about Moir's child sex piece, my visit to the tenement, the boy who took me to the new place.

'You went with one of the girls.'

'Who told you this?'

'A call was made. Anonymous call. You denying it?'

'Anonymous! Packy fucking Walsh, Fiona. Wanting me stopped. "Call off your boy." And that's what you're doing.'

'Did you go with a girl?'

I shielded my eyes. Her perfume was choking me, burning my nostrils.

'Well that was kind of the idea. Difficult to talk when there's a half a dozen people in the room.'

'Talk,' she said. 'Talk, that's good. Did you pay her?'

'What?'

'You heard.'

'Yes I paid her. Of course I paid her.'

'Your own money?'

'My own fucking money, Fiona. I'm not claiming it on eccies. I'm not putting it in my tax return.'

She stepped away from the window and sat on her desk. She crossed her arms and uncrossed them.

'Did you have sex with her?'

'Fuck this.' I stood up. 'I'm going to HR and I'm going to MacLaurin.' Hugh MacLaurin was our union rep, Father of the Chapel. 'You better have a good reason for carrying on like this. It's not illegal. In case you didn't know. Even if I paid her for sex, it's not illegal.'

'Well that's fine then. Knock yourself out. Top *Trib*

journo tours the brothels. That's a great look for the paper.'

'I don't know. Might put a few hundred on the Sunday.'

'Don't fucking push it, Gerry.'

I stopped in the doorway. Our eyes were locked, the stand-off stare.

'Tell me you got something then. At least tell me that.'

I held her gaze for another few seconds and slammed out into the newsroom.

When I got back to the flat Mari was crashed out on the sofa with Angus on her chest. I hoped there was still a beer in the fridge. Mari's *Christmas Crooners* CD was playing in the empty kitchen, a lot of swooping strings and festive suavity. I opened the last Sol and slumped onto a kitchen chair. According to Bing it was beginning to look a lot like Christmas.

I took a long pull on the bottle.

'You fucking think so?' I said.

Chapter Nineteen

McCallum and Stokes had their offices on Hope Street. Good address for a law firm, I thought, as I slogged up the communal stairs and took my seat in reception. Ian Ramage was running their in-house PR. I remembered him well from my first stint at the *Trib*. He was the one who got the biggest kick out of the Hey You's 'undercover' look, the one who stayed in character, even in the office, scuffed Sambas up on the desk, swigging Coke, rubbing his five-day beard and talking out of the side of his mouth in that nasal Clydeside whine. I wondered if he kept it up at home. You pictured him scowling at the telly, dousing a fag in an empty tinnie, cuffing his kids on the back of the head.

Now, though, he was striding to the double doors, polished loafers winking in the striplights. Clean-shaven, black suit and a soft-touch open-necked shirt, cornflower blue. Thin and pinched. I wouldn't have known him.

We stopped at Pret A Manger for takeout sandwiches and coffees and then walked on down, without discussing our destination, to George Square. A pale winter sun was squatting on top of the City Chambers. Despite the cold the benches were full, the office workers squashed together with their Greggs pasties and sandwich cartons on the little islands of grass. We sat side-by-side on the steps of one of the statues, an equestrian number, all hooves and helmet plumes.

Ramage sucked his iced latte with its straw, its see-through plastic dome. I shifted my hams on the cold marble step, stowed my turkey-and-cranberry wrap in the pocket of my Berghaus.

'Missed you at the funeral.'

'Right.'

He tore a bite off his sandwich, a shred of rocket hung from his lip and he pushed it back in with a twist of his thumb.

'You couldn't make it?'

He chewed down his bite of sandwich, sucked on the straw.

'I worked with the guy. It doesn't make me his friend.'

I nodded, took a slug of mocha.

'Does it make you his enemy?'

Ramage looked away across the square. He turned right round to face me.

'The fuck kind of question is that?'

'I don't know. You work with the guy for three years. Three-man team. You're too busy to go to his funeral?'

'And that's your business how?'

'I'm asking, that's how. I was his mate and I'm asking.'

Ramage was shaking his head, bulge of muscle in his jaw.

'I didn't like him. It happens sometimes. In fact, I think it might be happening again.'

I didn't say anything. We chewed our sandwiches to-gether. Ramage looked at his watch.

195

'How are things anyway?' he said finally. 'On the Quay.'

'Fine. Apocalyptic gloom. Hysterical laughter. It's like the last days in the Führerbunker.' I shrugged. 'Same old same old.'

Ramage laughed. 'Didn't you leave?' He frowned round at me. 'I thought you left.'

'I came back,' I said. 'Couldn't keep away.'

He took another bite of his sandwich. We chewed together in companionable silence.

'Glutton for punishment.' He stamped his foot at one of the red-legged pigeons that were encroaching on our space. 'I was glad to get out of the *Trib*. Glad to see the back of it.'

I kept quiet. Ramage shuffled back against the plinth, sucked down some more latte.

'I kept thinking I'd get my chance,' he said. 'Keep the head down, file your copy, the break would come.'

'Fat chance.'

'Yeah. Well. Slow learner, me. I wrote a piece about a year ago, a child-benefit scam.'

'I remember it. Govanhill.'

I did remember it. A Roma gang was trafficking kids up from England, registering them at local schools and claiming child benefit. The kids never showed up in school; they disappeared, back to England, back to Slovakia, and the gang collected the benefits.

'That's it. The Leeds and Bradford connection. Anyway, it was a decent story. And I did the running. I found the story, stood it up. I wrote the copy. My first splash. I was stoked, you know? I stopped off on the way home, bought some bubbles at the offy. I get up on Sunday morning and they've swapped the first two pars and given the byline to Martin Moir. *With additional reporting by Ian Ramage.* I thought: fuck this for a game of soldiers. That's when I knew: I'm never getting anywhere in this game.'

'Been there,' I told him. 'You're on a hiding to nothing. He's the name reporter. It's his byline that puts on readers.'

'Oh Moir was the talent, no question. In some way I didn't even mind. Moir could write. He had it all over me and Dom, as a writer. But getting stories? He didn't have the nose. Stomach either, come to that.'

'Yeah? I think he did alright, all the same.'

Ramage's latte ran out, his straw rasped in the empty carton. He burped. 'Think what you like. We fed him the stories – Dom Young and me. Everyone thought Moir was the golden goose. Like fuck. He was the wee runty bird in the nest – left to himself he'd have starved to death.'

Ramage's lunch-break was over. We stood up to go.

'Fuck is this guy anyway?'

He was craning up at the black prancing hooves, the bulging chest muscles, the plumed helmet.

'I don't know, Ian. Listen, there's nothing you worked on together, nothing that might give us a clue, some idea of what happened, what kind of trouble he was in?'

Ramage crumpled his sandwich tray, wedged it in a bin with his coffee carton.

'I'm happy to help. I actually am. But, Gerry: the guy

197

wrote exposés of gangsters. That was his job. You want to know who's happy Martin's dead? There's whole streets in this city, entire fucking postcodes.'

We walked back across the square.

'So you came back?' he said. He was smiling now, scornful and maybe a little bit jealous.

'The bad penny,' I said. 'Dog to its vomit.'

It's not a job. No one comes to papers for the job. It's not a career. It's Woodward and Bernstein. Your name on a byline. Your splash on the news-stand, the big black type in its lattice frame. It's Welles in his black fedora atop a mountain of bundled *Inquirers*. It's Redford's corduroy suit in *All the President's Men*. Break the news. Expose the facts. Tell the truth and shame the devil. That's why you started. The career, the mortgage, the school fees, the car; all that came later. And once you're encumbered with kids and cars and monthly repayments, that's when you weigh things up and that's the time – if you've got any sense – that you look round for something else. Even then, though, you'd linger a bit on your way out the door.

We walked up St Vincent Street. Sun in the windows. Hard yellow sky. Traffic fumes. At the corner with Hope Street we shook hands and swapped business cards. I was halfway across the junction when he shouted.

'Gerry.'

At the far kerb I turned. The green man was flashing, the traffic already pulling away. Ramage stood on his tiptoes and shouted something but it died below the engine noise.

'What?'

He tried again, his voice pitching higher.

'The stories he *wasn't* writing,' he shouted. 'Think about them.'

He turned on his heel and a double-decker ground past. When its orange bulk had passed he was gone, lost among the bobbing heads.

When I got back to the flat that evening Mari was lying on the living-room carpet watching the Disney Junior channel. Angus was asleep on her chest again. I put a cushion under her head and turned down the telly.

'Elaine rang.'

'Yeah? What about?'

'I don't know. She wants you to call her back.'

I took a Sol from the fridge and punched the number. It was Adam who answered. His bonhomie sounded a little strained and when Elaine came on I understood why. He'd been offered a job, a big promotion. In Aberdeen. They hadn't decided anything and they had a couple of weeks to make up their minds but they wanted to put me in the picture.

'Aberdeen? You're not serious, Lainie? You'll be wearing thermal underwear for ten months of the year.'

'It's a good job, Gerry.'

'But Aberdeen? Jesus. What does he do again?'

'Gerry, for God's sake. He's a hydraulic engineer.'

'Right, right. Not going to take it, though. Is he?'

'We're discussing it, Gerry. Like I said. I'll keep you in the loop. You'll be the first to know.'

Chapter Twenty

Tuesday morning. The cold stung my eyeballs, pinched my ears, itched the dry split in my lip. I'd overslept, felt like shit – the boy woke up twice, needing changed, needing a bottle – and the tiredness ran in shivers down my arms, across my back. I was out in the street, engine running, heater on, chipping at the windscreen with the plastic scraper. Late for conference. No stories. No leads. Cursing it out with every stab of the scraper. Fucking weather. Fucking country. Fucking job. Fucking city. Muffled music, the opening bars of *White Riot*. I shook one glove loose, and fumbled for the phone. Fingers stinging in the cold, get it before it goes to voicemail.

'What!'

Nothing. Not nothing – silence, somebody there. I tried again.

'Gerry Conway speaking. Who is this?'

'Mr Conway?' The voice sounded distant and thin. An accent. 'Is Mr Conway?'

'Who is this?'

'Gina.'

Who's Gina? I thought. Then she said her name again and it came to me. The red dress on the floor; goose-flesh under my palms. The smell of damp and the two-bar fire.

'Gina from . . . before.'

'I know who you are, Gina. Do you want to meet?'

We arranged to meet that afternoon at three, in a café on Kilmarnock Road. I'd just ended the call when the phone rang again. Driscoll.

'Duty calls, Gerry. Pitt Street at two. Body found in the West End. Murder.'

'Yeah, I'm actually onto something here, Jimmy. It's a story. Could be big.'

'Mmm!' Driscoll's mock enthusiasm. 'A murder, is it? Murder in progress?'

'No, it's—'

'Yeah. This is a murder, Gerry. You're the crime reporter. So there might be a school of thought that argues this should take precedence. Over anything. Be there at two.'

I took the phone from my ear and looked at it, as though expecting an explanation for Driscoll's rudeness. Then I stowed it in my pocket, pulled on the glove and started back with the scraper. Gina had withheld her number. If I didn't show up at three, if I missed our meeting, she might not get back in touch. But if I didn't show up at two to the Pitt Street press conference, I might not have a paper to write for.

Once the window was clear I drove Angus to nursery, signed him in, hung his jacket on his peg, watched him settle down at the puzzle table. As I hit the signal on my way out of the car park a man waved from an incoming car. It was the owner, fifties, shaved head, tight white goatee. He swung past in a black BMW X5, thirty grand's worth of car. I'd have paid for that in full by the time Angus started primary school.

'It's official, then,' he said. 'You're the new Martin Moir.'

I eased into a splay-legged lozenge of moulded tangerine plastic, nodding at the old hands behind me, MacCrimmon, Torchuil Bain.

'Not the new anything, mate. I'm the old Gerry Conway.'

We were in the conference room at Pitt Street. I was sitting next to Pete Gallacher of the *News of the World*.

'Yeah, speaking of Moir . . .' he was saying.

'I wasn't.'

'Aye, but speaking of Moir, I heard something.' I knew what was coming. I knew by the pitch of his voice, the way he wasn't looking at me. 'They're saying it might not have been suicide.'

'Who's saying?'

He shook his head. 'I know you were close, Ger. It's none of my business.'

He was checking his voice recorder, thumbing the buttons.

'It's rubbish,' I told him. 'He left a note. The Fiscal's satisfied, the police. It's rubbish, Gal.'

He nodded.

The pack shushed and shifted in their seats as a uniformed cop hustled into the room and took his seat at the table. A media-relations civvy was passing out copies of the press release. The cop took his hat off and set it on the table. His hair was white, the hat had left a ring around his head. He looked fat and ungainly in the new Strathclyde uniform, the black Lycra T-shirt, the zippered fleece. He stared morosely ahead while the handouts did the rounds.

'Gentlemen. Ladies. I'll keep it brief.' You do that, I thought. He lifted a sheet of paper, the same sheet we held in our hands, and started to read.

'A body was discovered in the early hours of this morning in a lane in the West End of Glasgow. A postmortem examination has confirmed the cause of death as multiple stab wounds. The victim, who has not yet been identified, was male, white, aged between thirty and fifty, with mid-brown hair. Anyone who was in the vicinity of Great Western Terrace Lane between 1 a.m. and 6 a.m. this morning should contact Crimestoppers on 0800 555 111 or the incident room at Partick Police Station on 0141 641 7331.'

He looked up, suspicious, truculent, as if waiting to be contradicted. Gallacher raised a hand.

'Was it sexual, inspector?'

The cop's eyes widened, as if the very notion were outlandish. He stared at Gal for a moment and then back across the heads.

'There is no evidence to suggest a motive of a sexual nature.'

'Mugging?' someone offered.

'The victim's belongings appear to be intact. We don't suspect robbery as a motive.' The cop put his hands on the desk, fingers linked. 'There is, however, another element to this investigation, one that we don't wish to over-emphasise at this stage, and I would ask you to resist unwarranted speculation in your reporting of this element.' We all sat up a little, shuffled in our seats, gripped our pens a little tighter. 'The victim was wearing a football scarf in the colours of Glasgow Rangers.'

The pack stirred.

'It's sectarian?'

We were picturing the headlines, the billboards, the spike in sales. The cop raised his hands, brought them down in a shushing motion.

'We don't know. We do not know. But, yes, at this stage we cannot rule out a sectarian motive.'

He looked around to check that we were finished, no further questions, gave a single nod.

'Thank you.'

He lifted his hat. The chairs scraped back.

'Was he tortured?'

The cop was halfway out of his seat, jamming his hat on his head. We all stopped where we were, frozen in postures of decrepitude, hunch-backed, knees bent.

Torchuil Bain of the *Mail* was still seated, finger in the air, conning his notes. He looked up brightly.

'Was he tortured, inspector? Is that why you can't tell the age?'

The cop settled his hat and zipped up his fleece. His face had coloured, darkened, stormy bulges purpling his jowls.

'The pathologist's report will clarify that. I have no further comment to make.'

The pack moved into a huddle, comparing notes, checking details. I pushed through and made it to the door. The inspector was halfway down the corridor, moving quickly.

'Inspector.'

He kept walking, turned his head slightly as I caught up with him. 'I have said all I plan to say, Mr—'

'Conway. Gerry Conway from the *Tribune*.' I held out a card. He didn't take it. We had reached a set of security doors. He was punching in a number.

'Inspector. How will this affect next Saturday?'

There was an Old Firm game in two weeks' time. They were always trouble. But now? After this? The inspector frowned, held the door for a moment.

'Well that rather depends on you fuckers, doesn't it?'

The door crunched shut.

This was the story, this was tomorrow's splash. Every paper in Scotland would put on readers tomorrow. Hightailing it back to the Quay and getting this down in a hurry should have been pretty far up my to-do list. Even phoning it in. But I didn't have time.

The car was in West George Street on a thirty-minute meter that had expired ten minutes ago. I set off at a sprint, jacket flapping behind. Let them ticket me, just don't let it be clamped. Don't let it be towed.

It wasn't. I threw myself into the Forester, hauled shut the door and gunned it down Pitt Street and onto the bridge. It was quarter to three, traffic filling all three lanes but moving briskly. I turned off at Junction 1, past the Burrell, the round tollhouse on Pollokshaws Road, and up into Shawlands.

When I reached Kilmarnock Road the schools were

letting out and I couldn't get parked. I got to the caff at ten past three, breathless, sweating. She was sitting at a window table, hands cupped round a steaming mug like a woman in a soup advert. A grey polo-neck sweater, jeans and brown boots. Brown leather flying-jacket over the chair.

I ordered camomile tea.

'You look different,' I said.

She smiled tightly. 'With clothes on?'

'No. I mean. Yeah. With your clothes on.'

She nodded.

'You look different also.'

'I look like shit.'

She laughed. 'This is what I mean!'

The waitress came with the china pot, the smoked-glass tea cup, pot of extra water, set them down in turn. She looked at the table and nodded, drifted off with her empty tray. I smiled at Gina.

'Is Helen,' she said. I nodded, mind a blank. 'Helen *Friel*.' I smiled again. She was angry now, her hands in tight fists on the table top. 'The girl who is killed.'

'Right. I'm sorry.' The prostitute. The body in the woods. I'd written the bloody story.

She sat back, sipped her hot chocolate. 'I know who.'

'You know who killed her?'

A workie came in, boiler suit tucked into his boots, looked around, stared at Gina as he clumped up to the takeaway counter. Our napkins fluttered when the door banged shut.

She gripped the mug tighter, nodded.

'Have you gone to the police?'

She shook her head. I glanced at the counter where the workie was looking over, caught his eye, held it till he looked away.

'Is it a punter? Do you know his name?'

'Is no punter.' The word in her mouth had a vicious, plosive sound, it took her accent to reveal the word's true meaning. 'No punter. Is Mr Walsh.'

'Walsh? Which one?'

'Thin one.'

The workie lifted a styrofoam cup from the counter, glanced neither right nor left, let the door swing back as he strode into the roadway. The waitress crossed to shut the door.

'Packy Walsh killed the girl, strangled her?'

'No. His friend. But Walsh is the guilty.'

I bought her another hot chocolate and she told me the story. She wouldn't let me tape her but I took notes as she spoke, filling three pages of my Moleskine while she spoke in halting English and gripped her mug, tapping its rim with a crimson fingernail.

It was a Friday night, she told me. Walsh brought his friends round on Friday nights, business partners, key lieutenants, eight or nine of them. The girls had to service them for free. There was one they all dreaded, a skinny bloke with glasses and red hair. He liked to choke the girl he was screwing, grip her throat till she spluttered and gagged, her eyes rolling white in her head. He would pay for his pleasure, unlike the others, double the going rate, but the girls drew the line, turned him down. All except Helen Friel, pushing thirty, six years on the game. She hadn't the looks of the other girls, she turned fewer tricks, she couldn't be choosy. Helen had the full house – the habit, the kid, the wastrel husband who showed up pissed to steal from her purse. So she went with Walsh's ginger mate on Fridays. She wore a silk scarf for the next three days but she went. And then one week she didn't.

It was late October. A football match had been played that week – it was Borussia Dortmund at Parkhead, I later worked out – and the visiting fans had been celebrating. The girls made a fortnight's wages in one night. Even Helen was flush. On the Friday, though, she'd caught a cold and her throat was sore. When Walsh and his cronies trooped in around midnight, she rose to go. *Where's the fire?* says Packy Walsh; *the fun's just starting.* But she picked up her cigarettes and lighter and stowed them in her handbag. Walsh was livid, raging. A hoor showing him up in front of his mates. Carol tried to intervene, the madam, but Walsh knocked her down before starting on Helen. He slapped her around, took his time, made it look good for his mates, for the other girls, until Helen picked herself up and stalked off down the hall with the red-haired man at her back.

Later they heard noises from the room, a man's cries, some crashes and bumps. When they poked their heads out of their own rooms and gathered in the hallway in their robes and kimonos, a man was stationed in front of Helen's door, barring the way. The girls were told to dress and go. Something had happened, something had gone badly wrong, but no one knew what till they saw Helen's face on the Sunday-night news. Glasgow prostitute missing, hasn't been home in two nights. The police came round but the girls didn't talk: no one was keen to be the next Helen Friel. When they found the body in woods no one was surprised. Carol started a story that Helen Friel had gone home that Friday. She'd gone out alone on Saturday night, walking the streets, and someone had abducted her, taken her off and killed her. Nobody believed it but nobody denied it.

'And you would testify to this?'

She nodded, knew the word. 'Testify.' She nodded firmly. 'Testify, yes.'

'And you're not scared?'

She shrugged. She was going home, she told me. She wasn't an illegal, she had paid her own way here. She owed no one anything. She wasn't being held against her will. She had made some money and now she would go home, back to her family, her mother and father, her little boy in Brezno. But she would talk to the police and, if needed, she would come back to testify.

I nodded. I didn't believe her. Good intentions. She might talk to the police before she left, but when she got back to her home town, to her little boy, would she want to come back to nail a Glasgow gangster? We needed to get it all now, everything she might remember.

'What about the man with red hair?' I asked her. 'Did you see him again?'

She shook her head.

'Glasses. Red hair. Skinny. Anything else?'

She pushed back the sleeve of her jumper, twisted a brown arm under the lights. Tracks? He was a junkie? No: she was clapping a cupped palm onto her upper arm. She repeated the gesture.

'A tatt? He's got a tattoo?'

'Yes!'

If she'd seen the tatt, maybe she'd been with him too. Had he hurt her too?

'Is OK.' A mind-reader. She gripped my wrist. 'I'm OK.'

'Good,' I said. 'I'm glad. The tattoo. What was it?'

She put her hand out like a traffic policeman: Halt.

I waited. She did it again, held the hand out, fingers together, in front of my face, watching my reaction. I shook my head, shrugged, I didn't get it.

'A hand,' she said. 'Red.' She tapped one of the roses on the tablecloth. Held the palm up again: 'Like this.'

I nodded. The Red Hand of Ulster. Good. Not the most unique of emblems in the West of Scotland, not the kind of design one could show around the tattoo parlours, hoping to trace your man. But something.

'And words,' she said. Her fingers traced a smiley mouth on her shoulder. 'Other language.' She shrugged.

I took her napkin, flattened it out, clicked my biro, drew the hand, the shield, the crown on top, the curved scroll underneath, filled in the words: *Quis Separabit.*

'Yes!' She patted the napkin. That was it.

Quis Separabit: Who Will Separate Us? He had a tattoo of the crest of the Ulster Defence Association. He was a UDA sympathiser, possibly a member – the UDA had a

210

Scottish Brigade. She gripped my wrist again, frowning, pointed at the napkin. She wanted an explanation. How to explain to a Slovakian Catholic the allegiance of a lowland Scot to an outlawed Ulster Protestant paramilitary force? I didn't try.

'Politics,' I said.

She gave me her number, the address of a flat in Battlefield. She was flying to Prague next Friday but was happy to talk to the police before then.

We shook hands on the pavement outside the café. I told her I would be in touch. I looked for something else to say, mark the occasion.

'You're brave,' I told her, stating the bloody obvious. I patted my heart – where I thought my heart would be – but she knew the word, she was shaking her head, looking at the pavement.

'If I'm brave,' she said, 'Helen Friel still here.'

*

I phoned Lewicki from the car.

'It's a start,' he said.

'Right. Don't go overboard, Jan.'

'That's the point, though, isn't it? What did she actually see? She saw Helen Friel leaving the room with this ginger charmer. Did she even see them go into another room together? It's supposition, Ger. Plus, a case like this, there's the character of the witness. A whore, basically. She a user too?'

'I don't know.' I pictured her clear eyes and skin,

thought back to the damp bedroom with the two-bar fire. Would I have noticed track-marks? There were no marks on the arm she had bared in the café. 'I don't think so. Maybe. Wouldn't you be a user if you lived like that?'

'It's what they'll argue. Prostitute, drug-user. Person of low moral character.'

'For fuck's sake, Jan. She's going to risk her life to testify against Packy Walsh. How much moral character do you want?'

'That's a commendably enlightened point of view,' Lewicki said. 'It would be nice to think that everyone will share it.'

'So we've got fuck all?'

'No. We've got a start. Now we have an idea what happened we can go back and talk to the other girls, prompt them, give them the hard word. But we need corroboration.' He paused. 'The fucking UDA?'

'I know. It makes no sense. The Walshes are Tims. And it's a Celtic game, not Rangers? Plus, it's the Neils who've got the Ulster connection, not the Walshes.'

'Aye but that was different. Maitland's thing was with the UVF. The UDA's a whole different ballgame.'

My mind flashed back to the phone call, the number on Moir's Post-it, the Ulster voice at the end of the line. Lewicki's trace had got nowhere but maybe this was connected.

'A Loyalist feud? Maybe he's Belfast, not Glasgow. He's over helping the Walshes. Is he hitting the Neils to hurt the other mob, the UVF?'

'Jesus, Gerry, who knows? The key at this stage is the

girls. We get even one of them to confirm this story, then we can move. If nothing else, we can charge Walsh for the assault.' He sniffed, cleared his throat. 'You writing this up?'

'Sensitively,' I said. 'With the tact and discretion that have come to be my hallmarks.'

Lewicki sighed, a long low sound that carried no hint of forbearance. 'Just don't fuck it up,' he said.

I bought a roll and square sausage at the baker's beside the Cope, a caramel latte from the Starbucks at the *Trib*, put my iPhone onto silent, unhooked my office phone. Half an hour later I filed it to Driscoll:

A prostitute whose body was discovered in woods near Duntocher in October may have been murdered in a Glasgow tenement, the *Tribune on Sunday* has learned. Helen Friel, 30, a recovering heroin addict, was assaulted in a southside brothel two days before her body was found, according to a fellow sex-worker.

The woman, who has agreed to give a statement to police, claims Ms Friel was punched and slapped by the brothel owner – a member of the notorious Walsh crime family – to coerce her into having sex with a customer known to be violent.

The *ToS* has passed this information on to detectives working within the elite Scottish Crime and Drug Enforcement Agency. An Agency spokesperson

213

thanked the *Tribune on Sunday* for its diligence: 'We are grateful to the *Tribune* for bringing this material to our attention. We will investigate these serious allegations with urgency and rigour.' Pressed on whether arrests may be imminent, the spokesperson declined to comment.

Ms Friel's body was discovered by forestry workers in woodland close to the A82 on 25 October. A post-mortem examination determined the cause of death as strangulation.

The Walsh crime family, headed by brothers Patrick 'Packy' Walsh, 52, and Declan 'The Woodpecker' Walsh, 48, controls the supply of cocaine and heroin to the south side of Glasgow.

Martin Moir, the *Tribune on Sunday*'s Investigations Editor, had been investigating the Walsh crime family before his sudden death on 22 October.

The last sentence would probably go – Driscoll would strike it, or Maguire would – but I chanced it anyway. I wanted Walsh to know that his card was marked, that another *Tribune* journo was on his case. Then I wrote up the press conference, the one we would splash with, the Rangers fan murdered off Great Western Road.

Chapter Twenty-one

'Is this an interview?'

Mari was watching from the kitchen doorway. I frowned at the mirror. Paul Smith suit. Lemon shirt, oxblood tie. Tan Loake brogues.

'It's called a suit. Type of men's apparel. Not sure you have them in New Zealand.'

'Oh I think I've seen them.' She slipped her arms under mine and tightened the knot of my tie. 'Yeah. Guy sold me a Holden, he was wearing one.'

'Aye? We'll all be selling cars if the paper doesn't pick up.'

*

The Jarvie Club was on Great Western Road, a terrace set back from the traffic, up on the hill with its own strip of road. The blonde sandstone portico was crumbling a little but the brass plate shone wet in the white sunless day. The door opened before I could ring the bell and a porter asked me to sign in, pointed to the stairs.

I climbed slowly, my leather soles slipping on the carpet, and thought about Haining. The first time I heard him speak was in 2005. The city was selling off council land, punting gap sites to developers at throwaway rates.

Most council leaders would have kept this quiet; Haining held a press conference. He brought us to an empty lot behind the Gallowgate on a blustery June morning. A lectern stood in the rubble, amid the wagging thistles and torn johnnies, the turds and the used syringes, and Haining gripped its sides with his big fists and glared out at the press pack, a wind from the river lifting his hair.

'At the start of the twentieth century,' he told us, 'this was the most densely populated urban area in Europe. This plot of land. Seven hundred thousand people lived in three square miles of Glasgow city centre. Families of five, six, seven, living in a single room. Worst rate of infant mortality in the developed world.'

He clamped his mouth shut, nodded slowly, scanned the heads.

'That's the challenge this city faced,' he said. 'A challenge with no parallel in this country, few in any others. Did we meet it?' He shrugged. 'We tried. We knocked down whole districts, put up a hundred thousand homes, shifted whole communities out of the slums. But a process on this scale, it's not neat and tidy. It's messy. It's piecemeal. You end up with places like this. Places where the slums were cleared and nothing went up in their place. Gap sites. Wastelands. Eyesores. And we know what happens then. The gangs take over. The junkies. Another bit of Glasgow gone to the dogs. But so what?' He spread his hands, hunched his shoulders. 'So what? We can't afford to build on them. It's out of our hands.'

He shook his head, studied the lectern. 'Not good enough,' he said, looking up. 'Not. Good. Enough. *We* can't afford to build. But—' tapping the lectern with a stubby finger – 'we know people who can. And if they undertake to build something useful, if they build houses or shops or businesses, this city will sell them the land. We'll bloody *give* them the land. Will we make money? No. Will we make this city a better place?' He looked around at the rubbled lot, the detritus of coke cans and smashed half-bottles, the dead bonfires, charred scuddy-mags. He leaned forward on one elbow, his lip curled in scorn. 'What do you think?'

It was classic Haining. Fluent bullshit, for the most part, but something winning in the delivery. No front pages came from that speech, it didn't make *Reporting Scotland* at half past six that evening. But that wasn't the point. He'd killed it as a story. There would be no ex-posés, no hostile headlines about the city flogging the family silver. He'd painted a quick fix as a moral crusade and stopped the Scottish press pack doing its job.

At the top of the stairs I straightened my tie, checked my fly. A shoelace working loose. Kneeling on the fleur-de-lis carpet I listened to the buzz from the Glasgow Room, through the double doors. People who knew what they were doing. People who belonged. I straightened up and pushed the door.

The room was packed, suits and dresses in loose groups, white-shirted waiting staff weaving between them. I faltered a moment, wavered, like someone who'd stepped off the kerb into oncoming traffic, scanned around for the drink, the bar, the waiters.

'Gerry!'

Haining was plunging through the bodies, burly, bear-ish, the big teeth bared in a chummy growl.

'Glad you could come.' The moist palm, meaty.

A girl appeared with a tray of champagne. For a moment I thought it was the girl from Temora Street, Gina; she had the same shade of hair, the same purple hollows under her eyes. I plucked a flute and tipped it back. Haining leaned towards me. His bulk created a private space, a little alcove in the busy room.

'I meant to say, Gerry. The piece in Sunday's paper: just the ticket. Get the facts down. Straight bat. No hysterics.'

'We aim to please, Councillor.'

'"Gavin", please! Councillor!' He laughed and steered me into the crowd. 'I mean it, though. Enough shit with these fuckwits without blowing it out of proportion.'

A trio opened up at our approach. Two men and a woman.

'This man writes for the *Trib*,' Haining announced. 'Watch what you say!'

Three broad smiles.

'Gerry Conway. Anna Vallance. Alan Goldie. Lewis Rush.'

'Pleasure.'

The woman was early thirties, flirty, flushed, she held her glass up at her shoulder, head cocked to one side. Her glass caught the sunlight; deep red print of her lips on the rim. I wondered which of the men was fucking her.

'Not bad,' she said, staring. 'About time we had some new blood. Any blood, in fact.'

The thin one shot his cuffs, frowned, flexed his shoulders. I stopped wondering.

The other man, Goldie, was in telly, head of current affairs at Baird. I'd known him when he was election officer for Labour's Scottish leader in the Nineties.

There were thirty people round the table. I knew some of them by sight. The bassist for a local band, just back from playing South by Southwest. A novelist with heavily gelled hair and a cream blazer with thick black pinstripes. I recognised the blazer – he was wearing it on the cover of his latest novel, *Heavy Sex*, which made it onto the Booker longlist. I spotted McMillan from the *Scotsman*, a best-selling historian, the presenter of a TV makeover show.

I was seated between the tipsy woman and an old gent in a dark suit and striped tie. The strip of marbled card at his place-mat said 'John Patullo'. He leaned across to read my own before clasping a massive hand round mine.

'Conway.' He settled his napkin. 'You're the newspaperman.'

'I'm a journalist, yes.'

He nodded. Above the blue checked shirt his wattled neck wavered.

'I was sorry to hear about your colleague.'

Had he known Moir?

'A capable man,' he said. 'I liked him a lot. Here.' He took a card from his top pocket and placed it on the table beside me: *John Patullo, OBE. Kentigern Consortium.*

The sound of pewter on glass. Conversations faltering, stalling, dying out around the table. Haining on his feet, smiling. He put down his spoon.

'Ladies. Gentlemen.' He spread his arms. 'Friends. I nearly said *Comrades*.' Little rip of laughter. 'As ever, pleasure, real pleasure to see you. As you know, I like to mix things up in these little gatherings and we have two new faces with us this afternoon. Lauren, could you give us a wave, please?' A smoky, cadaverous blonde across the table raised her hand like someone swearing the oath of allegiance. 'Lauren Trevelyan from Burnbank Media. Moved up from London last year. And we have our own Gerry Conway of the *Tribune on Sunday*.' I raised my hand. 'Gerry moved up from – where was it, Gerry? Mureton?' Laughter. 'You're both very welcome.'

He smoothed his tie with a fat hand.

'For the benefit of the newcomers, these events are social. There's no discussion paper, no agenda. Just bringing you guys together, in my opinion, is good for the city. Things will happen, ideas will emerge, if artists talk to bankers. If CEOs talk to filmmakers. If lawyers talk to journalists. Hang on, scratch that – say fuck all to journalists.' More laughter. 'Gerry, Brian: only joking.

'I think of these gatherings as a little investment in the future of our great city. I'm fortunate that my position allows me to bring talented people together. Sadly, one very modestly talented person has to be leaving—' he looked at his watch, 'right about now. Watch *Reporting Scotland* tonight and you'll see why. Enjoy your dessert. Enjoy the wine, the company. Talk to each other. And I'll catch you next time.'

And then he was off, patting shoulders, shaking hands,

on his way to the exit. Light smatter of applause and the conversations started up again.

After the meal, we moved to the side tables for coffee. Gold-rimmed cups and dice-sized cubes of tablet.

'Gerry.'

Allan Goldie at my shoulder, tight smile, eyebrows raised.

'You got a minute? You're not heading off?'

'No, it's fine.'

'Great.' He ushered me over to a table in the corner where we sank in the brown padded club chairs.

'I'm glad I caught you. Look, I'll get straight to the point, Gerry. We're commissioning a series of programmes about the referendum. Explore the issues, explain the process. Profile the key players. Leaders' debates, studio audience of five hundred people.'

I nodded. 'Sounds impressive.'

'It might be. That depends on the talent. Talent's you, Gerry. We want you to front the series.'

I looked away down the long high room, the sun in the tall windows catching the nap of a blue suit, a sheaf of feather-cut hair, a bright plug of gold in a long-stemmed glass.

'What about Dennis?'

Dennis Garvaghy was the channel's political editor. He'd fronted their coverage of every election since 1992. I'd sat up into the small hours more often than I could remember, watching his stern jowls announce Labour holds in Aberdeen North or Hamilton South.

Goldie grimaced. 'Oh, Dennis is Dennis. Dennis is

221

great. He's going through some *issues* just now, working things out. We're planning some changes at the channel. Look,' he held his hands up; 'I don't need a decision right away. The programmes won't be starting till the spring. Meantime, let's get you on *Spectrum* again, get the viewers used to that handsome mug.'

Spectrum was the Sunday-lunchtime politics show that Dennis had fronted for the past ten years and on which I irregularly – and to my mind ineptly – guested during my first stint at the *Trib*.

'OK.' He was on his feet now. 'We'll start the profiles with the "No" camp leader. Better the devil you know!'

He was grinning.

'I'm sorry,' I said. 'Who's leading the "No" campaign?'

The grin fell. He looked puzzled, gave a short laugh.

'He is.' He jabbed his thumb over his shoulder to where Haining had been sitting. 'I thought – I mean, Jesus, you're sitting here.'

I looked at the vacant chair, the napkin that had still to be removed.

'But he's not even in parliament. He's not an MSP.'

'All the better. He's not tainted. You've seen them, Gerry, the Party's Scottish emissaries. It's not the brains trust. They're not in government, they know fuck all about opposition.' He opened his arms. 'Meantime Haining's running a city with a budget of ten billion.'

'So the plan is, what? He leads it from outside parliament?'

'He runs the "No" campaign. Saves the Union. Hosts the Games. Stands for Holyrood in 2015. They win, great – he's in the cabinet, he gets the big job in a couple of years. They don't win, McKay stands down, Haining's in the big chair, wins next time. Look—' he checked his watch, 'we'll cover all this when we do the briefing. Keep in touch.'

I took the hand he offered, watched him slip back into the fray.

Chapter Twenty-two

'We invite you all to join us after the service for a cup of tea in the Gathering Area, which is reached through the doors on your right as you leave the church.'

She blessed us, impressively, with one hand held high. Then we all stood up as a man in a black velvet robe carried the big black Bible down the aisle, followed by the minister and the choir.

The Gathering Area was a modern, glass extension to the church, a kind of see-through transept. There were chairs along both sides and a serving hatch at the far end, where a woman in a scarlet cardigan was tipping tea into mugs from a big tarnished pot. Glasses of pale diluting orange caught the sunlight. There were small round tables with plates of biscuits and buttered fruit loaf.

I was chatting to a man with a name-tag reading 'Bertie' when the minister floated into my field of vision. She had changed out of her robes and was now wearing a blue Adidas tracksuit and chunky white running shoes. I had a cup of tea in one hand and a slice of pineapple loaf in the other. I swallowed the last mouthful, rubbed my palm on my jeans and shook her hand.

'Are you visiting the parish?'

A toddler with a custard cream held aloft careened between us.

'No. Yes. I grew up around here but I live in Glasgow now. In fact, though—' I fished a card from my breast pocket – 'I'm here for another reason.'

She read the card. 'Martin,' she said.

'I was Martin's friend, as well as a colleague. Clare's been trying to make sense of what happened and she's asked me to help.'

'Yes.' The minister nodded, as if this made perfect sense.

'I'm trying to, I don't know. Gauge his state of mind. What might have driven him to do what he did. I wondered if you might have time to talk to me for a little while.'

She nodded. That would be fine. She had Session in half an hour, but was I free that afternoon?

We met in one of the cafés on Bank Street, 'The First Edition', scrubbed deal tables and leather couches. It was the minister's suggestion.

'I thought you might feel at home.'

'Why's that?'

'Newspapers. The First Edition?'

'Right. Actually it's not a newspaper reference.'

'But what about—' she jabbed a thumb at the window; the offices of the *Mureton Standard* across the street.

'I know, but it's not that. It's Robert Burns. The poems. The first edition of his poems was published up the road.'

'Right. I never thought.'

The waitress arrived to take our order.

'About Martin,' I said, when she was gone.

'Of course.' The minister frowned. 'Look, this is – it's

a wee bit delicate.'

'The seal of the confessional?'

She smiled. 'Not exactly, no. As Presbyterians we like to go straight to head office. Cut out the middleman. But still. He spoke to me in confidence.'

'I was his best man,' I said. 'I'm Esme's godfather. I'm not out to cause any trouble. I'm just trying to find out what happened.'

She held my gaze for a second or two and then the espresso machine spluttered, an exasperated snort, and the minister sat forward in her chair.

'He came to see me before he died,' she said. 'About two weeks before. He was upset. I thought it was his marriage, maybe he was having an affair, or maybe Clare was. That's what it usually is. I sometimes feel I should give up the pretence and set up as a marriage counsellor. But that wasn't it.' She looked across at the *Standard* offices and then back to me. 'His problem was God. He was having, I suppose you'd call it a crisis of faith.'

'He'd stopped believing.' My guess was right; Martin's faith was as shallow as his Glasgow accent.

'No,' she shook her head. 'No. Quite the opposite. He'd *started* believing. His problem was too much faith, not too little.' She looked at me sharply. 'You're not a believer, Mr Conroy?'

'Conway.' I shrugged. 'I'm not not a believer.' I shrugged again. 'Hedging my bets.'

'Pascal's wager. Can I tell you something? Most people who go to church don't believe in God either. If you asked them straight out, "Do you believe in God?" then

226

they'd likely say "Yes", but that doesn't mean anything. They believe in God the way you believe in helping old ladies across the road. Mostly what they believe in is being nice. The religion of being nice.'

The waitress arrived with the coffees and the minister smiled up at her.

'I'm not knocking that,' she said. 'Nice is good. It's nice to be nice. But Martin had gone beyond that. He said he's seen things that made him know that good and evil were real. Heaven and hell were real. He'd seen evil things. He'd seen people who were going to hell for what they'd done. That's what he told me.' She shrugged. 'A faith like that isn't easy to live with.'

'Did he tell you what it was? What he'd seen that made him think this way?'

'He didn't elaborate. I guessed it was something to do with his work, with the stories he was writing.'

'What did you tell him?'

She stirred her coffee, frowned.

'I told him to pray. I told him these people needed our prayers. I said that no one was beyond the reach of God's mercy. That Jesus asks us to love our enemies. I told him it wasn't his disciples who were crucified alongside Jesus; it was two criminals. But the truth is—' she smiled and shook her head. 'The truth is, I was jealous of him. I wanted Martin's faith. I don't know anyone who's going to hell.'

There was a comeback to that but I let it lie.

We walked back to the church, along Bank Street. This was the nice part of town, the part they forgot to

227

improve. Cobbled streets. Low-lintelled shops from the time of Burns. Lime trees on College Wynd. We climbed the steps to the Laigh Kirk. In the elevated churchyard she stopped at a headstone.

'Have you seen this?' she said.

It was a Covenanting grave. John Ross and John Shields were buried there. Not their bodies; just the heads. They had been executed in Edinburgh after the Pentland Rising. Their severed heads were sent to Mureton to hang on the tollbooth. Another stone commemorated a group of Covenanters who were banished to the American plantations. Their ship foundered off Orkney and two hundred prisoners drowned, five Mureton men among them. We'd done all this at school, local history. She showed me a third stone, under a bare black tree: *Here lies John Nisbet, who was taken by Major Balfour's party and suffered at Mureton, on 14 April, 1683, for adhering to the Word of God and Scotland's Covenanted Work of Reformation.*

'Suffered,' I said.

'It means executed,' the minister said. 'Hanged, usually.'

'I know it does.'

'Sometimes worse than hanged. Tortured. Mutilated. Sometimes they chopped off the hands of the Covenanters and mounted them on pikes. Carried them through the streets in an attitude of prayer.'

We looked at the pale blue stone, the black letters.

'I'd say we've got a way to go,' I said.

'What's that?'

'Scotland's Covenanted Work of Reformation.'

She zipped up her fleece as the wind stirred the branches.

'I'd say so too.'

*

I spent the day in Conwick with Roddy and James, drove back late. The snow came on as I crossed the moors. I made it back to Glasgow by eleven. Mari had gone to bed. A bottle of Rolling Rock sat on the bookcase, a half-inch still to drink. Someone was kicking a can down the street, the smart repercussions oddly clear in the quiet night. Each kick produced a tumbling burst of sound, the sharp hollow rattle of a snare-drum. I thought of bright green turf under floodlights and the four shadows of each piper marching in formation through the centre circle. Midweek internationals at Hampden Park, the Strath-clyde Police Pipe Band taking the field at half-time. The drums were what thrilled me, not the pipes, the gunfire bursts of the snares.

Ramage's words floated into my head. The stories he wasn't writing. What did that mean? It sounded like pure Zen bullshit. The sound of one hand clapping. How did you know what Moir wasn't writing? The stories he wasn't writing were all the stories in the world. I tipped the last of Mari's beer down my neck and tiptoed through to check on Angus.

*

Next morning I rode the subway to St Enoch. A skinny kid in a Celtic top strap-hung in the half-empty carriage, glaring at the other passengers. He was cracking his gum, loud random snaps that detonated in the rattling carriage. I felt his gaze boring into my cheek but I lifted my eyes to the overhead ads.

The tabs had gone big on the West End killing. *Sectarian Slasher*. *The Hillhead Butcher*. The assumption was that the killing was random, that the victim had been chosen for his colours, picked off the street and driven to an unknown location. Slashed and stabbed. Teeth kicked from his mouth. Face smacked with iron bars, drubbed into paste. Dumped in the lane with his scarf still round his neck.

What would come first? That was the question the killing had posed. The second attack, or the reprisal? There are no Catholic areas in the city, no ghettos or enclaves. But there are churches and bars. Some of the Celtic pubs had fixed massive grilles across their windows. Two colossal bouncers stood like heraldic animals outside Molloys on the Gallowgate. Police had been drafted in from peripheral divisions for the Old Firm game. The Chief Constable had cancelled all holiday leave. It felt like Belfast after the Shankill bomb. That bilious lull. A city flinching, hunched for the blow.

And then, as quickly as it came, the trouble passed. I took the call from Lewicki.

'They've identified him,' he said. 'The guy in the lane, the Rangers scarf.'

'Yeah?'

'Name of Declan Coyle.'

'Not a Rangers fan, I'm guessing'.

'That's a safe bet.'

'One of ours.'

'I wouldn't say that, Gerry. One of the Walshes. A first cousin. High up in the firm.'

'Fuck.'

'Fuck is right. Well he took his sweet time but the fun starts here.'

'It was Neil?'

'The scarf was a message. Payback for Billy Swan.'

The train rolled into St Enoch. Dirty light. The yellow bricks. On my way past the Celtic top I swung back and snapped 'Boo!' in his face, made the closing doors, lunged for the stairs.

On Argyle Street the crowds were thick. The street vendors were busy, guys in leather jackets and Santa hats, selling perfume and Christmas paper from trestle tables. The Christmas lights twinkled on a parade of long coats and smart leather boots, bulging carrier bags. 'Seasonal' glam rock boomed from the speakers above JJB Sports. The city had forgotten about the murder, the headlines, the body in the lane. Now that it was no longer 'sectarian', it was business as usual. Another 'Ice-Cream War', a 'Tanning-Salon War' might be just around the corner, but these were like the wars on the telly, they didn't affect you.

I was wandering through the St Enoch's Centre looking for Mari's present when the phone rang again.

'Gerry. It's not sectarian.'

'I know, Fiona. It's Neil. I heard.'

'You coming in?'

'On my way.'

'And Gerry?'

'Yeah?'

'The Walsh piece: I don't like it. You're sure about the source?'

'Hundred per cent, Fiona. It's solid.'

I was heading for the exit, Jamaica Street, I would flag a cab. She still hadn't spoken. 'What does Driscoll say?'

'He thinks we should run it.'

'There you are then.'

*

I woke that night with a start, there was someone in the room. It was Angus, standing at my bedside shouting 'Max!' and hitting the duvet with a book. 5.17: *Jesus*. I turned on the bedside lamp and struggled into a sitting position, wedged a pillow behind my back and hauled the boy onto the bed, where he burrowed back against the headboard and clapped his hands as I opened his book. He slapped the open page. I cleared my throat and read him the story about a boy called Max whose bedroom turns into a forest. For nearly a week now Angus had been materialising nightly at my bedside (*my* side, never Mari's), the pink digits showing 4.37 or 5.12, tugging at the duvet and clamouring for 'Max!'. It got so I could read it with my eyes shut, reciting from memory the cadenced prose about monsters roaring and gnashing their teeth, while Angus turned the pages.

Once Max had returned from the kingdom of the wild things to find his supper waiting on his bedside table, Angus fell asleep. Lucky him. I gave it twenty minutes before padding through to put the percolator on. The first bars of molten pink and crimson were streaking the sky, lights coming on in the Kelvinside tenements. I thought again about Ramage's parting shot: 'Look at the stories he *wasn't* writing.' How did you do that? Stories were everywhere. The city seethed with stories. That's where Maguire was wrong: everything *is* a story, given half a chance. The stories Moir might have written? They were limitless, endless. Stories he *should* have written, stories we all should have written. It made me sick just to think about it. The stories we missed. The stories we never even glimpsed, because we didn't have the time or the money or the basic skills any more to do our job. It was like a tap left running, the stories we were missing.

Chapter Twenty-three

Joe was at my elbow, a ghost in the whisky mirror.

'That's your taxi, Gerry.'

A fat bloke in a patterned jumper was holding one of the swing doors, his car keys dangling from his pinkie. I held up a finger and drained my Lagavulin.

It was good to leave now. If I stayed any longer in the Cope I would say something stupid, something hard and wounding that would queer my future dealings with Maguire. Anyway, it's only when you're beaten that you need to say these things, and I'd won. The piece was out now, despite Maguire's bad grace. Driscoll had convinced her. I'd put the link on Twitter and my hack followers – @KennyFarq, @StephenKhan, @TorchuilBain – were busy retweeting it. The cops would have to move now; the Agency, the CID. They'd have to investigate Walsh. If they didn't move, I would call in my favours with the apparatchiks, get questions raised with the minister.

I was thinking all this as I weaved between the tables, nodding to the Saturday crew, Maguire and Driscoll in earnest cahoots at the other end of the bar, Neve McDonald queen-beeing in the sports boys' booth, the scruffy subs clustered round the dartboard. The paper was finished, we put it to bed two hours ago, it was out of our hands. This was the one point of the week when none of it mattered, the numbers, the imminent cuts, severance deals, the perfidious Yanks, the one point when we felt like a team.

My hand was on the open door of the cab before I realised something was wrong. The driver should have been moving round to get behind the wheel but he was standing by the bonnet, making sure I got into the cab. And there was someone behind me. I knew this the way you know it on a football field, when you're shielding the ball and you sense a challenge from behind. In the quarter-light of the cab I saw a blurry face looming at my shoulder and I spun, thrusting upwards with my elbow and felt it connect – there was a crackle of cartilage as his nose crumpled – and swung a left at the drooping head.

A rod of pain shot up my left forearm. The punch a poor one, a partial connect, but the man spun into the wall and sat abruptly down on the pavement, his head looping back and smacking the whitewashed brick of the Cope. The driver was moving now, a shape in my peripheral vision, but I stepped smartly back and bundled him into the bodywork – I could feel the powerful shoulders under the ribbed wool of the sweater – and saw him topple into the gutter as I turned.

The smart move now was to crash back through the Cope's double doors shouting blue murder but I turned and sprinted off down the Govan Road. The scrubby wasteground of the Festival Park was on my right but I ploughed on, under the fluttering Union flag outside the Blue Star Social Club. When I reached the main road I turned left – another pub, another Butcher's Apron on a pole above the door. I was sprinting past when it struck me that Cessnock underground wasn't far in the other direction, so I pulled up short and wheeled around and saw the yellow hyphen of a taxi sign. I was out in the street, waving my arms and when I bent to check that the driver wasn't the man I'd just encountered I hauled on the door and collapsed back onto the ribbed black seat as the door clunked shut.

'West End,' I told the guy. 'Clouston Street.'

The reds and whites of the brakelights and headlights wavered in the rear window but nobody was chasing us, shouting in the street, flagging us down. I was safe. I had made it.

For the next sixty seconds I focused on my breathing, let the juices flood me, the joy, the relief. A laugh bubbled out. I wanted to whoop and holler. I stamped the floor of the cab in utter fuck-you glee. Then I realised we were heading south, not north. I looked out for a street sign, spotted the boarded-up shell of the Clachan Bar. He had doubled back, we were heading down Paisley Road West.

'Hey!'

The driver ignored me.

'*Hey!*' I leaned forward, rapped the glass partition. 'I said Clouston Street. You're heading south!'

He glanced at me in the rear-view.

'Wee detour, sir.' He pulled out to pass a stopping bus. 'Someone wants a word.'

I looked around me. The red 'doors locked' buttons glowed in the dark. The cab was picking up speed now, bowling down the outside lane. I could see the lights of Ibrox Park off to the right above the tenements.

'What? Who does?'

The driver was nodding, he met my eyes in the rear-view. 'I think you know, mate.'

This was it. I thought, irrelevantly, of where I might have been headed if I had listened to Mari, if I'd stuck to politics, stopped trying to act the big man, bought a house in a nice tree-lined street in a quiet seaside town. Right now this seemed like important stuff to want. I wanted it too. I wanted a garden strewn with discarded scooters and waterlogged basketballs, a clamshell sandpit weighted with a brick, a set of goals with fraying nets, a wilting disc of grass beneath the trampoline. I wanted out of this cab, this city. I wanted out of this life.

Fuck it. I sat back. Getting out of the cab wasn't a challenge. You could try to kick the windows out or smash the partition, you could take out your mobile and phone the police, but what was the point? Packy Walsh wants to see you, he sees you. If not now, later.

On the fold-down seat in front of me, the big green 'G' in its nest of rings. I pulled it down, swung my boots up onto the padded leatherette. I felt like phoning Maguire just to hear her reaction. Not involved? How's this for not involved? I took out my makings and rolled a smoke. The driver watched in the rear-view. I lit up.

'You cannae smoke in here.'

'Is that right?'

Walsh had been involved in Martin's death. I hadn't said that in the piece but it was there between the lines. It was standing up and waving between the lines, blowing a big fat trumpet. And if Walsh had done Martin he could do me. I tipped some ash carefully onto the upholstery, rubbed it in with the sleeve of my leather. But he wasn't a mug. Packy Walsh wasn't about to start picking off *Trib* reporters one by one. This was a frightener. A warning. Nothing worse.

I held to that thought as the cab turned onto Dumbreck Road and then left onto Nithsdale. The big villas of Pollokshields loomed above their hedges, security lights shining between the trees. We swung left and then right and then slowed at a pair of gateposts. Someone must have been watching because the big steel gate slid open and we crackled over frozen gravel to the big front door.

The house was huge, Victorian, some nabob or tobacco baron's mansion. A row of floodlights was set into the path around its base and a greeny light splashed the pale sandstone walls. Two fat Doric columns buttressed the front porch, and a man stepped out from the shadows and tugged on the taxi door.

'This way, Mr Conway.'

He wore a black puffa jacket and a beanie hat and his breath streamed out in the cold. I dropped my smoke on the taxi floor and dragged my shoe across it.

'Your tip's on the meter.'

A wide lawn rolled away on my right, each whited blade of grass casting a shadow. I followed the puffa jacket across the tight gravel and up the broad stone steps. A brass bootscraper was set into the top step and I remember thinking that if I swept the legs from the big guy he might stove his head on the metal edge and I could make a run for it.

My knees shivered a little as we crossed the threshold but the whisky anchored me, burned in my gut like a glowing coal.

The door closed behind me. A man was rising from a chair, cut-glass tumbler in his hand.

He didn't look like his photos. The one you always saw in the papers was an old one. He had lost weight since then, his features were finer. He was wearing a dark-red silk shirt and stone-coloured chinos, and the hand he held out was small and neat, like a surgeon's. I shook it limply.

'Get you a drink, Gerry? Lagavulin, is it?'

There were two shelves of bottles above the bar and it looked like all of them were single malts. I spotted a Laphroaig, the crimson label of a Cardhu.

'I'm fine.'

'Suit yourself.'

He came out from behind the bar with the glass in his hand.

'Sit down at least.'

I sat across from him in a fat tan La-Z-Boy, its high padded arms hemming me in. I felt like a boy in his father's chair.

'Well it's nice to finally meet you.' Walsh sat down in a wing-chair, crossed his legs. 'Though I hear you've been claiming my acquaintance already.'

I think I may have opened my mouth at that point but I had nothing to say so I shut it again.

239

'Apparently I recommended an establishment in Govanhill to you.' He had seen the card I left with Gina. 'I don't mind,' he went on. 'I just hope you enjoyed yourself.' He sipped his whisky. 'I saw your piece on Sunday.'

'Yeah? Keep reading. We need all the help we can get.'

'Normally I'd go straight to my lawyer. He enjoys sorting these things out. Making people repent their rashness. But I thought we'd have a chat first.'

'Is that a euphemism?'

He laughed. 'No,' he said. 'No it's not. If I wanted to hurt you, you think I'd bring you to my house?'

'I don't know what you'd do, Mr Walsh.'

Walsh smoothed his shirt-front with a dainty hand. 'You're upset,' he said. 'You're hurting. Martin was your friend. I understand that. I liked Martin too. He did me a favour once. He was a good journalist.' *Better than you*, his look said. 'But he killed himself.' Walsh tapped the arm of his chair. 'That's what DS Gunn thinks, isn't it? The pathologists. You, on the other hand, have decided that I was involved. Why would you think that?'

He sipped his whisky, light catching the facets of the heavy crystal tumbler, a dark tint of scorn in his eyes.

'Yeah, that's a hard one.' I was riled now, could feel my forehead tightening, should have taken a breath but didn't. 'Martin Moir's on your case for the past two years. The last guy Moir went after was Walter Maitland. Now where's Walter Maitland again?' Walsh held my gaze. 'But hey, you're fine with that. You're not scared at all.'

'Why should I be scared?' Walsh stood up. I gripped the padded arms of the chair, got ready to spring to

240

my feet but he was only fixing another Macallan. He stoppered the decanter and lifted his glass. 'He'd been after me for two years. What had he actually done?' He spread his arms and looked around the room. 'I'm still here. Watty Maitland's up in Peterhead; I'm not. I'm nursing a twelve-year-old Speyside and enjoying our conversation. Martin wrote a lot of things, he made a lot of allegations, insinuations. How much of it stuck, Gerry? How much of it came to court?'

I wished I'd taken the whisky now, a finger or two of Lagavulin.

'No but he'd found something, hadn't he? Something that would stick. And you stopped him.'

'Oh, I see. He was *about* to get it right. He was just on the verge of something big when he's taken out of the picture.' Walsh laughed. 'He'd had a fair crack at it, Gerry. Two years. Maybe there was nothing to get. You ever think of that?'

'Could be. Could be you're a liar and you killed Martin Moir.'

'Well you print that, Mr Conway, and see what happens.'

'What, you're gonnae put me in a quarry?'

No rage, no snarling eruption. Just the cold eyes, the sour mouth. He tipped his head back till it rested on the stiff padded leather of his claret wing-chair and let his eyelids droop. When he opened them he kept his head tilted back, watched me through weary slits.

'What would you do if I told you I'd killed Martin Moir? I put out the word. I arranged to have him killed.

241

Would you want that knowledge?'

I looked at the narrowed eyes. All the bravado seemed to have left me and I didn't know the answer. Walsh sighed.

'Out of your depth, son,' he said. 'Your taxi's outside.'

I got to my feet and opened the door. The big guy in the puffa jacket detached himself from the wall and looked from me to Walsh.

'By the way.' Walsh was behind me, fixing another drink. 'The guy who saw the lassie in the close. You remember his name?'

I stopped in the hallway. I didn't turn round.

'His name was McClymont.'

I could hear the ice-cubes rattling the glass, the stopper coming out of the bottle.

'Aye. Grant McClymont. Ask your Polish mate about him.'

The fat bloke was leaning against his taxi, texting with one hand. He straightened as I came abreast but I walked on past him and down the gravel drive. The gate clicked and slid open. I zipped up my jacket and kept walking.

*

Next morning I logged into cuttings, called up Moir's stories for the past three years, everything he'd written since the day I left the paper. I put a half a ream in the printer and watched the stories sift out, stacked them on the kitchen table.

Mari and Angus were out at the park. I looked at the

242

clock: ten past eleven. So what? I took a Rolling Rock from the fridge, put some Muddy on the sound system, started working through the cuts. I sorted them into piles, according to subject-matter. A pile for stabbings. Smaller pile for rapes. Mari and Angus came back. Shootings. She put Angus down for a nap. Front companies; fraud. She appeared at the door in her running gear, hair up in a scrunchie, fixing the iPod earphones into place. Gang-related violence, the tallest of the piles. She raised her eyebrows at the three empty bottles and closed the front door with the softest of clicks.

It was geography. I spent two hours at the kitchen table and geography was the key, nothing else. Nothing connected Moir's recent stories, nothing beyond the location. His hunting ground had shifted south. For twelve months he'd barely crossed the Clyde. So what were the stories he wasn't writing? They were the stories about the northside and the East End. They were stories about Hamish Neil.

Chapter Twenty-four

'Back to the scene of the crime.'

Lewicki spun the wheel, took us deeper into the dreary streets. The water tower loomed above the grey maisonettes.

'What crime's that?'

'Take your pick. This whole estate's a crime scene. You know what that was?'

We were passing a newish apartment building in yellow brick, already streaked brown where the rivets had rusted, bled down the frontage.

'Surprise me.'

'The Bellrock.'

He pulled in to the kerb to light a ciggie and I studied the building, the little pocket of wasteground beside it.

The Bellrock Bar was one of the fabled Glasgow pubs, like the Saracen Head or the Vulcan Bar. It was Walter Maitland's shop. Two men had been murdered there in the late Nineties. They were picked up in another pub and brought to the Bell. The doors were locked, the shutters closed and the fun began. Teeth were pulled. Fingers smashed with hammers. Facial hair burnt off and noses scorched by cigarette lighters. The post-mortem revealed scalding to the head and upper body of both men in a pattern consistent with kettles having been emptied over them. Ligature marks on the elbows, wrists and ankles suggested each man had been tied to a chair. Both had been shot in the head.

'You know what happened there?'

'I covered it,' I told him. 'I wrote the story.'

Lewicki tapped the steering wheel. 'Well,' he said. 'X marks the spot.'

I also knew what happened next. Maitland had friends on the force. Though the wasted bodies were dumped beside an exit on the M8, they were linked back to the Bellrock Bar. His police mole gave Maitland the heads-up. He called his men out at midnight, trucks and diggers and bulldozers. He flattened the Bell, not a stone left standing, and trucked the rubble into the night. When the cops showed up to do the forensics, a riot squad with a battering-ram and the SOCOs in their moon-suits, the pub was gone, vanished. Just a raw patch of earth, a low wall filmed in brick-dust.

Lewicki killed the engine. Turned the key again to bring the window down an inch then turned it off again.

'You knew,' I said. No petulance, no tone of accusation; just a statement of fact. 'You knew about Moir.'

Lewicki looked out of his window, blew smoke though the gap. 'I had an idea.'

'How?'

'It was one of his stories.' He was still facing his window. I watched the back of his head. 'The Café Verona shooting, end of last year.'

I remembered it. A man had been murdered in a pizzeria frequented by the Walshes. Two men with scarves round their faces walked in and shot him in the chest as he ate linguine with his girlfriend. Four bullets. A junior Walsh lieutenant.

'What about it?'

'Well, your friend's report was commendably accurate. It was a little *too* accurate. He knew some things that we hadn't made public.'

'Like what?'

Lewicki turned to face me. 'Like the number of shots.'

I zipped up my jerkin. With the engine off the heater had stopped. Cold air surged in through the open window.

'But he spoke to the witnesses. Other diners.'

'Witnesses.' Lewicki grinned, shook his head. 'What would they know about it? I could take a gun out right now and fire six shots at that wall and you wouldn't be able to count them. A busy restaurant? The crowd, the panic, the echo. The shooter wouldn't know himself until he checked his magazine. But Moir knew. Four bullets. He also knew that the killers escaped in an SUV.' Lewicki nodded. 'Well, again, that was news to us. News to the witnesses. They *heard* the killers drive off but they didn't see them.'

A man had come onto a balcony, three floors up, gripping the railing as if he was planning to vault it.

'You're saying what, Jan? You're saying he was in on it, the hit?'

'I don't know. He knew about it. If he didn't know in advance he knew soon after.'

'Why would they tell him?'

'Make sure it gets a good show. And maybe a favour to Moir. Throw him a bone.'

The man on the balcony raised his arms in a stretch, locked his hands behind his head. He was wearing saggy black boxers and a V-necked dark green T-shirt.

'You ask him about it?'

'We pulled him in.'

'And what?'

Lewicki shook his head. 'Look at this eejit. T-shirt and drawers in the middle of winter. Prick. And nothing, Gerry. He denied it. Says he spoke to a witness at the scene, a wee boy in the street who saw two men leaving in an SUV. Says a witness in the restaurant told him the number of shots. He's lying through his teeth but what can you do?'

Moir was dirty. Moir was bent, bought, crooked. The prince of the *Tribune*. The boy king of Pacific Quay. Doing a scumbag's bidding.

'Hey. Don't take it so hard,' Lewicki was saying. 'They've got everything else. Lawyers, judges, cops, no shortage of cops. Why wouldn't they have journos too?'

Was this why I'd done it? I thought I was vindicating Moir's memory, tending the flame. But really what I wanted was to find him out, prove that Moir was just as shabby as the rest of us.

'I'm not taking it hard, Jan, I'm just, I cannae see what – look, you're going to have to explain this to me.'

'Explain what?'

'What he wants with a hack. A polis, yeah. A judge? All the better. Every home should have one. But buy a hack? We report things anyway. That's the job.'

Lewicki was frowning, a sour grimace, it pained him how slow I was, how much he had to school me.

'Think about it, Gerry.'

'I am thinking. Who even reads us any more? The best we can do is leave him alone. And put the bloody window up, I'd rather die of secondary smoke than freeze to fucking death.'

'It's not about him.' Lewicki chipped his smoke onto the pavement, shut the window. 'It's about the other guy.'

'What other guy?'

'Jesus, Ger, do you read your own paper? What was Martin writing for the past twelve months?'

'Crime. Gangs. The usual.'

'Crime where?'

I thought of the cuts on my kitchen table.

'Southside. Govanhill.'

'And who runs Govanhill?'

'Packy Walsh runs Govanhill.'

The man on the balcony leant to spit over the railing. He watched it land and went back inside. I knew all the answers to Lewicki's questions, I just didn't know what they meant.

'You see it now? He's not writing stories about Govanhill. He's writing stories about Packy Walsh. If the papers are all over Walsh, then the polis will follow. If the polis are tied up with Walsh, they can't come after Neil.'

'It's a diversion.'

'Pure and simple. Plus, if there's too much heat on the South Side, they can't trade. Where do the smackheads take their business?

'Okay. I see it.'

'The Neils are cute. They've got touts in the Walshes' crew, always have done. They give Martin stories about Walsh. Most of what they feed him is true, but sometimes they'll give him a ringer. See if he'll run it.'

'The girl. The child sex ring.'

'Maybe there was a child sex ring. Maybe there wasn't. Kids being abused, pimped out in Govanhill? Probably. But the guy McClymont fingered, Radislav Gombar – he wasn't involved. And the story Martin wrote was a fairytale. Just a bullshit story to keep the heat on Walsh.'

*

I cabbed it back to the Quay. On the way there we passed the site of the athletes' village. The signs on the hoardings had changed: I saw the outline of the lighthouse, the stylised beam of light – BELLROCK SECURITY. At the *Trib* building I paid the driver and trudged across to the revolving doors but I stopped in my tracks. I couldn't face it, riding up in the lift to the fourth floor, sitting at my desk, tapping out my bullshit stories. I crossed the concourse to the river, gripped the chill railings, closed my eyes as the wind stirred my hair.

How could he have done it? How could Moir have kept it going? Sitting in conference every Tuesday, filing his copy on Friday, reading his byline on Sunday: *By*

Martin Moir, Investigations Editor. And all of it fed to him by gangsters. All the splashes, all the page-four leads, just a ruse to keep the polis tied up with one hood and not another. I remembered Ramage's words. *Everyone thought Moir was the golden goose. Like fuck. He was the wee runty bird in the nest – left to himself he'd have starved to death.*

I turned and leaned against the railings. He'd sold us out, betrayed us. All the things he believed. And Moir did believe them, despite what he'd done, I was sure of that. Moir believed them even if no one else did. Though, what, after all, had he betrayed? The building rose above me, six stark storeys of smoked glass, and the big neon eagle on the roof. A hollow boast of a building. A statement that no one believed any more.

Chapter Twenty-five

The sounds of the river, the song of the Clyde. That's what comes back now, the river's jostling slaps and slurps, two inches from my head where it lay against the hull. All that summer we lived on a boat, a Loch Fyne skiff, berthed at Renfrew. Elaine's dad was a scallop diver but he'd cracked three ribs toppling from a bar stool on Paddy's Day so the boat was idle. We gave up our uni flat and moved in. I was eighteen, Elaine twenty. We slept in the bow, two curving bench-beds that met at a point. Every night, after a beggarly half-pint of Bass in the Harbour Bar, we would pick our way across the rubbled yard and climb down the rungs to the wooden pontoon. Stepping across a black half-yard of river I would pause with my foot on the gunwale. You could sense the boat's heft through the sole of your shoe; one flex of your ankle could tilt the whole craft.

We took her out once – the *Jessie Jane*, she was called – when Elaine's dad came to visit. Sailed her down to the Tail o' the Bank. Past the big container cranes at Greenock, out to where the river widens. The day was fine. The Clyde shone in its bowl of green hills. We stood on the little deck and spun around to take it all in. The mouths of the Gareloch, Loch Long, the Holy Loch. The estuary towns – Helensburgh and Greenock – looked trig and grey in the sun. On the way back we left the channel, took a short cut and grounded on a sandbank. For miles around us the Clyde stretched away, flat and blue in the failing light, and the *Jessie Jane* in the middle, grounded. We weren't stuck fast – the engine took us off and we motored back in the dusk with the cormorants flying low across our path – but I remember that moment, the sand grinding the hull, and the three of us on deck, on solid ground and out at sea.

I looked at it now, through the streaked windscreen. The grey firth, its skin shirred by wind. Dark hills dissolving in rain. I thought of what lay beneath, the ticking hulls, the warheads, the sleek black shapes that snagged the nets of trawlers. Why did he do it? I lit a Café Crème and turned the key to press the button, bring down the window an inch. Blade of wind in my ear, rain spotting the leg of my jeans. Was it money? Was that enough, was that all it took? Or was it the promise of all those stories, the thrill of his byline under the splash?

I knew that craving, knew what you'd do to feed it. I couldn't feel superior to Moir, not even now. We were none of us journalists, not any more, not properly. But it had cheered me, it had solaced me to think about Moir. Still answering the bell. Still coming off the stool. Digging out stories and standing them up. Better than the rest of us. Better than me. Tell the truth and shame the devil: that was why Moir had been going after Walsh. Not just to gladden a scumbag like Neil.

I chipped the smoke out the window, three-pointed on the gravel and left the lay-by, heading south. Out on the moors, the rain turned to sleet. I prayed for snow, great banking drifts that might trap me in the car till the news got better.

It was after seven when I parked outside the house. The curtains were parted to show off the tree, a fancy white one, swathed in silver tinsel. Globular baubles in hard metallic reds and greens, candy canes like the handles of umbrellas.

'Gerry.' She seemed pleased to see me, stood aside to let me enter, cocked her head for a peck on the cheek.

'The girls in bed?'

'More or less.' I could hear muffled shrieks from upstairs, bare feet pounding a hardwood floor. She turned away and I followed her down the hall.

'You want a drink?' She stopped in the kitchen doorway. 'I'm having one.'

'I've got the car,' I said. She looked at me. 'Yes, I want a drink. Small one.'

*

The living room smelled of furniture polish and coffee. The girls' toys were neatly stacked in bright plastic boxes along the far wall. The painting above the fireplace was new – a cool blue abstract with hard clean lines – and a photograph of Martin hung beside the bookcase, a studio portrait in black and white, a jumpered Moir smiling hopefully out, ten years younger. One of the overhead spots caught it full on.

'Here you go.' Clare was back with two brimming

glasses. I took mine in both hands.

'That's small? Jesus, I'd hate to see a big one.'

She smiled. 'There's an answer to that but I'll restrain myself. Saw you on the telly.'

'Aye.' I'd been on *Spectrum* at the weekend, pretending to know about the referendum.

'Martin used to do that. In the old days. Not staying?'

'Sorry.' I shrugged out of my jacket, dropped onto one of the sofas as the door burst open and Esme skidded in.

'Mum, Chloe's in my bed and she keeps rumpling around. Hiya Uncle Gerry.'

'Hiya, sweetheart.'

She backed onto Clare's lap, threw an arm up and round her mother's neck.

'You excited?' I jerked my head towards the tree.

She nodded rapidly, sat up straight. 'It's fourteen sleeps. Mum, is it fourteen sleeps? It's fourteen sleeps, Uncle Gerry.'

'I know it is, kiddo. I'm marking them off.'

'Alright, chancer.' Clare lifted Esme by the waist and set her down on her feet. 'Off. Tell madam to get to her own bed, or else.'

She skipped over to say goodnight and I kissed her cheek. Clare refilled my glass and sat back in the armchair, nursing her own. The blues, greens and purples played on her left cheek, on the skin of her bangled forearm. Christmas lights. I sipped my wine and tried not to feel like the bad Santa, though she must have known that to come unannounced like this, through the driving sleet, with a death-knock face, when the girls were in

254

bed, could bode nothing good.

She was ready now, waiting for me to speak. I set my glass on a coaster, nodded at the photograph. 'That new?'

She turned to appraise it.

'Had it for years. Just never got round to putting it up.'

'Clare, there's a guy called Hamish Neil.'

'I can read. I read the papers. My husband was a crime reporter.'

'I'm sorry. You know him, then?'

She was swallowing a gulp of wine but she waggled her head.

'Hamish Neil? No, of course I don't know him. I know who he *is*.'

'Well your husband knew him. Martin knew him.'

Her eyes above the wine glass gave nothing away. I leaned forward, draped my hand over my own glass, twisting it back and forward on its coaster.

'Knew him pretty well.'

She nodded, sipped her wine. 'Say it then, Gerry. Don't be shy.'

'He was on the take, Clare. Your husband was bent. He wrote stories for Hamish Neil, stories Neil supplied him with.'

I was staring down at the coffee table. When I looked up she was frowning.

'That's it? He got his stories from a gangster? That's your big revelation? Gerry, that's the job. That's how you do it.'

'This was a bit different, Clare. There was money

255

involved. He drew a wage. He wrote the stories that Neil wanted written. He wrote stories to order, for a Glasgow gangster.'

There were folds in Clare's brow, a deepening crease between her eyes.

'Why would he do that? Why would a gangster want stories?'

'He wrote about the Walshes, Clare. He went after the Walshes. Not every week, but enough to keep up the heat. The polis follow the papers. We're still good for that. You make something stink enough in the papers, the cops have to clean it up.'

I lifted the bottle, splashed some pinot into my glass. Threw it back, splashed some more. I'd to drive across the moors in the dark and the snow but I couldn't get through this sober.

'You mean it keeps them off Neil's back?'

'Yeah, but mainly it ties up the Walshes. You've got the cops camped out on the front lawn, it tends to restrict your movements. It's about the contracts, mainly,' I said. 'Martin was just doing his bit to clear the ground for Neil. Take out the competition. He'd probably have got them anyway.'

She was rubbing her wrist; the bangles shivered.

'The money,' she said. 'The twenty-six grand.'

I nodded.

'You said contracts?'

'The Games, Clare. The Commie Games. Building, demolition. Transport. It's all up for grabs. Security. They're all out to tender, there's plenty at stake.' I finished the wine and stood up. 'Anyway I'm sorry.'

She was nodding, still rubbing her wrist. 'How much?'

'What?'

'There's plenty at stake. How much?'

'I don't know.' I lifted my jacket, squeezed the pocket for my keys. 'Over a billion, I think. I don't know the exact figure. Big biccies anyway.'

She shook her head. Her eyes flicked round the room, took in the Linn, the wall-mounted plasma.

'Should have held out for more, shouldn't he? Sold himself short.'

She walked me to the door.

'Don't say that, by the way, Gerry. Pay us both the respect.'

'What?'

'"Sorry." You're not sorry.' We stopped in the hall-way. 'Coming to my door with your hangdog face.' She shook her head. 'He's off his pedestal now, isn't he? Bad as the rest of you. Worse. Got what you wanted.'

'I never wanted this, Clare.'

I zipped up my jacket and took out my car keys. I was waiting for her to open the door but she wasn't finished.

'Doesn't change anything,' she said. 'It doesn't mean he wasn't killed.' I'd hoped she wouldn't go down this route. 'Even if it's true, Gerry, even if you're right. Martin was on the take. Doesn't mean he wasn't murdered.'

'I'm thinking it does, though, Clare. I'm thinking a guy ties himself to the wheel and drives into a quarry, that's a guy who hates himself. Well, maybe now we know why.'

257

I let the door swing free as I walked down the path, the dull crump of snow under my boots. I had to scrape the fresh snow from the windscreen, run the engine for a minute or two. When I pulled away she was still standing in the doorway, backlit by the hall light. I didn't wave.

Chapter Twenty-six

The first thing I saw when the lift doors parted on the newsroom next morning was Niven and Maguire, choppers bared in rictus grins, a snapper crouching in front of them, angling for the shot. They each had a grip of an ugly, angular object, a kind of jagged plastic shield. The snapper stood up as I passed them and Maguire's smile slumped.

'Gerry.' I turned. Niven was already heading for the lift. 'Gerry, a word.'

Maguire was wearing a new suit, fitted, black, a skirt instead of trousers. Her hair was different. The object she was holding looked like some kind of trophy.

'Greater Glasgow tag-team champs? Scottish press corps mixed doubles?'

The curled lip, the hooded eyes. 'I thought you'd like to see this, Gerry.'

She passed me the thing, a jagged hunk of Perspex. It was shaped like the silhouette of Scotland. In frosted white, floating in the plastic ice, was the stylised nib of a fountain pen above a line of smart italics: *Martin Moir Award for Investigative Reporting, 2011.* I turned it over in my hands. She was waiting for my verdict. I passed it back.

'We need to talk.'

'What's stopping you?'

'Not here.'

She sighed, hefted the trophy in a scarlet-taloned hand and marched off towards her office. I watched her unaccustomed calves above the glossy black heels. In the office she turned and leant against her desk, arms braced. She raised her eyebrows at me. I closed the door and leant against it.

'He was working for Neil.'

There was no way to break it gently so I didn't try.

'Who was?'

I nodded at the trophy. 'Wonderboy.'

'*Martin?*'

'He was on a retainer. He was writing stories for Neil, bringing heat on the Walshes. Screw them over for the Commie Games contracts.'

She pushed away from the desk, lowered herself into a seat, rested her arms on the little round table, slumped down. I drew out a chair and sat down opposite.

'That's where he got the money, the twenty-six grand. The Linn hi-fi, the Lexus. He was bent, Fiona. I got it from a cop, drug enforcement, an Agency guy. They'd marked his card. A piece he wrote last year about the pizzeria shooting, he knew things the cops hadn't revealed. Details. The number of shots, that kind of thing.'

'What does that prove?' She raised her head.

'It proves he was bent. I'll sit on this for the moment, Fi, but if you're stupid enough to go through with this—' I jerked a thumb at the trophy.

The head drooped again, the arms sliding out till the

crimson nails clicked against the base of the trophy. A clang like a bell as it dropped into the metal bucket.

'Do yourself a favour,' she said. 'If you see Niven in the lift over the next few days, take the stairs.'

'I'm sorry, Fiona.'

'Merry fucking Christmas, Gerry.'

*

At the flat that evening I was re-reading *The Sportswriter* and waiting for my coffee to brew. Three heaped tablespoons of Blue Mountain were swirling around in the pot and the sharp dark smell was filling the kitchen. In some ways I should have been happy. Packy Walsh had been arrested and charged as an accessory in the murder of Helen Friel. DNA recovered from the forest where the body was dumped had placed one of Walsh's charmers at the scene: Radislav Gombar, the Slovak enforcer whose name had been linked with the phantom child sex case in Govanhill. The search was on for Mister Quis Separabit. Gombar had fled – presumably back to Slovakia – and Walsh was safely banged up in Barlinnie. But Walsh hadn't killed Martin Moir and I couldn't shake the feeling I'd been scammed. When I thought I was fighting for justice I was doing Hamish Neil's dirty work again.

I put my palm on the ball-shaped top of the plunger and pressed. It hadn't been the smoothest of days and I hoped that things would look a bit brighter after a hit of high-country Jamaican. At forty quid a bag, it was dearer

– and probably purer – than most of the coke in the city.

I looked at my watch: not yet eight. Still early enough to call James.

'Hey, Killer.'

'Hello, Dad.'

'How many?'

One of the many shitty things about working Saturdays was that I always missed his games. Adam took him instead. There was a whole cohort of teammates and touchline fathers who thought that James's dad was a skinny bald guy with a beard.

'Two.'

'You or the team?'

'Me. We won five-two. I got two.'

I fetched a still-warm mug from the dishwasher.

'The old left peg?'

'Yeah, one of them. And one with the head.'

'Brilliant. Who got man of the match?'

'It's "Player of the Day", Dad. Morgan got it.'

'The greedy one?'

'He scored three goals.'

'Yeah, he's greedy. Bet you made most of his.'

'I made one.'

'There you are. I'm proud of you, son. Is your mum around?'

I poured the coffee, black, bright, oily, the scent of bitter oranges. Elaine was calling to someone, her heels clacking on the kitchen floor.

'Gerry, yes. What is it?'

In the old days, when our separation was fresh, we

spent hours on the phone. We talked more when we'd just split up than we'd done in the last few years of our marriage. Elaine was diligent, solicitous, took my calls at all hours, soothed me, lulled me, talked me down. Not now.

'Hello to you, too.'

'I'm busy, Gerry, People here. What do you want?'

'Aye, OK. This Aberdeen thing. Where are we?'

'We?'

'I mean is he taking the job?'

She breathed through her nose. I knew the sound, not a good one.

'When we reach a decision,' she said, 'we'll let you know.'

'I don't get a say?'

'In what job Adam does?'

'In where my children live.'

In the silence I could hear voices, laughter, knives on plates, the sounds of civilisation. I could picture the dining room with its yellow walls, the blue vase in the alcove, the placemats with the phoenix motif.

'You get good access, Gerry. You see them every weekend. It's pretty bloody generous, actually.'

'Is that a threat?'

'What?'

'It might not be so generous if I don't toe the line?'

'No! No, Gerry. Your access is good, that's all. Whether we go to Aberdeen or not, that won't change. Look, I'm in the middle of a dinner party. I can't do this now.'

She rang off. No, access wouldn't change. Everything would stay the same. Just add a round trip of three hundred miles whenever you want to see the boys. I had little enough time with them as it was. Now every Sunday I'd be up at the crack of dawn, hauling the Forester up the A fucking 90.

I yanked a carton of milk from the fridge: empty, a pissy dribble at the bottom.

'Ah, did you not get milk?' There was a girlish quiver in my voice. I put down the book, marched to the living room, shaking the empty carton.

'What's that, sweetie?'

'I said there's no bloody milk.'

She looked up from her drawings. 'Well you better go and bloody get some then.'

I would have slammed the door if Angus hadn't been in bed. I grabbed my old leather and clattered down the stairs. I hadn't worn my leather in weeks and when I zipped it against the evening chill and plunged my hands in the pockets I felt a small object nestling under a packet of tissues. I traced it with the ball of my thumb, the surface ridged, scaly, it was Moir's fish, the little key-ring charm that used to hang above his desk. I brought it out, bounced it on my palm as I crossed Kelvin Drive, when something struck me. I stopped on the bridge, under a streetlight. I hooked my finger into the key-ring and pulled on the fish's tail. It came apart with a click. Glinting in the yellow glare as I held it to the light was a slim metal tab, a half-inch blunted blade.

Back at the flat, Mari glanced up from her work as I booted up the Mac, plugged the stick in the slot.

'Where's the milk?'

'What? I'll get it later.'

NO NAME: the device appeared on my desktop. I double-clicked and waited. A little box came up on the screen, framing a string of jpegs and Word docs and pdfs. I clicked on one of the jpegs. A man leaving a shop. He had the smug, furtive look of the illicitly photographed. Curly hair, broad nose, the shadowed frown-lines; it was Hamish Neil, in a white T-shirt and dark jerkin, a chunky watch catching the light. Through the plate-glass windows on either side, where the sun's reflection didn't blind them, were wreaths and bouquets. A street number – 137 – was visible at the top of the photo. Next photo: Neil again, leaving the florist's, this time in a V-neck Lyle and Scott sweater (you could see the yellow eagle at the chest), shoulders hunched against the rain. In neither shot was he carrying flowers.

For the next twenty minutes I clicked through the photos. Most of them were Neil. Leaving the florist's, leaving what looked like a hotel, leaving a tenement building. In some of the shots, a fit-looking woman – thirties, dark bobbed hair, sunglasses – was leaving the same buildings. Were these photos from the cops? Had Moir been doing his own surveillance?

The pdfs were scans of documents – bills, receipts. There were invoices from Laurelbank Retirement Home in Bearsden, the monthly accounts for Mrs Margaret Strain, Mrs Joy Glendinning, Mrs Norma Ross, from March of last year to October of this.

'Shit.'

'What's this?' Mari was at my shoulder. She squatted

down on her haunches, arm on the back of my chair.

'It's Martin's,' I said. 'I think he might have been clean after all.'

It was a dossier. Moir was building a dossier on Neil. Was that what this was? Had Moir been playing a double game, courting Neil to uncover his secrets, getting close enough to hurt him?

Lewicki answered on the fourth or fifth ring.

'You never hear of a home life, Conway? It's nine o'clock on Saturday night.'

'That's the weekly jubilee, is it? Set the clock by you?'

'You've got a dirty mind, Conway. We're watching a movie. Beer, tattie crisps. Homey things. Normal things.'

'Aye. Well it's homey, normal crims I'm calling about. Hamish Neil. Moir was keeping a dossier on him. I think Moir was clean after all.'

He picked me up within the hour. I was walking up Great Western Road when the Saab pulled in ahead, no signal. I'd copied the files onto my MacBook and I passed Lewicki the pen-drive.

'And you got this how?'

'Had it all along, Jan. Took it as a keepsake when I cleared his desk. Thought it was just a key-ring.'

We drove right out Great Western Road, through Anniesland and Knightswood, clean out to Clydebank. Parked in an empty business-centre car park. Lewicki fetched a laptop from the back seat. He worked through the files and photos, grunting now and then. I lit a Café Crème and watched the lights of Inchinnan across the river.

A grin kept stretching my lips so I could hardly smoke my cigar. I felt absurdly pleased that Moir was clean. I'd been wrong. We'd all been certain that Moir was gunning for Walsh and that Packy held the key to Martin's death. We'd been facing the wrong direction, stuck on the Clyde's wrong side. We should have been looking north, not south – to Cranhill not to Pollok. But I'd been right, too: Moir had kept the real stories hidden. Hid them so well that we nearly missed them. His real target was Hamish Neil but he never got the chance to see it through. I felt bad for doubting him. The only thing now – not for my sake or for Clare's or the girls' or Neve McDonald's but for Martin Moir himself – was to finish the job. Starting with the cleanskins – this florist, this retirement home.

'It's good.' Lewicki shifted in his seat, frowning at the screen. 'The florist's a front, we know that. The nursing home too. But the bills are new, the invoices. They'll turn out to be ghosts, would be my guess. If we can tie Neil to these dockets we might have a crack at this. Sit tight for the minute, I'll check with the tech boys tomorrow. Fucking Moir.' He shook his head. 'Should have known he'd never have done it, break the ninth commandment.'

Chapter Twenty-seven

'Chrysanths are always nice.' The woman waved a vague hand at some buckets by the till. 'Or—' She peered around the shop, distracted, forlorn, a hand poised in the air, like someone who's just come into a room and forgotten what she came for. 'Or orchids?' Her fingers tapped the tissue-paper backing of a window display where three vulgar blossoms hung in waxy, drooping folds.

'I hate orchids,' I said. 'The smell.'

'Not everyone's taste,' she said brightly. 'What's the occasion?'

She was fair, late forties, a heavy-set sensual woman with a smoker's crimped lips. She moved among the displays with a buoyant grace. She wasn't the woman in Moir's photos.

'I'm visiting my aunt,' I said. 'She's in a nursing home in Bearsden.'

'Bearsden's nice.'

'Laurelbank Retirement Home.' I lifted a Mackintosh vase, checked the price on the base. 'Do you know it?'

She had her back to me, scanning the arrangements along the back wall. 'I don't think so,' she said. 'What about a plant? They last longer.'

She smiled at me over her shoulder.

I bought some yellow carnations.

Laurelbank was a whitewashed villa with red tiled roofs
in the sleepy streets behind Roman Road. A smiling teenage girl in a white nurse's tunic answered the door.

'I'm here to see my aunt.' I brandished the carnations.
'Mrs Glendinning.'

'Come in.'

She slipped behind the reception desk and smiled
afresh, as if greeting me for the first time.

I waited.

'The name again, sir?'

'Glendinning.'

Her manicured fingers rattled the keys. The name on
her name badge was 'Katya'. She grimaced at the screen.

'I'm sorry, we don't appear to have a resident of that
name. Are you sure you have the correct . . . facility?'

I nodded. 'This is the place.'

'Well, I can't see it.' The smile was back. 'Why don't
I get Mrs Cole? I haven't been here long. Mrs Cole will
have a better idea.'

She disappeared through a swing door and I leaned
across the counter to steal a glance at the screen but it
was back at the homepage and I moved smartly across to
stand beneath the bucolic landscape that hung above the
empty fireplace: a man in grey on a hillside casting a fly,
a chill-looking dawn mirrored pink in the river.

'You're looking for Mrs Glendinning?'

The woman who stepped out from behind the counter
and strode towards me was wearing a smart dark-blue

two-piece. The suit had a mature, even matronly cut, but the body underneath it was good, and the woman's eyes and the two-inch heels on her court shoes suggested she knew it.

'That's right.'

'I'm very sorry, but Mrs Glendinning left us in August.' The woman's hands were clasped beneath her chest and she was nodding slowly.

'She died?'

'Oh no!' The lips twisted in a waspish smile. 'No, the family took her away.'

'Do you have an address?' The address on Moir's invoice was a PO box in Edinburgh.

'For the family? I'm afraid not. They were moving away. Down south; Cornwall as I understand it. They were taking Mrs Glendinning with them. What did you say your connection was, Mr— ?'

'Moir. Martin Moir. I'm the nephew.'

I watched the eyes for a reaction.

'Martin *Moir*?'

'That's right.'

'And do you have an address where we can reach you, Mr Moir, if something, if something turns up?'

'I'm afraid not.' I put out my hand and she grasped it lightly, absent-mindedly. 'I think I may be moving soon too. Thanks for your help.'

The receptionist was still rattling the keys as I pushed back through the doors and into the street.

I drove round the block and parked a little farther down the street on the opposite side. I smoked two roll-ups, enjoying the weak, low sun on my half-closed eyes. In twenty minutes a white Porsche Cayenne pulled up outside Laurelbank and a slim brunette in jogging gear – three-quarter-length black leggings and a fitted, waterproof vest with fuchsia panels – slipped down from the driver's side and bounced across the gravel on her spotless white Mizunos. When she tossed her hair on the top step I was ready with the iPhone and snapped two shots before the door closed. The short bobbed hair, the Jackie O sunspecs: it was the woman in Moir's photos. I tossed the iPhone onto the passenger's seat and headed back to town.

Lewicki phoned that evening. He had a colleague, Callum Kidd, who wanted to meet me, pass on some data. There were front companies the Agency knew about, even if they couldn't yet prove them to be fronts. As of now they'd decided to share their intelligence with public bodies – local councils, health trusts, licensing boards – to prevent them awarding contracts to firms with criminal links. Kidd was prepared to show me the list.

The next afternoon I drove to Lock 27, picked my spot in the empty car park. The pub had yet to open but the chef stood smoking by an open fire-door, the wind rippling his thin checked trousers. There was no one else around. I thought it might be more conspicuous to ignore him so I jerked my chin as I headed for the towpath and he raised two fingers of his smoking hand, blessed me with his cigarette.

I was heading east. Low sun. The frozen grass sparkling, like something sprayed with silver paint. A jogger was powering towards me, the sun at her back, a silhouette of legs in black Lycra. I stepped onto the grass and she rasped past, jiggle of blonde ponytail, a swivelled eye.

The second bench was empty. I wiped a glove across the perforated metal, wiped the glove on my leather jacket. I was five minutes early. The Forth & Clyde was freezing over, two wavy lines of ice jutting out from either bank, a stripe of standing water in the middle. I could feel the bench through my jeans, the frozen metal, a dull itchy chill on the backs of my thighs. But the sun on my face had some heat and I closed my eyes to savour it. When I opened them a dog was rooting in the weeds at my feet, a boxer, its dainty waist twisting back and forward as the scents drew its nose. The man attached to it stood uncertainly, a pained half-smile on his long face. He wore a short jacket of houndstooth tweed, a scarlet scarf. He held the leash in a brown gloved hand.

'Conway? Gerry Conway?'

'Aye.'

I gave my hand to the dog, let it snuffle and lick, the blunt snout bumping my fingers, then took it away as the tailless rump shuffled up to the bench, the leg lifting. The man looked on with pursed lips. He didn't look like a dog person. Was the dog even his? Was he a cutout, I wondered? Was this the cop?

'I've got something for you.'

He took off his gloves, hunched his shoulders to reach into his inside pocket. I took a folded paper from his hand, stowed it in my own breast pocket.

'Alright?'

I nodded. He was nodding too. A swan slid into view behind him on the black strip of water, like something on a rail. We needed a form of words to finish this, to bring the transaction to a close.

'Be careful, alright?'

I tapped my pocket.

'Won't let it out of my sight.'

He shook his head.

'No, I mean *you*. You be careful.'

'Okay, I will.'

He looked off up the towpath and back at me. He was deciding whether to tell me something. A cop, I thought. He's the cop, not the cutout.

'Hamish Neil finds out we gave you that?' He shook his head, tugging at the gloves, flexing the fingers. The dog watched his hands. There was something else, something behind his words. He turned to leave and I grabbed his forearm, the wiry tweed.

'Hold on. How would Hamish Neil find out?'

He held my gaze. 'Hamish Neil's got a habit of finding things out.'

'A rat?'

I thought he hadn't heard me at first.

'It could be.' He studied the towpath. 'Aye. We think so.'

I looked across the frozen water, the solitary swan slow-moed back into view. Did swans not come in pairs?

'You mean he'll know about this? Our meeting? Hamish Neil?'

'Just be careful,' he said again. He tugged hard on the

273

animal's leash and crunched off up the frozen path. The dog's cropped tail wagged like a finger.

'Hey!'

He stopped. The dog turned at my voice and they both stood and waited.

'Why the canal?'

He shrugged.

'I live near here. It's where I walk the dog.'

He strode off, the dog trotting beside him in the frozen grass, rooting for smells. I tugged the paper from my pocket, two sheets of A4, stapled, folded in quarters. A printed list of company names and their registered addresses. *Citywide Cabs, Skyline Scaffolding, Greene Group, Judd Construction.* The usual fronts – cabs, builders, demolition. Then the others. *Sunset Boulevard Tanning Salon, Flowers By Genevieve, MacKay's Coaches.* Two hairdressing salons. Cash businesses, Lewicki had told me. Any place you can fabricate clients, phantom customers. Laurelbank Retirement Home was there, and a fitness club in Bothwell.

Would Maguire publish the list? I wasn't sure. But she would publish the fact that the list existed, that we had it in our possession. That in itself should get the Justice Committee excited, spook Neil's cleanskins.

Then I turned the page and the words swam up, *Abacus Nursery, 15 Jeffrey Street, G12.* I closed my eyes, flinched as from a blow, opened them, read it again. I was breathing through my nose, I could hear the snorkeling of air as if I was under water.

274

Chapter Twenty-eight

I started for the car, pulling out my phone, scrolling for the number. It went to voicemail, the stupid, upbeat message: *Mari, Gerry and Angus are having too much fun to come to the phone. Leave your number and we'll call you back!*

'Mari.' I cleared my throat. 'Mari, are you there? You need to pick up Angus from nursery.' I tried to keep my voice even but it buckled, broke. 'Now. As soon as you get this. Call me.' I tried her mobile; it rang out.

The chef was gone, I looked at the empty wall where he'd stood, thinking, *This is what you'll remember, this scene will live with you forever if something's happened.* Then I turned the ignition, put the Forester in drive.

It was the feeling you have when you've lost a child, when a toddler wanders off in the shopping mall, when your first frantic search draws a blank and your brain circles back round the words: lost, gone, dead. You enter this zone of abeyance, a poisonous lull. If something has happened, it's happened. The time you let slip, the six or seven minutes when you weren't watching, will happen again. They have already happened to the boy; now they will happen to you. You will find out what your next card is: do you get your life back or will fate, God, chance, take it away?

I drove down the Crow Road, onto Great Western. I drove like an old lady, drove as if there was a tray of eggs on the back seat. Keep as quiet and still as you can, and nothing bad will happen. Neil's voice came into my mind, as if he was sitting beside me in the car. *You can't keep a thing safe, you don't deserve to keep it.* Onto Byres Road. Dowanhill. I turned the wheel left and right and swung round corners till the building loomed up, the nursery with its yellow sign, the artwork in the windows, coloured cellophane, the smiling bears and happy tigers.

I'd held it together till now but when I reached the car park panic swelled. I sprang from the car, keys swinging in the ignition, door agape, and plunged towards the steps. A mum was coming out with a red-haired toddler, a wee girl, maybe two years old. She was tugging a hat from her head and she chucked it on the ground and the mother stooped to lift it.

You're supposed to let the door click shut and then press the buzzer – it's a security thing – but I slammed past the mum and into the hallway, lunging for the tweenie-room, bracing myself on the jamb. The heads looked up from their toys and games. In a corner, two kids were asleep on beanbags, the little bodies sprawled as though they'd fallen from a height. Music was coming from a portable CD player, a nursery rhyme with tinny percussion. A boy in a pinny at the water tray pointed at me and said, 'Angus!' I heard the click from the supervisor's knees as she rose and came towards me, frowning.

'Angus is gone. He's away already. Did she not tell you?'

'What? Who?'

'Your wife phoned. Your sister picked him up. You've just missed them.'

The room seemed to buckle, to bulge in random places: the suds in the water-tray, a curly blond head, the crest on the supervisor's polo shirt. I lurched through to the baby room, the pre-school room – frantic, calling his name – then spun out onto the steps.

And then I saw it. Three-pointing in the street: the black Beamer X5, the tinted windows. I ran for the Forester, hauled the door shut, stamped on the gas. At the car-park gate I saw braking tail-lights, the Beamer turning right onto Great Western.

My hands were shaking as I sped up the street and signalled right, waited for a break in the traffic. All down Great Western I kept the black tailgate in sight. St George's Cross, onto the motorway, spurt of speed, crossing three lanes, rush hour starting. Blue signs overhead, Kilmarnock, Prestwick Airport. The South. I ran through the possibilities. South Side, Ayrshire, the ferry to Ireland, straight down to England. I looked at the fuel gage, the needle bumping 'F'. Good: I'd filled up last night, coming back from the five-a-sides.

The Kingston Bridge looped us over the Clyde, the river molten yellow, sun fizzing on the Armadillo. I was right on the tail, no cars now between my front end and the tinted rear window. The Beamer left the motorway at Junction 1, zipping past Pollok Park. I kept on its bumper through Shawlands, into Newlands, the big sandstone semis, plenty of trees. Then a furniture lorry swung out of a side street and I jammed the horn with the heel of my hand, mounted the pavement, cleared the rear wheel by a tenth of an inch.

When I turned the next corner the Beamer was swinging to the kerb, brake lights flaring. There was a space right behind it but I put the foot down to get alongside, wrenching the wheel to swing my nose round, blocking it off. The belt slapped my chest, slammed me back in my seat as the Forester bucked on its chassis but already I was out, sprinting round the car, yanking the door, two fistfuls of shirt, hauling the guy from his seat, shouting for my son. The driver's head was bucking in slow-motion, his arms flapping as the seat belt held him. A child was crying, screaming, I couldn't see the child.

I dropped the driver and hauled on the rear door. The eyes swung round, the pink screaming mouth; a blond boy, not Angus, not mine. I frowned at the child and my temple exploded, dropping me onto one knee, my cheek bumping the bodywork. I staggered up and back. The driver stood swaying, mad eyes, mouth yawing, the fingers of one hand clenched in the other.

'I'm sorry.' I backed up, hands high. 'My son. I thought you had my son.'

He lashed out, made a clumsy orang-utan swipe with his good hand as I ducked past him and into the Forester, punched the locks, found reverse, found drive, away.

Barrelling down the street I could see him in the rear-view, planted in the roadway, legs apart, cradling his broken hand.

My head was pulsing with pain as I turned onto

Kilmarnock Road. My Hugo Boss specs were hanging askew – a leg had snapped when the driver lamped me – and the eye on that side was closing. The bump to my cheek had gashed a gum and blood was pooling in my mouth, slipping down my throat like brassy phlegm. But my chest wasn't heaving. The mist had cleared. The ball in my stomach was gone. I was thinking straight. When my phone rang I fished it calmly from my pocket.

'Gerry?' Mari's voice was small and scared, a voice I'd never heard before. 'Have you got him? I got your message.'

'No.'

'You want me to go?'

'No. I've been. He's not there.'

I thought I'd lost her for a minute but her voice came back, smaller than ever.

'What do you mean?'

'I'm in the car. Hold on.' I tossed the phone on the passenger seat, pulled out of the traffic, into a side street, parked.

'Mari, look. Listen. I met a cop today, a detective. He gave me a list of companies that Hamish Neil's involved in. The nursery was on it, Abacus. Hamish Neil owns Abacus. He knows I'm doing the story, he knows the cop was meeting me. When I got there Angus was gone. They told me you had phoned and that my sister had picked him up.'

Silence. A little hiss that might have been Mari catching her breath. I haven't got a sister.

'Gerry this isn't funny. Tell me this is a joke.'

279

'I'm sorry. Mari, listen—'

'Someone's got our son? A *gangster's* got our son? What are the police doing?'

'Can't call the police. It's Hamish Neil, Mari. He might do something stupid.'

'Something stupid? Something fucking *stupid*? He's taken our son.'

'I'm calling Lewicki. I'll call you back.'

The charge was now under five per cent, a sliver of red in the battery icon. I scrolled to Lewicki. Voicemail. Fuck. I left a message.

There was nothing to do but drive.

Twenty minutes later I parked behind Mari's Outback. Took the stairs four at a time, tore the pocket of my best blue jacket as I yanked free the keys. Was I hearing things, I wondered, or did something else make this noise, the noise of thumping feet, but here he was, tearing through from the living room, his straight wide smile, his long-sleeved T-shirt with 'It's Not Fair' stitched on the front. He thumped into my arms and I hoisted him high and hugged him, swinging him round in the tight little hall, laughing. His kicking feet caught the overhead light and the shadows swung drunkenly over our dance. When I stopped, breathless, smudging his neck with a kiss and lowered him to the floor, Mari was framed in the kitchen doorway – spent, haggard, sick. She turned on her heel. The boy laughed at the slam of the living-room door.

When the shouting was over, the tears and the rage, she told me what happened. After I called her from the car, Mari was frantic. She tried to phone the nursery but the line was engaged. Before she could try again the phone rang; it was the nursery manager calling to apologise. There'd been a mistake, she said. The girl in the tweenie room was new, confused, she'd got Angus mixed up with another kid. Angus never left – he'd been away having his nappy changed, he'd been in the changing-room all along. Mari drove to pick him up.

That night, when Angus was in bed and some sort of cookery showdown played at an unthreatening volume on Channel 4 and the air in the living room seemed to ring with aftermath, Mari held a ladybird-patterned vest by its tiny shoulders and told me she was taking Angus to New Zealand. She was kneeling on the floor, folding the boy's clothes and placing them in piles on the sofa. I closed my eyes for a moment and opened them again. We'd talked about this. Her parents hadn't seen Angus since just after his birth, when they flew over and stayed with us for a month. It would be good for Angus to see them again, good for Mari to be with her folks. We'd talked about it but nothing more. Now she was going.

'Two weeks before Christmas? If you even get a flight it'll be an arm and a leg.'

'Right. Let's expose our son to the vengeance of a fucking sociopath because the flights are too dear. I'm booking it tonight.'

She bent to her work, something implacable in the crown of her head, the fierce symmetry of her centre parting. On the TV an anxious bespectacled man tossed a handful of scallops into a flaming wok.

'Okay. We'll talk when you get back.'

She didn't say anything.

'When are you coming back?'

She carried on folding the clothes, laying them out on the bed. She didn't look up.

'You're not going to answer me?'

She looked up, back at the clothes.

'Ger, you need to sort this out. I can't have this. I can't have my son threatened, in danger.'

'Your son?'

'Ours. No, fuck it, mine.' She was angry now, she threw the crumpled T-shirt back in the basket and jabbed her thumb at her chest. '*My* son. Mine. He's your son when you learn to keep him out of danger. The bare fucking minimum. Keep him safe.'

You can't keep a thing safe, you don't deserve it.

She was right. I hadn't kept him safe. I'd failed him. The boy was hers now more than mine.

In a minute or so she stopped folding and came round behind my chair. Her hand cupped my jaw, slid round my neck, drew me in.

'I'm sorry.' She kissed my ear. 'I didn't mean that.'

'No, you're right.'

'No I'm not. But, Gerry, it's the best thing. He can't go back to nursery anyway. Not now. He's better away from here.'

Quis separabit. I nodded, pulled her back into me, held her. As I pressed my lips to her hair Angus started crying. She clapped my back twice and went through to lift him.

Chapter Twenty-nine

'You're a lucky man,' Haining said. 'I was on my way out. Five minutes later and you'd have missed me.'

His raised eyebrows measured my narrow escape. I gripped the hand that emerged from a glinting white cuff and we bumped shoulders. It was like the clasp before a bout. There was a chair in front of his desk and I took it.

'I need some information.'

Haining was settling back behind his desk and he froze for a second, his elbows locked on the arms of his chair, like a man on the parallel bars. Then a smile quenched the scowl on his face and he eased himself down.

'Gerry Conway, the emperor of small talk.' He was shaking his head, smiling as if to himself. 'Can I at least offer you a coffee?'

I was done with fucking about. My family was flying to New Zealand in two days' time. I didn't know when I would see them again. The only way to get them back was to put a stop to Hamish Neil. We were publishing the list of Neil's fronts in Sunday's paper. For now, this sack of creash was going to do his bit to help.

'I need the names of the successful bidders for the Commonwealth Games contracts.'

He goggled genially. He leaned forward with his elbows on the desk and smacked his knuckles into his palm a few time before spreading his hands.

'Anything else?'

'That's it.'

'Really?' He waved an expansive hand. 'You wouldn't like the details of my own contract: salary, terms of employment?'

'I imagine they're adequate.'

'Okay,' he nodded. He sat back in the chair and crossed his legs, dragged a big hand through his hair. 'Maybe you'd like to enlighten me, tell me what the story's about.'

'I'm not writing a story,' I told him. 'Not yet.'

'Uh-huh.' His attempt to stay genial and composed was sending little pulses down his jawline. He squared his shoulders, rolled his head like a boxer loosening his neck muscles. With some effort, a little hoarsely, he asked: 'What, then; idle curiosity?'

'I'm taking it to the police. I've got a contact in the Agency; when you give me the information I'll pass it on to him.'

The last gleam of bonhomie had been extinguished. We faced each other in the big square office and Haining looked at me with honest contempt.

'What is it you think you've found out?'

'I haven't found out anything. But you know what I'm going to find out. The bidders are fronts. The money's going to Hamish Neil.'

He gazed off, not at the window, where the pigeons burbled and pecked along the balustrade, but at a window-sized painting on the opposite wall. It depicted a covered arena, its yellow pennants twisting in the wind, rising in triumph above tiers of A-frame chalets, while sleek faceless citizens – mostly in couples or family groups – enjoyed the verdant walkways. It was an artist's impression of the athletes' village.

'There's one thing that gets me,' Haining was saying. He was frowning at the illustration and I thought for a moment he had spotted a flaw, a glitch in the artist's vision. Then he faced me with a look of savage puzzlement. 'Why aren't the cops asking this? The fuck are you doing here?'

I shook my head. 'They don't have enough evidence to move on this yet. They can't come down here asking questions.'

'But you can.'

I shrugged.

'So you're the message boy?'

'I'm doing a favour,' I said.

'Oh yeah? Could you do me one?'

'It's you I meant. I'm doing you a favour. If you go ahead with these contracts you're finished, fucked.'

Haining ran his tongue across his teeth. He tapped his fingers softly on the desk.

'Maguire know you're here?' he said quietly. 'Threatening elected officials. Defaming them, spreading lies, hearsay? Of course she doesn't. Go home, Gerry. Some of us have got work to do. Even if I wanted I couldn't tell you the names. The contracts haven't been awarded yet. There *are* no successful bidders.'

'I mean the lowest bidders. The ones who're going to get the contracts. I also need the timing of the bids, relative to the others.'

'Excuse me?'

'Who was the lowest bid. Who was the latest bid. I'm guessing they're the same.'

Haining smoothed his tie with a big flat hand.

'You know how much it's worth, that information? How sensitive it is?'

'You want to read your website, Councillor.'

'Sorry?'

'The deadlines have passed. I checked the web this morning. Have the deadlines passed?'

The big jaw swivelled in acknowledgement. 'Most of them.'

'Then it's worth fuck all. Except to you. It might be worth something to you, if you're smart enough to use it. When do you announce the winners?'

'The new year. Three weeks' time.'

He was staring at the desk, breathing through his nose. The noise seemed to fill the room.

'Good. Then your question's wrong. It's not how much the information is worth, it's how much the city's image is worth, the city's good name. Look, you announce the successful bidders in three weeks' time. I start digging, the cops start digging. If there's dirt we'll find it. You think we won't?'

He didn't look up from his desk.

'Then you've given contracts to gangsters. The Games are tainted. Your shot at First Minister's fucked. You tell us *now*, we've got two or three weeks to dig. If we find anything in time you can cancel the contracts.'

He looked up. 'And if you don't?'

'Oh we keep on digging. But this way, if something turns up, you're covered. You cooperated with the authorities, you did all you could.'

'And if I don't tell you?'

'Then there's a nice big space on the *Trib*'s front page with your smiling face on it. You knew about the police's suspicions and you did nothing.'

He didn't waste time complaining. He didn't cast up his favours to me, or the Friday lunches, the spot on the *Spectrum* show. He pushed his chair back and yanked on the knot of his tie and flipped his top button with a vindictive thumb. He crossed to the window and rested his knuckles on the deep wooden sill.

'I'll need some time,' he said.

I joined him at the window. The fog had thickened and swelled, filling the square, obliterating the lunchtime strollers. Only the statues – black and dully lustrous – were still visible. Just below us a figure in a top hat and frock coat was jabbing his cane at the insubstantial ground. On the far side Queen Victoria steadied her horse amid the shifting mist. And above it all, teetering on his column, with a plaid across his shoulders and a novel in his fist, was Sir Walter Scott.

Our breath whitened the window as if the fog had seeped inside.

'I can't email it,' he said.

'And you don't want me coming back here twice in a week.'

He looked at me sourly. I fished a card from my breast

pocket and wrote my home address on the back. 'Send it there.'

'I'll need a couple of days,' he said.

'Fine.' I tapped the card into his breast pocket. 'If I don't hear from you by Friday, you might want to give Sunday's paper a miss.'

I jogged down the marble staircase, thinking of the picture on Haining's wall. You would like to live in a city like that, with its pastel shades, its green indeterminate trees, its slender strolling citizens. A year ago, Haining had been the Pharoah of the Clyde, captain of the city's fate. Then in May the Nationalists took five of the city's eight seats. Haining's empire was hanging by a thread and no amount of Carrara marble or Spanish mahogany could hide that fact.

I pushed through the revolving doors into the bright muffled light of the square. I lit a Café Crème, set off through the milling shoppers. At Queen Street Station I stopped and looked back. Across the square the City Chambers rose from the snow like the palace of some Doge or Viceroy. Domes and balustrades and columns, all the Second City pomp. White sky mirrored in the Chambers upper windows. It was too far to see, but I could picture him there, the Chevalier, the lost leader, looking out across a square named for a foreign king, the statues of another country's heroes.

Despite my frozen feet, my throat, the press of Christmas shoppers, I felt good. I had struck a blow. The old Ulster euphemism – *returning the serve* – came back to me. I had returned the serve. My cigarillo landed with a *tsk* in the puddled slush. There was nothing I could do until Haining's letter arrived and then everyone could get to work. Me, Lewicki, the Agency.

A rockabilly three-piece was busking at the top of Buchanan Street, beneath the green statue of Donald Dewar. A crowd had gathered and I joined its outer edge. A flat-topped double-bassist in a cut-off checked shirt with the collar turned up was spanking his machine, his hand bouncing like a flail, the low notes burbling up beneath the sharp loose click of the strings. A hunched drummer stroked a skeleton kit with his brushes, and the clean jabbing licks of the frontman's Gretsch sliced through the wintry air. 'Stop the Train' was the number they were playing and the simmering rhythm stayed with me as I climbed the steps to the Buchanan Galleries.

I had barely thought about Christmas but now, for the first time that year – and maybe for many a year – something in me lifted at the piped music, the golds and the silvers, the rich metallic reds, the thick foxy ropes of snowy tinsel. I wanted to shop, I wanted to align myself with the bag-toting crowds. I wanted a toy for Angus. Maybe it was the buskers' song but I wanted a train, an old-fashioned wooden affair and I found the very thing in a boutique toy shop on the upper level. An engine of white sanded wood, its funnels and wheels slicked a thick glossy red, with hook-and-eye carriages and sickle-shaped segments of tongue-and-groove track. 'I do,' I told the woman when she asked if I wanted it gift-wrapped, and her perfunctory smile couldn't stop me adding, 'It's for my son.'

289

Chapter Thirty

I came home early the next day. Flat empty. Stink of shit in the kitchen. I pulled the bag from the sleek metal bin, tried not to look at the blue translucent nappy-sacks, tied it and carted it down to the green. Back upstairs I ran the tap till steam was rising from the sink and then washed my hands with pink surgical scrub. I dug in the freezer for the silver package. I put a filter in the plastic cone and spooned it in, three dollops, watched the grains darken and liquefy as I tipped in the water, waited for the smell to fill the kitchen, masking the savour of shit. When I caught myself standing at the window, glooming out over the empty back court, I picked up the phone and sat down heavily at the kitchen table. I had her on speed-dial but I punched in the number.

'Hello?'

'It's me.'

Silence. She never made things easy. I'd envisaged a brief bout of small talk, an opening skirmish, but Elaine always knew when something was wrong.

'What is it?'

I took a sip of coffee and started. She didn't interrupt. I told her about Moir, his involvement with Hamish Neil, the dossier on his pen drive, the nursing home in Bearsden, the phantom residents, the meeting with the cop on the canal towpath. I told her about the nursery, the chase, the fight, the sudden reappearance of Angus. I told her about Hamish Neil, the kind of things he'd done, the kind of man he was. When I caught my breath the silence was back. I winced into it, waiting for the crash. Her voice, when she spoke, was surprisingly calm.

'But you're in Politics,' she said.

'Yeah, but I got embroiled in this thing, this story and it got, I don't know, out of hand. I'm sorry. I don't think he'll do anything.'

'Embroiled? You mean your editor commissioned it?'

'Aye. Well, no, it wasn't—'

'You did it yourself. You sought it out.'

I didn't answer.

'Oh, Gerry. Jesus wept. Gerry Conway saves the world.' She snickered, a harsh snapping sound. 'Try saving your sons next time. Your own flesh and blood. Try starting with them.'

*

She called back that evening. I was changing Angus's nappy when the phone rang and I knew it would be her. She was careful to make clear that it had nothing to do with my phone call that afternoon, with the things I had told her.

'Although, to be honest,' she said, 'it does rather vindicate our decision. Anyway, it's a chance we can't pass up, is what we feel.'

She was waiting for me to speak, give my blessing.

291

'It sounds like a good job,' I said. 'A good move. I'm sure you'll be happy.'

'Thanks, Gerry. We will. And the boys, too. A new city. Good schools. And of course access won't be a problem. We're both very happy for you to come up at weekends, stay with us. Take the boys down to Glasgow. Whatever.'

'That's great, Lainie,' I said. 'It means a lot.'

*

Mari spent that evening packing. They left two days later. I drove them to the airport. Snow in blackened ridges at the kerbside. Cops with guns at the terminal building. I left them in Departures, saw them join the line for security, Mari with the passports in her free hand, the boy waving when she told him, his little fist flashing open and shut.

On the way back I punched the button for Radio Scotland. *Newsdrive* had started, Mhairi Stuart intoning the headlines. *Referendum . . . Commonwealth Games . . . Helmand Province.* I hit the button again, drove home in silence.

The next day I had barely sat down at my screen before Maguire called me through. I'd written up the Agency story, the fifty-odd companies that were fronts for Hamish Neil.

I knocked on the glass beside her open door.

'Sit down, Gerry.' She was frowning at her screen. She had the boss face on, the bad-news face.

'Oh, Fiona. Tell me you're kidding.'

'Just sit down.'

I didn't sit down. If I sat I was conceding a point, losing ground before we'd begun.

'Don't fucking start this, Fiona—'

'Sit down, Gerry. We got it legalled last night. They're not happy.'

'They're *lawyers*, Fiona. They're meant to be not happy. That's their job, stop us doing ours.'

'You may remember the last time we took a flyer on a Conway story.' She pushed her glasses onto her head, rubbed a hand up and down her face. 'Reporter lost his job. Guy called Conway.'

'We're not naming all the companies. We're not doing the full list.' The cops had warned us that naming the companies could cause problems: the next time someone rejected a bid they could be open to reprisals. But I'd identified four firms with directors connected to Neil and we were naming all of those.

'We're naming four companies. We're naming Neil. We're identifying Hamish Neil as the gangster, the king-pin.'

'Fiona, that's the point. And it's not us, it's the police. We're just reporting it. Hamish Neil is a gangster. Stop fucking press. The companies he's involved in are fronts for organised crime. That's not fair comment? What definition of fair comment does that not meet?'

A bottler. Maguire was a bottler. Rix, for all his failings, was never like this. Rix would have run it, Rix would have come through. What were we here for if not for this? She must have read this in my face, she was shaking her head, mouth pursed, pure rancour.

'Say it then.'

'What?'

'Rix would have run it. Stormin Norman.'

'You're saying he wouldn't have?'

'Rix was three years ago, Gerry. Rix was when we had cash. When we had sixty thousand readers. When we could afford to make mistakes.'

'It's a mistake to tell the truth.'

'When you're going to get sued it is, yes. When you're nearly out of business it *is* a mistake. You seen the numbers? Forty-one, Gerry. Forty-one thousand people are buying the paper.'

'Making money for the Yanks. Is that what we're here for? Well it better be more than that because we're not making any fucking money. We can't go after Hamish Neil we might as well give up now. You used to be a journalist, Fiona. What would you call yourself now?'

'Are you finished?'

'We're all finished, Fiona. If this is the script, the whole thing's finished.'

We published the piece in the next day's paper. I tweeted the link, waited for the onslaught.

*

That evening the phone rang as I was making dinner, a tin of minestrone. Take the whole lid off; Elaine had drummed that into me. She'd seen it on the telly, a nature programme; when the tins end up on the dump, the little animals – the mice, the rats, the foxes – they push their heads in, trying to get the food. Then they're stuck, necks against the serrated edge. Tear their heads off trying to get out.

I left the tin half-opened.

'Conway.'

'Gerry, it's me.'

'Hey!

It was Mari. She was voluble, lit up, eager to spill out her news. The flight had been fine – anyway, bearable. Angus slept in his bassinet for most of the first leg. Mari's parents met them at Auckland and they were now ensconced in the big Mission Bay villa with the harbour view. They'd been to the beach that morning – it was summer there, of course – and a freak wave had knocked Angus flat as he paddled in ankle-deep water. She described her horror as the wave concealed him from view and the speed with which he scrambled up, too shocked to cry, shaking himself like a dog and glaring at the innocent Pacific. His grandad had bought him a 'boogie board' – a kid's surfboard – and he held it on his lap all the way home. He'd made friends with a neighbour's little boy and Mari's sister was arriving in two days' time from Oz, with her twin girls. A proper Kiwi Christmas, a sausage sizzle at the house and then out to Piha for beach cricket with the cousins. As she rattled on I felt a strange inertia grip me. It was all I could do to muster an interested grunt as each wave of talk withdrew.

'Hold on,' she said at one point; 'here he is. Who's

this, Angus? It's Daddy. Say "Hello Daddy".'

The boy came on – I heard the delicate slurp of his breath – and when I finished my sing-song riff of greeting he pronounced 'Dada!' in his thick-tongued, definitive way. Mari prompted him with questions and he repeated the words he knew, like someone underlining a text. 'Did we go to the beach?' 'Beach!' 'Did Angus ride in the car?' 'Car!' Then she remembered something.

'Oh, Gerry. He's got a new word. Listen to this. Angus, what did we see at the shop?' Then she whispered the word and he said it.

'Raddit!'

He said it again, more forcefully: 'Raddit! Raddit!' They had stopped off at the pet shop on the way back from the beach and Angus had been allowed to handle one of the rabbits. I could picture his delight as he patted and prodded the creature, its tail-like ears, its trembling nose. As Mari related the anecdote I could hear Angus in the background, repeating his new word with propriet-ary glee.

I was playing five-a-sides that evening so it wasn't until after nine that I was alone again and back in the flat. I switched the Christmas lights on, sat in the gloom with a mug of Rooibos, let the silence swamp me. The Rooibos was missing something. I rectified that, put the Lagavulin back on its shelf. I thought about the call from Mari, the boy's voice. I thought about Hamish Neil, Hamish Neil opening the paper, Hamish Neil reading my words.

He would kill me. If it came to it, he wouldn't think twice. If he didn't kill me he would kill Angus or Mari.

He had killed Moir and made it look like suicide. Would I be any harder? I wasn't short on motive. Broken marriage. Girlfriend leaves him. Three sons he doesn't see. Job in the shitter. Okay, I told myself; leave it at that. He had men who would do this, who would kill at his bidding. He had friends on the force who would cover his tracks.

That afternoon at work the messages had started. On the work email and then on my Twitter feed. I watched them come in:

Cranhill Boy@bigboysrules3h
@GerryCon
U know what happens to bhoys who tell tales out of school. #onedeadjourno

And then the others:

Squarego@Squarego1h
@GerryCon
Someone needs to teach u some manners u lying Fenian Scum.

Squarego@Squarego28m
@GerryCon
27 Clouston Street. Second floor left.

Thank Christ Mari and Angus were away. I texted Lewicki – *More shit on Twitter. Posting my address now. Can you check it out?* – and logged out.

You had the idea of making a difference. You had the idea of standing alone against the villains. I thought of the brochure that Elaine had sent me for the school in Aberdeen: *The aim is for boys to leave this College as men of integrity and conviction. We want them to learn to have the courage to stand, alone if necessary, for what they believe is right.* But the people who stood against Hamish Neil weren't left standing for long. Walter Maitland. Martin Moir. Packy Walsh. Declan Coyle.

And I wasn't standing alone. I had Mari and Angus. I'd already lost one family. I couldn't lose another. I had to fix this. One way or another, I had to finish things with Neil. I wanted them back, my partner and child. I wanted our life to pick up where it left off, the days to assume their familiar rhythm, but I knew, as I tipped another finger of whisky into my empty mug, that we'd already gone too far. Simply calling a halt wouldn't do. I couldn't just contact Neil and tell him it was over, I'd suffered a change of heart, I was backing off. A forfeit would be payable. Some penalty or levy. And I knew what the forfeit would be. I would have to get involved, come onside, work for Hamish Neil, as Moir had done or pretended to do. I would have to go over.

Would that be so bad, I wondered, if it meant getting Mari and Angus back? But it wouldn't end there. Either it would never end or it would end as it ended for Moir. I'd started this thing and now I had to see it through. Not everyone could come out of this with their shoes shined and their premiums paid. Only one happy ending was on the table and I planned to make it mine.

Chapter Thirty-one

They'd been gone less than a week and already the flat was like a shantytown. Too big for the bin, the pizza boxes were stacked on the breakfast bar, grease marks blooming on the white cardboard. Used coffee filters sagged on the draining board, their insides spilling like fresh soil. A thin stink rose from the bin. Shirts and T-shirts were scattered on chairs, newspapers littered the table. The whole flat was a disgrace. Fuck it. I hauled to my feet, marched through the rooms snapping on lights. The least I could do was keep the place in order. What if Mari and Angus came back tomorrow? They couldn't come home to a mess like this.

I would start with the kitchen.

Books and papers among the dirty cups and glasses. The folder from Callum Kidd, Lewicki's Agency contact, was open on the kitchen table. The *dossier*, you would call it. A book was lying across the pages and its spine, when I went to lift it, was underlining a telephone number. My fingers froze in the air above the book. The number seemed to swim up from the page. It was a mobile number and the last four digits – 1969 – formed the year of my birth.

In the living room I yanked the drawer of my desk and rummaged. As I hurried back to the kitchen I was flicking through them, Martin Moir's little pile of Post-its. I found the one I wanted and slapped it down on the table. Snap.

The number in the folder was the number on Moir's Post-it, the number he'd been called from on the night before he died.

It took me half an hour, but I got through to Callum Kidd. I stood in the call-box on Queen Margaret Drive and used the alias we'd agreed on.

'Mr Campbell,' he said loudly. 'How can I help?'

I suppose I was excited and it was a minute or two before I could make him understand what I wanted.

'It's a hand-written mobile number on the last page of the folder,' I told him again. 'Someone's obviously scribbled it down and it's been photocopied along with everything else. Have you got the folder there?'

There was a bit of rustling and banging, the booming of a filing-cabinet drawer.

'Aye.'

'There's a number on the last page.' I waited for him to find it. 'Whose is it?'

The pause went on a little too long.

'What is this? What have you found?'

'Just tell me whose the number is.'

'I've no idea,' he said. 'What's the deal here?'

'Look, I think I've found something but I want to be sure.'

'Give me your number,' he told me. 'I'll call you back in five.'

I stood outside the call-box in the chilly dusk, hands

plunged in pockets, shuffling my feet on the sparkling ground. The schools were out and lassies in long tartan skirts and sensible shoes drifted past in twos and threes. Starlings had massed in the lee of the bridge, a great black cloud that swivelled and turned like a localised storm.

Though I knew it was coming the phone made me jump.

'It's to do with Hamish Neil,' Kidd was saying. 'It's a number we had under surveillance. One of Neil's guys. But it's dead now, defunct.'

'What was the name?' I said.

'The number's defunct. The guy himself's dead. We're not even sure if this was his phone.'

'The name.'

'He was shot in October. Neil's enforcer. It's Billy Swan. Now what's your interest?'

'I'll call you back.'

I didn't go home. I walked on down Queen Margaret Drive, over the bridge, into the gardens. A man in green overalls was pushing a barrow of potted plants. 'Gates shut in half an hour.' He nodded at the little silver placard in the middle of the path: *Winter closing*. I gave him a thumbs-up, carried on into the Kibble Palace, the heat, the dripping ferns, little island of summer in the Glasgow cold.

Why had Swan phoned Moir? As I walked the stone-flagged aisles, past the greenery and the marble statues, I tried to make sense of it. I thought back to that Saturday in Maxton Park, the cops standing guard beside the in-cident tape, the little knot of watchers in the rain. No one questioned why Swan had been killed. The Walshes wanted to hit Hamish Neil. Swan was close to Neil, he was easy to get to. A click of the mouse would tell you where to find him at 2 o'clock each Saturday. Swan was the softest target. Nothing personal, as they liked to say in Belfast.

But maybe it *was* personal. Maybe Swan was killed for something he'd done, not just for his closeness to Neil. Something he'd done or was planning to do. I stopped beside a statue, a nude in white marble, a young man crouched on a rock, hiding his head in the crook of his arm. Cain, the placard told me: 'My Punishment is Greater than I Can Bear.'

Had Swan been killed by one of his own? Was he help-ing Moir get the dope on Hamish Neil? Was he phoning Moir to warn him they'd been rumbled, that Neil had made them? I thought again of Swan's photo in the paper, the bleached, tipped hair, the silver sleeper in the ear, the silly grin. A ned, I had thought. A grinning thug, a tool in the hands of a man like Hamish Neil. But maybe that was my own blindness. Maybe I should have looked harder.

Back at the flat I booted up and Googled Billy Swan. Apart from reports of the shooting – my own, gratify-ingly, right at the top – there was little to go on. He'd been acquitted two years back on a charge of serious assault (there was a brief court notice in the online *Scots-man*), and was profiled as a 'feared enforcer for northside kingpin Hamish Neil' on a Glasgow gangland website. But mainly the results were match reports in which Swan frequently featured as matchwinner: *with the Ayrshire side pressing for a leveller, Billy Swan slotted home a late penalty to put the game beyond Kilbirnie's reach*; or, *Billy Swan unleashed a trademark piledriver to sink ten-man Wishaw and bring the points back to Maxton Park*. Most of the reports had the same byline – Fraser Wylie – and appeared in *The Clydesider*, the city's local freesheet.

When I sat across from him the following afternoon, Wylie looked as though he, too, had been a player. Forties, fit and balding, his hair shaved close to the skull, he wore black jeans and a checked Ben Sherman shirt. We were in the *Clydesider* offices in the East End, a cheerful, low-ceilinged oblong cobwebbed in Christmas bunting. A parcel stood on Wylie's desk, a big square box with a red silk bow, a present, I assumed, for the Labrador-hugging girl of six or seven on his screensaver.

On the phone that morning when I set up the meeting I told him I was doing a piece on gangland killings. I understood that he was the only journalist on the scene when Billy Swan was shot.

'I actually stood beside him for most of the game,' Wylie told me now. 'The shooter. Of course you don't notice people at the time, but I remember his cap was pulled down really low and he didn't seem to be shouting for either side. He must have drifted round to the other touchline at some point because he was there when Swan went across to get the ball.'

He stopped then, watching it happen once more through narrowed eyes. He frowned.

'I told the cops all this, gave them a description. What is this, the *Trib*'s idea of a seasonal feature? Goodwill to all men?'

'Just to some of them,' I said. 'Goodwill's in short sup-ply for these fuckers. When did it happen? I mean, what time in the game?'

'Late on,' Wylie said. 'Maybe fifteen minutes to go.'

I nodded. 'Good game, was it?'

'Good game?'

If the question fazed him, Wylie didn't show it. He pouted, hunched his shoulders. 'Actually it was pretty poor, to tell you the truth. Scrappy. Not much shape. It had nothing-each written all over it.'

'And how was Swan playing?'

He looked at me sharply. 'Aye. Well, that was the thing. He was having a nightmare. A total stinker.'

'And that was unusual?'

'Unheard of,' he said. 'Swan was best player on the park every game I saw him play. Best player in the league, to be honest, but he had, well, other commit-ments that stopped him playing at a higher level. He tried out for Rangers, did you know that?'

'I did, yeah.'

'Well that gives you an idea. Touch, vision, the lot. Everything Blackhill did went through Billy Swan. Hard too, fought for every ball. Course it didn't hurt that most of his opponents were shit-scared to put a tackle in, but still. A battler.'

'But not that Saturday,' I said.

'He was shit.' Wylie shook his head. 'Yard off the pace. Wasnae interested. He was on the edge of everything, getting pushed off the ball. Looked like he'd never seen a ball till that afternoon.'

I nodded. Wylie spread his hands. 'Nobody said anything, because, well, because of who he is. But you could
see them shaking their heads, the Blackhill lot. They
were getting ready to sub him. The coach was calling him
over but he was out of earshot on the far touchline.'

'Okay,' I said. I wanted to be clear. 'So Billy Swan had
a bad game. It happens.'

Wylie shook his head. 'Yeah, that's how the cops took
it. *We don't want the match report, son. Just give us the
facts.* But this is the facts. I've watched Billy Swan for
three seasons and I've never seen him play like that. He
looked like a ghost, you know? He was playing like a
man who wasnae there. Like he knew something was
wrong.'

'You think he knew what was coming?'

Wylie sat forward on his swivel chair. His eyes were far
off again, flicking back and forth as if reading something
in the empty air.

'I was watching him at the time,' he said. 'Swan was
that kind of player, you'd watch him walking to take a
throw-in. He was standing with his back to me, waiting
for the guy to kick the ball to him, and something
happened. His shoulders slumped. I think he saw the gun
and his shoulders just slumped. He wasn't mad or desperate, he wasn't scared. He was just resigned. He knew it
was coming.'

Wylie's eyes came into focus and he looked at me
again. 'I'm not stupid,' he said. 'I know that counts for
nothing. But I know what I saw and I know what it
means. Swanny's number was up and he knew it.'

Chapter Thirty-two

The next day I drove through to Holyrood for First Minister's Questions. It was the last FMQ before the recess and a skittish, end-of-term ambience had established itself in the legislative chamber. The air of pantomime, never far from the proceedings, was stronger than ever and a knowing tone pervaded the scripted exchanges, the Presiding Officer's stern remonstrations, the jeers of the hooting backbenchers. There were questions about the referendum – the date, the wording of the question, who would be eligible to vote. And behind these were the bigger questions. Would the Union survive? Would an ancient nation recover its freedom? Would three centuries of British history be put out to pasture?

I couldn't care less. I had questions of my own. Why had Swan phoned Martin Moir on the day they both died? How were the two deaths connected? What would Haining's letter reveal about Hamish Neil's fronts? And behind these questions were bigger ones. Would Mari and Angus come back? Would the trace of apple-blossom shampoo on my pillow fade away or be replenished by a sleeping ash-blonde head? Would my son grip shyly to his mother's legs when he saw me in the airport, or would he tear across the concourse to where I knelt, down on one knee with my arms spread wide like a lover bursting into song?

In less than an hour it was over and the MSPs were streaming out like schoolkids. There were no headlines here, nothing worth writing up. I should have stayed in Glasgow and watched the podcast. I packed up my stuff and headed out, down the broad stairs to the Garden Lobby. Some of the stalwarts were massing at the tables – Torcuil Bain from the *Mail*, the *Scotsman*'s Kirsty Mitchell, Gallacher from the *News of the World*. They'd be off to Jinglin' Geordie's shortly, get the beers in, make a day of it. I waved across and kept walking. I'd parked the car at Dynamic Earth and I walked up the hill to fetch it, headed for the bypass and the M8.

I had almost reached Moodiesburn when my phone chimed once, a text, a jolting buzz beneath my heart. Then it chimed again, and another, two more in quick succession. It was like raindrops before a downpour. At the fifth or sixth I reached down, punching the button for Radio Scotland.

. . . have given no reason for the shock decision, beyond citing the 'stress of running a city with a budget larger than many third-world countries'. Mr Haining, who only last week hosted a party fundraising event attended by celebrity donors, was seen by many commentators as a future Scottish First Minister. He was also expected to lead the 'No' campaign in the referendum on independence. It is understood that Mr Haining has resigned as a councillor as well as from his post as Leader of Glasgow City Council.

Fuck. My eyes flickered shut for a second or two. When I opened them I saw the city skyline, the silhouette

307

of John Knox lording it over the East End dead.

Maybe it wasn't so bad, I told myself. Maybe he put it in the post before he resigned. And maybe Mari and Angus will come home and Elaine won't move to Aberdeen and Celtic will win the Champions League and we'll all have hot muffins and cocoa for tea.

In the *Trib* car park I made some calls. Haining himself had gone to ground; Bluestone Media – my old bolthole – was handling the fallout but they weren't in the mood to give exclusives to former colleagues.

I bumped into Neve McDonald as I left the lift. 'Maguire wants you,' she said as the doors slid shut.

'Hold me back.'

*

Maguire and Driscoll were in Maguire's office. I closed the door behind me. Maguire held up a hand and nodded at the screen. There was a special bulletin. A council spokesman read a statement, fielded questions from the shouting pack. There was footage of councillors arriving for an emergency session, brushing past the camera crews with frowns and brusque no-comments. A shot of the pack encamped outside Haining's flat, a stony-faced reporter doing his piece to camera. I think until I saw this footage I somehow assumed it was all a mistake. For so long Haining had been the coming man, the dauphin, the leader-in-waiting, his future assured. You forgot at times that his future had still to happen, that things could still go wrong.

'OK.' Maguire aimed the remote, killed the sound.

'Where are we? What are they saying at George Square?'

'Not a lot. Bluestone's handling it.'

Maguire frowned. 'That was your mob?'

'Bluestone? Aye.'

'Speak to them?'

'Yeah.' I shrugged. 'No favours. Party line. Strains of office, intolerable stress. They know it's bullshit, they know I know it.'

Maguire nodded. 'Can't reach him direct?'

'Fiona, I had lunch with the guy a couple of times. Three, I think. Me and about thirty other people. I'm not his buddy.'

Haining's silence was deafening. It resounded through the newsrooms of Glasgow and Edinburgh, where his big meaty voice had always held forth at the end of a phone, dispensing soundbites and sometimes sherrickings to the nation's hacks. It boomed through the studios of Baird and the Beeb, where Haining had breezed through pre-records and live links and sandbagged fellow panellists guesting on *Crossfire* or *Spectrum*. Haining had always been close to the media. He cultivated journalists, confided in them, sought their advice. He made you feel special, brought you into the panelled office in the City Chambers, with its framed eight-by-tens: Haining and Blair, Haining and Brown, Haining and Clinton. You felt like his friend. And now it was payback. For all his shrewdness and guile, it turned out Haining was a desperate innocent. He thought we would play along. We would all keep quiet and sit on our hands and let him recover in peace.

What was stress? That was the question we pondered, in the newsroom, in the Cope, over the next two days. A euphemism, certainly, but for what? Women? Money? Horses? Drugs? Or did stress take the form of Hamish Neil? Had the contracts been given to Neil's fronts and was Haining too frightened to tell us? We were running a book in the office, and on day three the drugs crew were cheering. A council spokesman revealed that Haining was in rehab. The phrase 'chemical dependency' was used. It emerged that Haining had been visited by two Agency cops who warned him that city criminals possessed mobile-phone footage of the council leader snorting coke.

Never forget where you come from. That was one of the dreary by-laws of Scottish politics, Scottish life. For Haining it meant bunkering down in his little East End shtetl, chumming round with the boys he'd known since primary, nodding to the players on the street, the old faces, the hard kid from Bellrock Street who'd made a name for himself. They were exact contemporaries, Haining and Neil. They'd gone to different schools – Neil to Cranhill Secondary and Haining to St Gregory's – but the scheme wasn't large and they'd grown up together. As kids they played on the Sugarolly Mountains – the brown heaps of chemical tailings dumped beside the Monkland Canal – and battled with rival young teams from Springboig and Ruchazie. They rose in their different spheres, watched each other's progress, kept tabs. Two lads who outgrew the district but never moved.

The cares of office. The head that wears the crown. They had that in common, the two Cranhill boys, but only one had the antidote, the stress-buster, the wee bags of happy dust. Among friends. Old pals act. Except one of them's thumbing 'record' on his phone while the other one's filling his nose.

Over the next few days, the story exploded. The big boys from London arrived, turned their overcoat collars to the George Square squalls, delivered their lantern-jawed pieces to camera. The word 'disgraced' had crept into the reports. *Disgraced former council leader, the disgraced politician* . . . And the stories kept coming. Strathclyde Police had interviewed another of Haining's colleagues. An ex-con had been given three-quarters of a million to run a drop-in centre for troubled kids in Shettleston. A twenty-four-year-old man from Cranhill had been questioned about the supply of drugs to Mr Haining.

Opposition parties were demanding an audit of all the city contracts awarded under Haining's stewardship. *Commonwealth Games contracts will be a priority, said Nationalist group leader Colin McDaid. We must safeguard the legacy of the Games; we cannot afford for an event like this to be tarnished.* Haining's style of governance – the forthright 'presidential' manner so often saluted in sympathetic profiles – was coming under fire. Councillors who'd happily basked in Haining's charismatic glow were suddenly restive, stung, rehearsing their outrage. Haining was arrogant, they complained, high-handed and unaccountable. He governed by cabal. No one knew what he was doing. He was out of control, he had to be stopped.

I'm not his buddy. My words to Maguire came back to me. I knew what they'd be saying, Driscoll and the others, in the canteen, in the Cope. Conway knew: that would be the rumour. Conway must have known. He knew about the coke habit, the connection to Neil. He had the story and he let it go. Too busy doing white lines at the Jarvie to do his fucking job.

At the flat one night I was sat at the kitchen table with Moir's little pile of Post-its spread out in front of me. The first three were lists of figures: times or prices, I still didn't know. Three of them were telephone numbers, one of them Swan's mobile. Finally there was the luminous pink square with the letter 'S' in ballpoint and then 'FC 7.30.' I set the pink Post-it beside Swan's telephone number. 'S' could be Swan. Maybe Moir had arranged to meet Swan at 7.30 some day, not long before he died. Maybe the same night he ended up in the quarry. But what was 'FC'? Another man's initials? Football Club? Was Moir meeting Swan at the footie ground, the clubhouse at Maxton Park? Did he even attend the match, was he standing on the touchline when Swan was shot? But that was mid-morning, ten or half past, not 7.30.

I put the Post-its back in a pile and thought again of the quarry's black water, the car park with the split-log buttress, the sad little pub on the banks of the canal and that was when it flashed on my brain. *Forth & Clyde.* 'FC' was the canal. Moir was meeting Swan at the canal, in the hotel on the Forth & Clyde. But Neil had found out. Neil had confronted Swanny that morning, or the night before, and Swan had told him everything. That was why Swan was out of sorts on the Maxton Park turf. And that was why Swan had tried to call Moir on the night of his death. With Swan shot and Moir in the quarry, everyone who'd been out to get Neil and wasn't a cop was dead. Everyone except me.

For the next few days I tried to lie low. It was quiet in the flat. I came home in the blue afternoons, in the failing day, reluctant to switch on the lights or close the curtains. I moved through the rooms, white walls shining blue in the gloaming. The flat was a museum of failure, each room a separate exhibit. The Angus Room. The Big Boys' Room. The Mari and Gerry Room. Lost civilisations. Their artefacts and tools. A broken toy. An empty cot, the stripped mattress propped against the radiator. The bed my son's mother no longer slept in. A guitar going mutely out of tune, a plectrum wedged in its slackening strings. Recreation of a typical family home. I passed through the rooms like a tourist.

The kids would build a fire some nights, over on the wasteland. You'd hear the whoops and drunken laughter, the battle cries and shrieks. A ruddy glow amid the trees, dark shapes aflicker. Something primal in the scene, a berserker frisson. On those nights I sat in the dark and waited for the hiss of leather on the stone stairs, the knuckle on the door.

But when it came, the day was bright, a sunny Monday morning. I was crossing the hall when I heard it, a slap more than a knock, a palm blattering, bouncing the door on its hinges. I hadn't heard the buzzer, but I knew that this wasn't a neighbour. I padded up to the spyhole. Even through the coiled glass I could sense it. Something in the stance, in the set of the shoulders. One of Neil's men. Retribution. I thought about phoning the police, pushing a wardrobe against the door, but what was the point?

I turned the mortice. The man straightened up as I opened the door. Slim, not tall, his hands hanging loose at his sides. Black army-surplus jacket, frayed jeans and white tennis shoes. A satchel-style bag worn crosswise on his chest. There were flakes of snow in his short dark hair.

'You Gerry Conway?'

I was almost grateful. I drew the door wide and ushered him in, led him down the short hall. What did I think – that actions have no consequences? That you could go after Hamish Neil without Neil coming after you? This was what it came down to. This was how it was slated to end, in my own living room, a man looping a strap over his head and dumping the bag on the hardwood floor. He bent his knees slightly, mimed sitting on the couch.

'Go ahead.'

'You don't know me,' he said, moving a cushion from behind him. 'But you'll know my old man.'

Did Neil have a son? Was this how they did it, the young blood avenging the father? But the age didn't fit; this guy was early thirties, too old for Neil's son, and too finely featured: that nose, that pointed chin could never belong to a scion of Neil's.

'I'm Walter Maitland,' he said. He half-stood and

stuck out a hand and I bent to grasp it.

Maitland's son. Walter Junior. Relief shunted home like a steroid, flaring the airways, dilating the veins. He wasn't from Neil: I wasn't the mark. He hadn't come to kill me. He was the one who fled to Ireland when his father went to jail. Although 'fled', it now struck me, was not the locution one would naturally apply to the man who sat on my couch like a fight-ready flyweight, his hard tight body completely at rest, my head mirrored twice in his unblinking eyes.

He ran a hand through the snow-damp hair, wiped it on his jeans.

'You got five minutes?' he said.

*

I'd heard of him, of course, Walter Jr, the gangster's brat. I'd seen old photos in the *Record*, a pudgy sneering kid on the High Court steps, acquitted on a charge of possession. And I knew the narrative that attached to his name, the city's collective wisdom about Maitland's boy. How he'd been a nothing all his life, dwelt in the shadow, tried to live up to the name. The only kid in the playground who'd never been in a fight. The kid they all hated and feared but never rated. The new bike, the first car, the riverside apartment: all of it laid on by dad. First screw, too, you'd imagine, some hand-picked call-girl in a honeymoon suite, high above the traffic. Everywhere he went, in the pub, in the scheme, guys vying to stand him a round, slip him a booster, the wrap, the baggie, one on

315

the house, mate. The gold card, the red rope, the compliments of the manager.

And then, in the snap of a handcuff, it's over. Maitland inside, Neil in the big chair. Regime change. Suddenly the sons are vulnerable: the near in blood, the nearer bloody. The kid brother in England, the college student, stays put. Walter Jr shits himself, packs a holdall, jumps a midnight Seacat to Ireland. I pictured the shifty eyes, the white face sucking down a whisky in the forward lounge, the holdall at his feet. But the guy who sat on my sofa, lean, honed, self-contained, with the glitter of winter beading his hair; this guy had changed.

He'd been in Belfast four years. I learned later from John Rose, the *Trib*'s Belfast stringer, that Walter Jr had hooked up with a Shankill Road team, friends of his father, ex-UVF. There was no special treatment. They gave him a job. He did it well. Worked his way up. First time in his life he was pulling his weight, his own man. Once a month he flew to Aberdeen to visit his father in Peterhead. He got in touch with some of the old guard, Maitland's lieutenants, men who'd gone over to Neil but still held a flame for the old regime. One of them must have mentioned me. Now he wanted to know what I had on Neil, what my angle was.

'You knew Martin Moir?' he asked me.

I shrugged. 'I did. Worked with him. Mates with him. Knew him well.'

'And Billy Swan, you've been looking at that, digging around.'

'Aye.'

The slim hands rested on his knees. The gaze didn't waver. 'It was Neil, wasn't it? Both of them.'

I shrugged. 'Looks that way.'

'They'd been talking,' he said. 'Is that right? The polis had turned them?'

'That's the theory,' I said.

I looked away. I could feel Maitland's gaze on the side of my face, the eyes drawing mine back to his.

'What do you think?' he said.

Outside the window a seagull lighted on the rim of a satellite dish. It cocked its head and fixed me with an orange eye before launching itself into space.

'I don't know. It's possible.'

I looked at the man on my sofa. He didn't need to know what I knew. If Moir and Swan had been grassing on Neil it wouldn't have troubled Maitland. He was only concerned about how it would play. If Swan was a grass, then Neil was right to kill him. But if Swan was clean, if Neil had killed him out of spite or after some petty squabble, then the rest of Neil's crew might see things differently. They might agree with Walter Maitland Jr that Hamish Neil should be stopped.

But that wasn't the way to stop Neil and I couldn't give him the answer he wanted.

'So you can't help me. No matter. Thanks anyway.' He gathered the strap of his bag in a fist and hauled to his feet. I shook the proffered hand. He was nearly at the living-room door when I spoke, blurted it out like a nervous kid.

'I could meet him,' I said. 'I could set up a meeting.'

317

'With Hamish Neil?' He held the door open. 'What good would that do?'

'Somewhere public. Somewhere he feels safe. Just him on his own.'

I let it sink in.

'You got somewhere in mind?'

Chapter Thirty-three

Startpoint Street. Newhaven Road. The same names flashed past. I'd been touring the scheme for ten minutes, driving in circles. At every turn the high flats striped the windscreen, white against the inky sky. Gantock Crescent. Sumburgh Street. The plan was to find a pub and ask directions from there. The plan had a flaw. There were no pubs in Cranhill. No pubs, no shops, no bookies. Just the blank white faces of the maisonettes.

Cranhill. Hamish Neil's kingdom was a Fifties scheme, squeezed between the motorway and the old Edinburgh Road. Cottage-style four-in-a-blocks, for the most part, but up towards the motorway stood the high flats, triple towers lapped by seas of grass.

Bellrock Crescent. Skerryvore Road. I swung through the tight streets, slowing for the speed bumps, scouting for shops or a café, anything that looked like a main drag. A big off-stage burble of thunder rolled over the car, and then it started: with a noise like a great tearing of paper a wall of water toppled onto Cranhill. The rain crashed on the Forester's roof, slopped across the windscreen, overwhelmed the wipers. I pulled over. Water fizzed on the bonnet, sparked and boiled in the roadway. Sodden roses bloomed on the maisonette walls.

I turned on Radio Scotland and waited for the rain to

stop. The weather came on, then the news, Haining still in the headlines.

'. . . *Deputy First Minister Noreen Telfer today announced an enquiry into the sale of public assets by Glasgow City Council. The move comes as fresh allegations emerge concerning the conduct of disgraced former city council leader Gavin Haining. Our political editor Derek Urquhart has more.*'

'*Yes, Mhairi, the latest revelation concerns the sale of council land during Gavin Haining's tenure. It's been alleged that vacant lots in the East End of Glasgow, sold at knock-down prices to developers, were then bought back at inflated sums as part of the city's preparation for the Commonwealth Games.*'

'*What sort of sums are we talking about, Derek?*'

'*Significant, Mhairi. In one instance alone, a block of land sold for the nominal sum of one pound sterling was bought back by the Kentigern Consortium – the city's arm's-length construction company – for six hundred thousand pounds. The Commonwealth Games athletics complex will be built on the site.*'

'*That's a tidy profit. Do we know who the vendor was?*'

I remembered Haining at his press conference, standing in the rubble, selling off the gap sites. *Sell them the land? We'll bloody give them the land.*

I punched the button, killed the news. Do we know who the vendor was? It might not be the name on the invoice, but the vendor was Hamish Neil.

The rain had stopped. Everything looked stunned and fresh, like the first day of creation. The railings sang in

320

the sparkling light, the tarmac threw up a molten glare. I sat in the car and smoked a Café Crème and watched a ginger cat high-stepping through the sparkling grass. I flicked the cigar end at its hind quarters and watched the cat clear a garden wall in a single fastidious spasm, its little bell tinkling. Then I turned the key and pulled away slowly, tyres hissing on the slick tarmac, turned another corner.

An old guy was walking a Westie. I slowed the car and bumped the horn with the heel of my hand. The old boy tugged on the red leash and crossed the grass verge. He stuck his head into the car.

'You're far from home, son, a motor like this. Lost your way?'

'Something like that. This a dry district or what? Youse all signed the pledge?'

The old guy laughed. 'You're looking for a pub? Good luck. Social amenities arnae the strong point round here.' He grinned, a dainty row of dentures. 'Don't get me wrong. You can buy drugs, son. That's no problem. Anything you want. Try buying a loaf of bread. A can of beer. Apart from that thieving bastard up on the Crescent there's nothing. You have to go out to Easterhouse or back into Parkhead. Either way it's a three-mile trip, an hour on the bus to get there and back. Fucking liberty, son, it's—'

'The Crescent?'

He pointed back the way I'd come.

'There's a Paki shop up the road there. Straight on and first left, across from the high flats. I'm no a racist, son, but the guy's at it. Fucking comedy prices, no kidding ye.'

'Yeah?' I keep a pack of B & H in the glove compartment; I took it out now and offered him one, lit it with the dashboard lighter.

'Very civil, son. A white man.'

'I'm actually looking for a friend of mine. Guy I used to know. Lives around here.'

'Oh aye?'

'Aye. Name's Hamish Neil.'

The old guy straightened up, yanked the Westie's leash. He spat on the grass verge. 'Cannae help you there, son.' He set off down the hill.

I three-pointed and headed back the way I'd come. Up the street and round the corner was a short parade of shops. A hair salon, a post office, a superstore. The electronic beep when I crossed the superstore's threshold brought the owner's bald head up from the *Evening Times*. I knew the answer before I asked.

'Sorry, pal. Never heard of him.'

The rain was back on. Some boys were messing about in the bus shelter outside the shops.

One of them stuck his head out of the entrance.

'You OK there, big man? Got what you need?'

He bobbed his head a little and chafed his fists together. 'Step into the office, sir. We'll fix you up.' Laughter from inside the shelter.

'Yeah, thanks mate, no. What it is, I'm looking for Hamish Neil.'

The boy's hands dropped to his sides. He reared back

as if a bad smell hit him. He swung back into the shelter.

'Do you know where I can find him?'

I had a folded tenner between my fingers. I jiggled it like a cigarette. I was in the shelter now, and the boys looked at each other and back at me. Four of them. Early teens.

'Anyone know where he is? Hamish Neil?'

They were standing with their backs to the blurry Perspex walls. One of them was propping himself up with a blue Adidas training shoe. He was kicking the shelter in a steady rhythm. The whole frame juddered with his kicks.

They didn't answer. Four blank faces, four sour stares.

'Where's your back-up?' one of them asked.

'I'm not a cop.' I shrugged. I reached inside my jacket and the nearest boy gripped my forearm. He held it tight as I brought my hand out with a business card between my fingers. The tallest boy reached for it. 'I write for the *Tribune*. I'm a journalist.'

'A *journalist*?' The boy spun the card at my face and stepped up close. 'Are you fucking thick or something?'

'It's not like that,' I said. 'It's not a story. I need to speak to him. I did him a favour a while back and I need to see him again. He knows who I am.' I stooped for the card, held it out again. 'He knows who I am.'

'Hey.'

An older guy was crossing the road, bulky, built, a short leather jacket and cropped black hair. He pointed a key over his shoulder and a black SUV squealed and blinked. A Lexus RX. The man's frame blocked the doorway of the shelter. I knew him from before: Neil's driver. He looked at me but spoke to the boy. 'What's the score here?'

The boy jerked his head at me. 'Guy wants to see Mr Neil. Says he knows him.'

'You know Hamish?'

I nodded. The man took the card from my fingers. He turned it over and frowned.

'So what?'

'So I need to see him.'

'What about?'

'I'd rather tell him.'

He looked neutrally at me, breathed through his nose, fingered the card.

'Stay here,' he told me. His index finger tracked along the line of boys and then jabbed at me. The boys shuffled closer, formed a loose circle around me.

'What happens if I run for it?'

The tall boy poked my paunch, lost his finger to the first knuckle.

'We'll catch you up when you get to the kerb.'

Smart cunt. The others laughing.

In five minutes the Lexus driver was back.

'Know the Water Tower? Down Bellrock Street?'

'I'll find it.'

'He'll meet you there in half an hour.'

He crossed to the Lexus. The sun had come out above the high flats. The day was turning out fine. In my rear-view as I pulled away the bus shelter pulsed like a heartbeat.

On the corner of Bellrock Street and Skerryvore Road is a great stone slab on slender concrete pillars: Cranhill Water Tower. Monumental and futuristic, it looks like a memorial for a war that hasn't happened yet. There are spiky railings all around the base. I was leaning against them when the black RX drew up across the street. Neil got out alone, wrapping his overcoat around him, picking his way through the puddles.

'Come on.' He strode past me up the hill. 'We'll go for a walk.'

I looked doubtfully at the Forester.

'Safe as houses, Gerry. Come on.'

We climbed up the hill towards the high flats, Neil moving at pace, his overcoat flapping.

'So you're back in the game.'

I shrugged. 'So to speak.'

'That's good news. I want to tell you, Gerry, I don't share the current despondency surrounding newspapers. A good newspaper will always be wanted. The public needs to be kept informed.'

A smile nipped at the corners of his mouth. I didn't say anything.

'You know what Jefferson said? About papers?'

I sighed. 'Surprise me.'

'Thomas Jefferson. He said if it was up to him, if he had to choose between a government without newspapers or newspapers without a government, he would choose the latter.'

The sodden grass was darkening my trouser-ends, water was seeping into my shoes.

'Yeah? And who'd benefit from that equation?'

'I think we all would, Gerry.'

'Well, if you feel that way, Mr Neil, maybe you could help us out, take out some ad space in the *Trib*.'

He smiled. 'Mine's more of a word-of-mouth business, Gerry. But a nice thought. Anyway, what can I do for you? You here to give me right of reply? Am I your splash on Sunday?'

I shook my head. 'You're not my splash any Sunday. Not any more. You know why I'm here. I'm over my head. I want to end it. I want it over. My girlfriend, the boy. I can't have them hurt.'

He was nodding. We had come to a stop at the foot of a slope, a green bank of turf. Up there were the high flats, the three big towers at the heart of the scheme. Neil jerked his chin at them.

'Used to play up there. On the Suggies. Heard of the Suggies?'

'Vaguely.'

'The Sugarolly Mountains. That's where it was. The motorway over there was the canal, and where the high flats are was the Sugarolly Mountains. Great days. I used to play here with my brother. Used to steal our mammy's tea tray and slide down the hills. Chemical tailings it was. Hazardous waste, basically. Whenever it rained this brown stuff came oozing out but nobody bothered. No one told us it was dangerous.'

He turned to face me. 'That's all it takes sometimes. Someone to point out the danger. Tell you to stop.'

'I have stopped,' I said. 'That's what I'm saying. I have

stopped. I'm back on Politics, as of now, this week. I'm finished.'

'That's good, Gerry.' He was prodding at the sopping grass with the toe of his shoe, clear water bubbling up like a spring, cresting the glossy black. 'Thing is, you'll appreciate, I'm going to need some assurance. A little token of your change of heart. Goodwill gesture, you might call it.'

He turned and started back down the hill. I caught him up.

'And this would involve what?'

'Nothing much. Write a couple of stories. Man in my position, I get to hear things. People tell me stuff. I could set you up with a couple of stories. Help you out. That's all. Do you a favour.'

We were almost back at the cars. I looked up at the water tower, the columns black against the green sky, the great stone slab like some megalithic tomb.

'Didn't work too well for Martin Moir,' I said. 'That arrangement.'

'You're not Martin Moir.'

He pointed his key and the car shrugged into life with a yellow blink, an electric yelp, like a dog rousing itself.

'By the way, what makes you think I would hurt you?'

'What?'

'You said it just now, you can't have them hurt. Who's hurting anyone?'

I remembered the panic on the towpath, the chase from the nursery, the hollow hour when I thought my son had been taken.

327

'Yeah, you've never had a cross word, Hamish, not with anyone. Those guys in the tanning salon must have firebombed themselves.'

'You know what happened there?' Neil was shaking his head, disappointed, the tight mouth. 'I tried to do it the smart way. Take the old man out of the picture with a minimum of fuss. But fuss is what people look for. If there's no fuss they think you're milky. You're not for real. They take liberties. So you have to do it anyway, what you should have done at the start. You're only putting it off.' He opened the car door, shrugged out of his overcoat and tossed it onto the passenger seat. 'I took that lesson to heart, Gerry.'

'You mean you'll be making a fuss over me?'

He smiled. 'No. I don't mean that at all. I mean I'll do what it takes to protect what I have. Like anyone would. You got a card?'

I gave him one. He took out a pen and wrote a number on the back. 'Get me on that. Once you've made up your mind.'

'I'll give it some thought.'

'You do that, Gerry.' He grinned, settling himself into the padded leather, reaching for the seatbelt. 'Weigh up your options.'

*

I phoned him next day from the box on Queen Margaret. I wanted a meet, just the two of us, sort out the details, get this thing settled. Someone would be in touch, he told me. No, I said. Here's how it is. I deal with you, not with your underlings. I don't come east. We meet in public, in the daytime, at a place of my choosing. You give me the details and I leave first.

'That's very organised of you,' he said. 'Did you have a venue in mind?'

'There's a place out west,' I said. 'They're big on music?'

'I know it,' he said. 'What time does the big music start?'

'Around four o'clock tomorrow.'

'I'll see you then.'

Chapter Thirty-four

Ceòl Mòr is a pub on the Great Western Road. It stands on the corner with Byres Road in a big converted church. It was Maitland's suggestion. I knew Neil would get the reference – it means 'big music' in Gaelic. Neil was Highland, his mother from Portree, a native speaker. Ceòl Mòr was perfect, Maitland told me. Fine and private. Dark, low-ceilinged, full of snugs and booths.

When I finished the call to Neil I called Walter Jr to tell him it was on. But then I had the whole evening to mope around the flat and think about what I was doing. If Walter Jr killed Neil I was free. Neil couldn't harm my family, he couldn't force me to work for him. But was that the end of it? Walter Jr would be grateful, no doubt. But the man who helps you kill another man owes as much to you as you do to him. Maybe Walter Jr would get to thinking that I should help him in other ways. And maybe once his gratitude wore off he'd start to think of me as the man who put Walter Sr away and not as the man who fingered Hamish Neil. As I watched the bonfires on the wasteground flickering through the trees it seemed to me that what I needed was a way to take the pair of them out. I had one more phone call to make.

Next afternoon I stood in the living room with a cup of tea, watching the boys. They were sitting at my computer, heads together, Roddy and James, playing Minecraft. They were here for the next two days. Elaine was still wary but I told her I'd squared things with Hamish Neil, the danger was past. They were supposed to be in school but there were only two days till the Christmas vac and I persuaded Elaine that they could skip them.

At quarter to four I took them out for a walk. They weren't happy, shrugging into their jackets and zipping them up to their necks, tucking their chins into their collars as we fought against the wind that barrelled down Clouston Street.

'Do we have to, Dad? It's too cold.'

We walked down Queen Margaret Drive to the junction. The sun was setting at the foot of Byres Road. The smell from the brewery was heavy in the air. As I stood at the crossing, gripping James's hand, I watched Ceòl Mòr from the corner of my eye. Lewicki's men would be in there by now, sitting in booths or perched at the bar, hanging over the sports pages or pretending to be busy with their mobile phones. Three of them, Lewicki told me. Firearms specialists. Marksmen.

The beeps sounded and the green man flashed. As we crossed Great Western, I glanced at the parked cars, the shop doorways. Lewicki was around here somewhere, waiting with reinforcements, though not in the pub: Hamish Neil would have made him in a second. The cops in the pub were to bide their time. As soon as Walter Jr drew his weapon they would do their thing. Before he knew where he was, Walter Jr would have three Glock 17s pointed at his head. He would drop his weapon and lie down on the sticky pub floor while an officer yanked his arms behind his back and snapped the cuffs and arrested him for the attempted murder of Hamish Neil.

That would take care of Maitland Jr but what about Hamish Neil? Neil would be unharmed, though he might require a stiffener, a generous draught of the nearest single malt. And once he'd downed it he'd have some thinking to do. He'd know that Maitland would never have moved on his own. Maitland would have cleared it with Neil's own crew. Some of the old guard, the men he'd inherited from Walter Sr and maybe some of his own guys too, had turned against him. The way I saw it, Neil now had two choices. He could purge his own crew and weed out the traitors. But this would get messy and he'd never know for sure who was on his side. The other option was to cut his losses, cash his chips and take a slow boat to Magaluf or Malaga or wherever superannuated villains were holing up these days. Either way, he'd have too much on his plate to pay much attention to me.

'There's nothing to *do*.' Rod was lagging behind. 'This is *bor*ing.' He would keep on like this, in a voice like someone scratching a balloon, until you lost the plot and shouted him down. Or you could bluster him out of it, chivvy him round.

'Rubbish,' I said. 'Brisk walk. Fresh air. What more could you want? A growing boy.'

'But where are we *going*?'

James looked up too, waiting for the answer.

'I don't know. A walk. Listen, we make it as far as the University Café I'll buy you a slider.'

'Can I have a tub?' James was serious now, establishing the conditions. 'Can I have a tub instead of a slider. And strawberry, not plain.'

'Course you can. Alright, Roddy?'

'Fine.'

There were carol singers outside Hillhead Underground, a proper choir, eight or ten cheery souls in matching red scarves, a conductor in a Santa hat. Shoppers paused to listen. A spirited version of 'God Rest Ye Merry, Gentlemen' was under way, the basses angry at the back, frowning and blustering, the sopranos joyful at the front, open-mouthed like fledglings. I gave the boys a pound coin each to drop in the Marie Curie bucket and that's when I heard the sound, faint at first, a distant sob from Dumbarton Road, then suddenly loud as an ambulance slalomed through the stalled traffic. The carollers flinched, kept their eyes on the song-sheets, eyes and lips growing desperately expressive as their voices were overwhelmed, before the ambulance passed, its loud sarcastic whoop dwindling towards the Botanics. Almost immediately, two police cars came slashing past, lights flashing Christmassy blue in the dusk.

I felt it in my chest, like the bass at a gig, a thumping note, panic. This was it.

'Right guys,' I said. 'Change of plan. Come on.'

James sensed my agitation, felt for my hand. I tugged him through the shoppers, moving too fast, I could feel him skipping to keep up. I had a flashback of him as a

333

toddler, Elaine and I holding his hands, hup-two-three and then the lift, the little legs cycling the air, *Again! Again!*

'Dad, what is it, Dad?' James was craning to look in my face but I stared straight ahead, kept up the pace. 'What's happened, Dad?' He was still at that age, his dad knew everything, his dad could answer all questions. Roddy snorted.

'Don't be soft, James. How's Dad supposed to know?'

A knot of shoppers was outside Ceòl Mòr, a craning crowd, the ambulance and cop cars parked askew in the street, blocking the traffic on Great Western Road. A uniform was out in the roadway, waving on the cars and buses; another one guarded the door of the pub.

I fumbled for my press card. I held it up for the cop on the door.

'Gerry Conway. *Tribune on Sunday.* Can you tell me what's happened?'

He looked at the card, then down at the boys. The blue lights flickered across his young face, the set mouth.

'There's been an incident, sir. A statement will be released in due course.'

'Bad one, is it?'

He looked at the boys, back at me, frowning.

'Not at liberty to say. Sir, I'd get the kiddies away from here, it's not, it's not suitable.'

Another car pulled up, two men getting out, suits and ties, Lewicki and a shorter colleague, moving slowly, stopping in the roadway to take it all in, the scene, the crowd, the short guy hitching his trousers.

'Thanks,' I said to the uniformed cop. 'Come on, guys.'

I caught Lewicki's eye as we passed, he looked down, gave his head the smallest of shakes. The two detectives were making for the door, taking their time.

'What happened, Dad?' James was still anxious, he wanted an answer.

'I don't know, son. An accident. Maybe a person collapsed in the pub, a heart attack. The ambulance was there to help them.'

'Three cop cars?' Roddy whistled. 'Some accident.'

I felt the rage, out of nowhere, turned on him, crouched on the pavement, hands on his shoulders, my back to James. 'You think that's smart?' His white shocked face. 'Frightening your wee brother? Think you're the big man? How would *you* know what's happened?' I knocked his shoulder with the heel of my hand. 'Smarten up!'

'All right!' He shook himself free, scowling, the jaw tightened, Jamie scared now, fighting tears. Fuck it. I stayed kneeling on the pavement, chin on my chest, let my eyes close. One boy hurt, another scared, and who knows what had happened in the pub. Nice work, Gerry. First fucking class. Leave things better than you found them.

In the flat I closed the front door and leaned against it, closed my eyes. I felt I could sleep standing up. I pushed myself off with my palms and stumbled through to the living room.

'Guys, look, I'm sorry. I'm sorry for shouting. You want to do something, play a game? Want to play the Wii?'

They were rifling through the DVDs. They looked up,

heads together, looked at each other. 'We're fine, Dad.'

When they were small, when they'd wanted me to play with them I was too busy, too tired. Now that I was ready to play it was too late, they didn't need me.

Through in the kitchen I slumped at the table, let my head cant forward onto folded arms. I thought about phoning it in, alerting the desk but I couldn't lift my head from my arms and I didn't know what to tell them. They would know soon enough, I figured. We would all know soon enough.

It was six o'clock before Lewicki answered his phone.

'Well that was a fun afternoon. Thanks a fucking million for setting that up.'

'What happened?'

Lewicki snorted. 'What happened? They missed him's what happened.'

'Missed him! How?'

A long exhale. 'They fucked up, Gerry. They're still waiting for Maitland to show when this blonde at the bar pulls a gun from her purse and starts unloading into Hamish Neil.'

'A woman?'

'Well that's what they think. Finally one of them gets a round off and takes the shooter down. When the smoke clears Hamish Neil's slumped in the booth with a chest full of holes and Walter Maitland Jr's on the deck, blood pumping from a leg wound and a blonde wig on the floor beside him.'

'Aw, Jesus, Jan. They were supposed to stop it. They were supposed to step in.'

'Yeah. Well. You cannae always legislate for skinny trannies wi' guns in their purse. Anyway, fuck it, it's a result. One dead, one in the Bar-L. What do you care, your worries are over. You're laughing.'

He rang off. I didn't feel like laughing. A man was lying dead in the city morgue. Not the best of men, you could say, but which of us was? A man who wouldn't be dead if I hadn't phoned him.

Later – it might have been ten minutes, might have been an hour – I lifted my head, groaned to my feet. The boys would need something to eat. There was a sign saying 'Poison' on the fridge door, a magnet with an 0800 number, the emergency helpline. Who to call if a family member ingests a toxic fluid. Did we have these as kids, poison hotlines? We never swallowed any bleach or weedkiller. Does it make it more likely? Does the presence of the number on your fridge door attract these sorts of events, call them into being? I peeled it off, dropped it in the bin. There was ham in the fridge, a wodge of pink slices folded like banknotes, a puckered tomato in the salad drawer.

I took the sandwiches through. The boys were still busy at the screen. My Fender was resting against the bookcase. When I picked it up something rattled in its innards. A plectrum. Angus liked to post them through the hole. They had all done this, all three of the boys, they had all gone through that stage. I held the guitar by the body, turned it under the light, peering into its coffin-like depths till I saw the little triangle of white. I shook it into position and then spun the guitar upside down. The plectrum dropped noiselessly onto the carpet.

Chapter Thirty-five

'Beat you to it.'

Jimmy Driscoll at my elbow, pink shirtsleeves, shaking his head, the wry smile.

'Sorry, Jim?'

'Maitland's boy. With Hamish Neil. Another couple of weeks and you'd have got him. We had a book on it. I said you'd get him in the New Year. Like you got Packy Walsh. But young Maitland got there first.'

I straightened up from the screen, clicked away from Torcuil Bain's flatulent 'Death of a Godfather' splash in the *Mail*.

'Well, the boy's keen. Or maybe he wanted to hook up with his old man again, the Dads and Lads unit at Peterhead. You seen Maguire?'

'Upstairs, mate. Listen, she's spoken to the Yanks. You're safe, Ger. We both are. Maguire's moving up. Sixth floor.' He grinned. 'I'm getting the big chair.'

He was stoked, so boyishly pleased that it felt churlish not to grasp his hand, clap him on the back, tell him he deserved it. The big chair. The paper would founder within two years, five at most, but Driscoll was happy.

*

The morning of the funeral was cold and dull, thunder-heads massing, dark over Riddrie. I knotted the tie in front of the hall-stand, the tie I'd worn at Swan's, at Moir's, got in the car, headed east. Outside the church I watched the mourners file out, collars turned to the cold, took my place in the line of cars heading east to Riddrie Park cemetery. Shrunken islets of dirty white, the residue of last week's snow, lined the pavements. It was Burns Day, the butcher on Provanmill Road had a window display of haggis and tartan, a portrait of the Bard watching the cortege pass. The pace was glacial, the hearse an old-fashioned horse-drawn affair. After five minutes of nose-to-tail I signalled, pulled out, and powered up the line, ignoring the pink shocked faces at the windows.

In the cemetery I found the grave they'd hacked from the wintry earth. A tarp was draped over the banks of soil and weighted down with a couple of planks. An unmarked cop-car was parked nearby – I spotted the extra aerial – and when the driver's door opened it was Lewicki who hauled himself out, zipping his leather and stamping on the cold gravel.

I took off my glove to shake hands.

'Finished at the kirk?'

'Aye, they're on their way.'

He nodded, sparked a roll-up. It was too cold to stand still so we walked together down one of the paths. A game was under way on a municipal pitch beside the cemetery, two pub teams hacking around on the chewy turf, urgent shouts, breath pluming in the frozen air. We

339

watched it for a minute.

'The cop at the locus, the boy on the door, the uniform. Works out of Maryhill. Tells me a journalist showed up, straight after the shooting. Didn't catch the name but describes him. Pushing six feet. Glasses, dark hair.' He sniffed. 'Two wee boys in tow.'

'Aye?'

'That was fucking stupid, Gerry.'

I couldn't argue. We watched the game until the dull purr of low-geared engines reached us across the head-stones.

The undertaker, in striped trousers and a morning coat, a top hat swathed in crepe, preceded the hearse down the cemetery drive, two white horses in blinkers and harness, black showgirl feathers bending in the wind.

Behind the hearse came the lacquered black limos. The cars crunched to a halt and the widow emerged, the gymrat, a sleek leg pointing from the limousine door, a hand holding a hat against the wind. She swayed over to the graveside, tanned, the Jackie O sunnies, the short fur coat, spike heels catching in the gravel. A heavy, rougher-looking woman held her elbow, the sister or the sister-in-law; she gave me the hard eye as she passed where I leant against the Forester, lighting a Café Crème.

The mourners shuffled into place around the grave. DAD, SON, HUSBAND: the floral tributes were lifted from the hearse. Three undertakers took the coffin by the handles and laid it on the tarp, on top of the planks, then stepped back, hands clasped over their groins like foot-ballers in a defensive wall. The Saturday traffic ground past on the Provanmill Road. The sun was sinking behind the Red Road flats as the minister started to speak. His voice was lost in the wind, overwhelmed by the footballers' shouts, the reedy peep of the referee's whistle. I left before it was over, walked to the car without looking back.

I wrote it up and Maguire gave it a show. Not the splash – Neil wasn't that important any more – but a nice page four lead with a new photo byline. There was a picture of Clare on page five, standing next to Niven and Maguire as she presented the Martin Moir Award for Investigative Reporting to a student journalist from Aberdeen.

Two days later I was pulling into the short-term car park at Glasgow Airport. The flight wasn't due for another half-hour. I bought a *Guardian* and sat in arrivals with a latte and a glazed Danish. Soon they would come through those double doors, my partner and son. I turned a page, tried to focus on the sports reports.

My mobile buzzed on the table. It was a voice I couldn't place – Irish, Ulster – wanting to thank me.

'Who is this?'

'It's Davey, Gerry. Davey Moir.' The cousin at the funeral, the one who spilled the drinks. 'Look, you did a good job. We want to thank you, the family does.'

'Thank me for what?'

'For helping with Martin. For finding out the truth.'

Was that what I'd done?

'Right. Holding up, are they? His mum and dad?'

'Yeah, they're OK. Listen, that thing I mentioned? With Martin's da? Your man was involved, Hamish Neil.'

He told me the story as I watched the arrivals board refresh itself, the flight from Heathrow ticking up the screen. Ronnie'd been on a job, Martin's dad, the DI in the Royal Ulster Constabulary. One clear spring morning in 1993 he was waiting at the port of Larne. For months they'd been working on the same job: cutting the UVF's supply line. They knew the Blacknecks were getting guns from Scotland and now they had a lead. The target is a lorry on the ferry from Stranraer. A cattle truck. They know what they hope to find. Beneath the truck-bed, under the hooves of the beasts, the shifting flanks running in shit and piss, will be a palette of crates. 'CORNED BEEF' will be stamped on the lids but the actual goods will be wrapped in oily rags, the latest consignment from Walter Maitland, the Blacknecks' Scottish armourer. The lorry disembarks and they tail it through the sleeping streets, stop it on the edge of Larne.

They're taking the driver down from the cab when an armoured car pulls up out of nowhere. Four Brits, one in civvies. The civilian's brass: clipped Sandhurst tones, MI5 or Special Branch. He takes Ronnie aside, tells him the arrest's not going to happen. We need you to let him go. Bigger picture. Ronnie's raging, months of work are slipping down the pan, he goes for the Brit, swinging punches, his own boys have to pull him off. Two days later he's back in uniform, bumped down to sergeant.

'But how was Hamish Neil involved?'

'Neil was the driver. Neil was making the drop.'

I'd known about Maitland, the Special Branch deal, how his handlers let him boss Glasgow so long as he

342

briefed them on Belfast. I should have known that Neil was in Belfast too. He might have been in on the deal. But the deal didn't work. The deal didn't save Maitland from Peterhead jail and it didn't save Neil from Maitland's boy.

I thanked Davey Moir and rang off. It was too late to worry about any of it now. A plane came down in an italic slant, bumped onto the tarmac, shuddered to a halt. It wasn't theirs, but theirs would land soon. Mari would come through those doors with the boy in her arms or holding his hand. She'd be full of her news. I had news of my own. I tapped the folded schedule in my pocket, the sheet of particulars from the estate agent. I'd seen a place, a house with a garden, sea view, not far from the city. I'd spoken to the vendor. It needed a bit of work – the tile on the front step was loose, the doorbell clanked like a chisel on stone – but we could live with that.

Acknowledgements

The person who helped most with this one – who made the whole book possible – would rather not be named. You know who you are and how deeply you're owed.

Stephen Khan and Lindsay McGarvie again shared their knowledge of the newspaper trade.

Lee Brackstone and Derek Johns showed me how to rescue the first draft.

For help and advice of various kinds I would like to thank: Katherine Armstrong, Michael Downes, Wendy English, Ronnie Fyfe, Colin Gavaghan, John and Nikki Hall, Michael Harlow, Paula Hasler, Peter Kuch, Linda Shaughnessy, Dougal McNeill, John Stenhouse and the Stuart Residence Halls Council.

Valerie McIlvanney and the four boys who share our house had a lot to do with this too, and they know how grateful I am.